THE BEAUTIFUL YEARS

A cry came from over the ploughed field, lonely and plaintive. Two male lapwings were flying above in erratic flight, then flinging themselves downwards toward the ground as though they would die with joy. He watched them, feeling sad and yet happy. He could see their broad wings as they turned, then 'see-o-weet', 'see-o-weet', calling to their mates walking on the damp furrows below. Behind, the sun was going down, and the sky was a lake of draining crimson yellow.

For a long while the boy watched them, then he began singing to himself. It was not one of the songs or hymns that he knew and was wont to pipe as Biddy vamped on the piano when his father was out of the house, such as *Won't you come home, Bill Bailey, won't you come home?* or *On Richmond Hill there lives a lass* — all learnt under the same instruction — but an improvised chant in a minor key, sad and wistful as the lapwing's song.

The Flax of Dream

THE BEAUTIFUL YEARS
DANDELION DAYS
THE DREAM OF FAIR WOMEN
THE PATHWAY

THE
BEAUTIFUL
YEARS

Henry Williamson

'The sun shone there for a very long time,
and the water rippled and sang . . .'
RICHARD JEFFERIES, in *My Old Village*

THE BEAUTIFUL YEARS
ISBN 0 600 20684 X

First published in Great Britain 1919
by Faber & Faber Ltd.,
First paperback edition 1967 by
Faber & Faber Ltd.,
Hamlyn Paperbacks edition 1983
Copyright © by Henry Williamson

Zenith books (Hamlyn Paperbacks) are
published by The Hamlyn Publishing Group Ltd.,
Astonaut House, Feltham, Middlesex, England.

Printed and bound in Great Britain by
Hazell Watson & Viney Ltd.,
Aylesbury, Bucks

TO
THE MOTHER
AND TO
THE FATHER

CONTENTS

THE BEAUTIFUL YEARS

SAVE FOR the moan of a little wind under the door and the regular and laboured ticking of the old grandfather clock in the far corner there was silence in the room. The moan became a wailing shriek as the rush of wind came with sudden force against the house, dying again and mumbling as though its anger had gone and left only misery. But the fiercer draught up the wide chimney breathed new fire into the flame-split logs, whose tawny energy had gone long since towards the stars: with a rustling tinkle the embers subsided and a wan flame hovered like the ghost of their former blaze; rising in silence, it seemed without heat and without light, it sank again, and the tock-tock-tockle-tack! of the clock impressed itself upon the pain-dulled mind of John Maddison, sitting so still and afraid in the deep arm-chair.

Then something that had been a vague shadow for a long, long time on the hearthrug, rose up, yawned, and shook itself. With a pad-pad of feet it came to John Maddison, and stared at him in the dimness. His master stroked the soft ears of the spaniel, whose eyes shone dull and glazed in the ember-light. When John Maddison ceased his mechanical action, the cold moist nose of the dog Fidelis was rubbed against his hand solely as indicating grateful thanks, and not in an endeavour to canvass for more pleasure. Then his tail thumped on the floor, for his beloved master, so silent and fearful, had whispered that he was dear old boy.

The door shook on its loose iron hinges, the moan rose to a wail again; an open but unread newspaper trembled and lifted on the floor; the wind thudded on the chimney-top.

Through the window came the rustling of the walnut by the edge of the lawn, and a deep bubbling cry quavered from its branches.

Fidelis looked up, cocking his ears; the cry came again, hollow and indefinite.

His ears flopped and became silky, for his beloved master had whispered that it was only the old wood-owl calling to his mate.

But in the kitchen Big Will'um looked at Biddy the cook and shook his head.

'Means bad, missus.'

Big Will'um was silent again, then took another bite of his meat pasty, thinking that he was very wise to be so respectful always to Biddy.

'Jinny Oolert came when granmer died, Big Will'um.'

'Ah, missus, I minds it.'

Biddy went to the fireplace and took an iron off the stove. The wood-owl was still crying; to her ears it sounded more insistent, suiting the wind that rushed every way and swayed the two black yew trees near the pump.

A tear fell on to the blouse, and with a faint hiss became part of the atmosphere as the hot iron slid over it. She wondered when the blouse would be worn again by the dear sweet lady upstairs, lying so still and pale while Jinny Oolert had come with the warning.

Big Will'um uncrossed his legs and Biddy scolded him for the noise his iron-shod boots made on the tiles. Big Will'um murmured that he was sorry, and wondered if he should go. He looked at the stars but dimly seen through the window, and thought that the night would be rough later on.

The owl hooted again.

They heard footfalls, rapid but light, coming down the stairs: a knock on master's study door: a low voice: and the footfalls of two people going up the stairs.

'I believe her be a-go!' said Biddy, and sobbed.

14

PATERNITY

Big Will'um breathed hard and his eyes opened very wide; he sat without a movement. In that part of the country it was a tradition that the continued hooting of those silent night hunters, the owls, near a house or cottage with sickness, was a sure portent that Death would come in the night.

The night clothed itself with great inscrutability and cloaked its stars with clouds that came with the wind from the west; the windows shook and the trees seethed outside. After a time Big Will'um lumbered off to his cottage by the cedar tree, with the news that Jinny Oolert had come again and again to the house and it meant but one thing.

The brown owl grew silent just before midnight. Maybe it felt hungry and had flapped into the darkness after rats and field-voles, or that its object in hooting had been achieved; again it may have been frightened when it heard the anguished cry that came from under the trees when the light in the sick room had been put out, and the figure of a man had blundered out of the house into the garden.

SEVEN YEARS OLD

A sturdy man, in tweed coat and cap, cord riding breeches and old leather leggings, left Skirr farmhouse and walked across the field towards the distant beech wood. He carried a hurricane lamp; the wind was gusty, and the flame trembled, but maintained its yellow glow. Some lapwings that had been crouching beak to wind in the centre of the field, rose with plaintive cries and swept with the gust, which caught their broad wings and hurled them along.

Under the beech trees the ground was sodden, for the month of January, just passed, had been a wet one even for the time of year. The blast tore at the black branches of the trees which stood out barely against the gray clouds.

Soon he passed through the wood and came to its farther edge. Here the field in front sloped gradually downwards; and close up against the trees a low shelter had been erected of hurdles stuffed with hay, and divided into a number of pens, each consisting of three sides and a roof which shook with the wind, yet resisted all effort to whirl them away. Two dark figures were attending to something lying on its side within one of the pens; the man who had just arrived went up to them, his hurricane light making the blackness beyond more absolute.

'Evenun', zur. Thissy be still-born.'

One of the men turned and spoke; his companion was busy with the dead lamb.

'How are they going, Jacob?'

'Fairish, zur. Dree double couples in last hour.'

The ewe that lay upon her side raised her head and gave a

deep ba-a-a to the wet limpness that she was so eager to caress. But Big Will'um had removed it, and was engaged in a curious job. Taking his sharp knife from his belt, he slit the dead lamb down the stomach, and commenced to peel its skin off, as though it were a rabbit. While he was doing this a little boy crept into the circle of light and watched him with eager fascination. Quickly and surely Big Will'um flayed the limp thing, and taking one of the lamps he went to a pen a few yards away, removed the hurdle that did duty for a door, stooped and picked up one of the lambs in his huge hands. The ewe made a rumble of anguish, but feeling that one of her most precious little ones was still snuggled against her, she lay down and contented herself with the beat of its tiny heart. Big Will'um placed the lamb, bleating in feeble protest, upon some hay, and proceeded to cover it with the dead thing's skin. All the while the little boy was watching with interest, which held him in silent wonder up to a point when his curiosity overcame his fancied conviction of utter nonentity.

'Please, Big Will'um, what are you doing?' he inquired, in a thin treble.

'Hullo, miboy!' said Big Will'um, glancing at him, straightening his back and taking some string from a waistcoat pocket —a waistcoat made of moleskins, the boy noticed, with envy and admiration.

'Hullo,' replied the little boy, watching him eagerly as he tied the coat of the dead lamb to the back of the other. 'Is it cold?'

'No, no, midear! Look ee naw, 'tis for that ould ewe to tend.'

'Oh I see,' said the eager child, wondering what the shepherd's mate meant.

'Is that knife sharp?' he asked next.

'Ah!'

'So's thissy!'

'Doan't ee cut ee wi' 'ut, then!'

'Pouff, I've had three before this one. This is a proper pig-sticker—a hunter's knife.'

He produced it from his pocket, and opened an enormous blade.

'Not bad, eh?'

'A gude 'un, thaccy!'

'If I stuck it under your fifth rib it would kill you, easily! Is it going to rain?'

'Afore long I reckon.'

The extra coat had been secured to the back of the lamb; he shut his knife with a snap and fastened it to a swivel on his belt. The boy looked at the belt with the same admiration as he had noticed the waistcoat, and made a resolution to procure one as soon as he had enough money saved up. He thought with joy of the eightpence hidden in a tobacco tin up his bedroom chimney—the belt would probably be two shillings. Then there was twopence due the next day—his weekly income; and probably threepence from the grocer if he could sneak some more empty jam jars and take them to the shop—perhaps he might manage even fourpence! It was a beautiful belt!

Big Will'um carried the lamb to the ewe, who was calling in deep sorrow for something she missed so much. She sniffed at the damp bundle, all floppy legs and loose tail, and bleated with satisfaction, while the lamb with the extra coat tied to it buried its head in her soft body with an instinctive action.

The little boy watched it and felt a curious gentleness inside him as he did so.

'Big Will'um?'

' 'Es, midear?'

'D'you think Mr. Temperley would let me take one home for a pet, later on, I mean?'

'But wot 'ud ee do wi' it?'

'Oh, I should like to nurse it. They are so sweet, aren't they, Big Will'um?'

'Sweeter when um bigger, wi' mint sauce, Li'l Will'um!'

Someone called the shepherd's mate, and he squelched over the sodden field to the circle of men around the lamps. Mr.

Temperley was giving instructions before going back to his supper. He feared rain in the night, and the period of yeaning in February was as important to him as the hay crop in June or the harvest of wheat in August.

The small boy followed his friend, Big Will'um, wondering meanwhile if he would be sent to bed supperless if he were caught out so late without permission. But this possibility was dismissed by the knowledge that Biddy, the cook, would hide a decent slice of cake and a glass of milk in the cupboard behind the rocking-horse, that was now regarded with kindly tolerance, as he was no longer a child, and therefore ignored engines, soldiers, and rocking-horses. The soldiers, indeed, had disappeared that winter, having been melted down to form bullets for his catapult. Biddy had made a great fuss when he was engaged on this secret and important business, declaring that the smell of burning paint would ruin her oven and fill the house with poison fumes. These complaints had received scant attention, for Mr. Maddison was in London, and his son had traded on the knowledge that Biddy's kind heart would prevent her from reporting him a bad boy on his return.

The boy joined the others, but stood at a distance. Every word spoken was listened to with the greatest attention, to be given out later on with embellishments, to Biddy. Mr. Temperley was speaking to Jacob, an old man with gray hair, and had not yet seen the listener. The others, their duties for the moment finished, were talking about the possibility of bad weather, and whether the frost would come and bind the water-meadows as it had, so Big Will'um's father had told him, forty odd years ago. Then the lambs had all died, and most of the ewes as well.

'That was t'time,' growled a farm-hand with his back bent by many years' work in the fields, 'when old Granfer Brown shot five girt geese in t'same evenun' in Varmer John Smith's long meadow.'

The little boy came nearer. Geese, wild geese. Five, all at

once. Oh, if only the frost would come and send the geese to Rookhurst again!

He thought of his seventy-three round catapult bullets, all smooth and deadly, in the washleather bag hidden under his bedroom floor, and wondered if he might be able to kill a wild goose when the frost came. Father had forbidden catapults, and therefore it had been necessary to take up the carpet in his room, remove a floorboard, and make a secret hiding-place for it. He had sawn a length off the board and fixed a hinge to it, so that it resembled a miniature trap-door. The trouble was that Biddy, or worse, his father, might discover it, for it creaked when trodden upon. But what was Big Will'um saying now?

'I doan't reckon as you can say that a man be mazed because ee doan't see eye to eye wi' 'un. I reckon as how young Jim 'Ollomun be peculiar like, but not so as you could call 'im mazed.'

The others said something to Big Will'um, but Little Will'um was no longer listening. He was imagining a tall man with long arms and legs whom everyone said was mazed. No one knew where he came from, but some said that he was left by the wandering Romanies, and old Granfer Will'um, who sat outside the inn all the summer, held the opinion that Jim Holloman was a proper Gipsy. Willie thought it a shame to call him mazed, as some of those nasty little village chaps did. Jim Holloman hurt no one, he only slept out of doors most of the year and wandered about on the hills and in the wood by himself; doing odd jobs at farmhouses, chopping wood, sweeping out the stables, and anything else, for a glass of ale or a slice of bread and cheese. He rarely spoke to anyone, except to say yes or no, or ask a simple question.

'Hullo, young Will'um! I didn't see you. How long have you been here?'

'I don't know, Mr. Temperley. What lovely lambs. I saw one having another's fur tied on it. Where's Jack?'

23

'At home, where you ought to be. How's your father?'

'Father is quite well, thank you, Mr. Temperley. I say!'

'What do you say, young man?'

'Do you think we shall have some frost, and the geese will come?'

'I hope not.'

'Oh, I do.'

'Why?'

'Because I am sure I shall kill one with my new cat——' He paused, remembering that Mr. Temperley was in league with Father against them having catties, and Father had said that it would be his painful duty to whip him if he ever caught him with another.

He turned round, and with a nervous good-night, disappeared into the darkness of the beech wood. Mr. Temperley chuckled to himself.

'Funny little devil,' he thought, 'queer little devil.' Then he remembered the boy's lonely life, with no brothers or sisters and no mother, alone in the house with his father and a housekeeper. The young lambs were raising thin and plaintive cries from the pens, and he grunted to himself as he thought of the child going back to that gloomy house, having stolen out, no doubt, without permission.

Meanwhile the boy was slipping on the wet leaves under the beech-trees, wondering if his father would find out that he had sneaked away without first asking. He could hear the plover calling as they passed overhead, and the loneliness of their cries made him wonder if they too longed for the spring to come. The wind threshed through the bare branches, and a few drops of rain were flung against his face. He broke into a run, pausing to climb slowly up an incline that led to the field beyond, from where he could see the lamp in Jack's house far away on the right and his own straight in front.

A dark figure loomed up as he ran over the grass, and he

stopped in fear. For a moment only though: it was Jim Holloman.

'Hullo, Jim. Where are you going to?'

'To the spinney.'

'Is it going to rain?'

'Fear so.'

'Hear the plover calling?'

'Ay. Beginning to feel the spring. There'll be eggs on the moors soon, shouldn't wonder.'

'Won't you get wet if it rains, Jim?'

'No, miboy. Got a fire, and a good hut.'

The boy asked his questions with great rapidity, hardly waiting for the man's replies. All the while he kept shifting his feet, as though desiring greatly to ask something, but dared not to. Suddenly he said, almost breathlessly:

'Jim, may I come and cook some spuds on your fire, please? You don't mind, do you? I wish I had a hut! Have you seen the lambs?'

The man looked at him and laughed softly to himself.

'May I, Jim?'

'Yes, miboy, of course you can. Maybe I'll have a leg of a rabbit for ee, too.'

'Oh, thank you so much! I'll get a pie from Biddy for you! I'll come to-morrow! Good-night!'

He turned round and scampered off, wild elation in his heart at the thought of crouching over a blazing fire in the crowstarver's hut, while the potatoes were baking in the embers and a rabbit sizzled on top. A rabbit strung on a green stick, just like a Red Indian would do it. Oh, Jim was a fine chap, even if he was only a crowstarver, and said to be mazed!

Soon he reached the garden railings, climbed them, and crossed the path. Through the mist he saw the yellow light in father's study. Creeping quietly over the grass, he peered through the window. By the fire sat father, deep in an arm-chair, reading. In the light of the shaded reading-lamp he could see his face, with its sombre expression and long beard, brown, but with gray streaks in it. Old Fidelis lay at his feet; then the dog looked up at the window and wagged his tail.

His father sat so still that the boy in the garden thought he must be almost asleep: he never turned over the page. The flames of the fire leapt up as a log crashed, and made darker the panelled walls. Old Fidelis rose on shaking feet and after undulating his body slowly to remove any dust, looked at his master's face, it being supper time.

Mr. Maddison, who had been listening, turned and saw his son in the garden, rose from his chair and went to the window. Fidelis waddled after him, but the face had disappeared. Mr. Maddison opened the door, and followed by the ancient spaniel, walked into the kitchen half a second after his son had slipped upstairs.

'Is Willie here, Biddy?' he asked in a quiet voice.

'The li'l lamb be in bed, zur.'

Biddy the cook and housekeeper began to shovel some more coal on the fire, making as much noise as possible.

'I thought I saw him in the garden a minute ago. You mustn't encourage him, you know, Biddy. He's wild enough as it is. Also, aren't you wasting coal?'

Biddy made a great noise with the coal before answering.

'He's a good little lamb, zur——'

But he had left the kitchen, and only Fidelis was looking at her, his bleary eyes telling her plainly that it was his biscuit time.

Mr. Maddison walked softly upstairs, and coughing before he did so, opened the door of his son's bedroom. The room was very quiet, except for the somnolent breathing of a still figure apparently asleep in the large bed in the corner.

'Are you asleep, Willie?'

No answer.

He sat down on the side of the bed; wearily his son raised his head and with sudden alarm appeared to perceive his father.

'Not—not time to get up, Father?' he wheezed, as though

disturbed from deep slumber. Tiredly he yawned, but remembered just in time that if he stretched his arms his father would see the sleeves of his coat.

'Willie!' sharply.

'Yes, Father?'

'Did I see you in the garden just now?'

A pause; then miserably:

'I don't know, Father.'

'What were you doing out so late at night?'

'I don't know, Father.'

'Do you know anything?'

'I don't know, Father.'

'Very well then, I will get the cane. That will give you something to whine about.' He rose from the bed and went out of the room. The figure lay still, his world suddenly crashed. Father was going to thrash him. Should he undress quickly and swear that he wasn't in the garden at all? Oh, father was going to thrash him!

He began to whimper.

His father returned and sat down on the bed again. 'I've told you before, my boy, I won't have lies told to me. You must learn to answer like a man, and also to obey. What were you doing in the garden at this time of night?'

The boy lay silent; only the sound of the wind drearing through the leafless trees and striving to break the hasps upon the window.

'Answer me, Willie!'

His son lay with his face buried in the pillow.

'Seeing the lambs, please, Father.'

'Didn't I say you were not to go out?'

'Yes, Father.'

'Very well then.'

A sob came from the boy's throat. His father saw that he was fully dressed.

'Take down your trousers. Don't keep me waiting!'

His father gave him six cuts with the cane; before and after each one his son screamed in fear, as a rabbit will when it first realises that it is caught in a trap.

'Now, my boy, perhaps that will teach you not to tell lies!'

When the father had gone into his study again, Biddy crept upstairs with a glass of milk and four jam tarts. But Willie did not want them, neither would he speak to her. She knelt down beside the bed and tried to put her arm around his thin little body, but he would not respond. With anger in her heart—for he was a gentle child with the brown eyes of her dead mistress —she tried to comfort him, but he remained unresponsive.

Mr. Maddison sat before the fire in the arm-chair, his hand trembling slightly as it held the archæological book at the same page. He looked out of the window, now splashed with the rain that beat an intermittent tattoo, and a fear came into him as he thought of his child ill with pneumonia, and then, perhaps, Death! It was like a flint arrowhead in his heart to whip the little chap, but he mustn't go out at night—he was all he had, and he might lose him! He was always sneaking out at night: it might lead to bad habits later on. As it was, the boy was a confirmed liar!

A scraping at the door, and old Fidelis implored admittance. He opened it, and the spaniel heaved slowly across the carpet, to sink almost immediately into a condition of pleasant drowsiness before the fire. After a while he stirred uneasily, feeling, in that intuitive way of old dogs, that his master was unhappy. With an effort he rose, pulled himself together, and sidled up to his chair, placing his head on his master's knee, and looking at his face, and whining, as though saying: 'Master, I missed a nice walk, for young master wouldn't take me with him, but pushed me away with his foot as I had got half-way through the door.'

He stood on three legs and began scratching. Flicking his left ear with his hind foot, he knocked against the table leg; then slunk away, for 'Shut up, damn you!' his master had harshly cried.

Chapter 2

ONE MORNING Willie had been invited to go to Jack's birthday supper, and the time before he would run towards Skirr Farm seemed never so long. He walked under the elm-trees while the sun was going down; they were bursting into blossom and covered with a rufous haze, as though the spirit of sunlight were loath to leave the bloom it had called forth. High above the ploughlands a lark was singing, for he too, felt happy, and a small flock of great titmice, a family of six, were searching for grubs in the elms. He listened to the wheezing and chattering among themselves: the father bird whistled, and the boy shouted. He did not know why he shouted, or why the lark sang, but it was for the same reason that the lambs on the hill-side that he had just left jumped into the air and flung their heads about as though they were mazed. Suddenly he was quiet and listening intently.

A robin sang on a dull brown furrow in the field behind the elms. The lark had dived to earth, and was chasing a crested rival, the tomtits were silent. Alone sang the robin on his dull brown furrow. It appeared to the boy that he sang sadly, as though he remembered the legend of his red breast, and how the stain came there long ago. Biddy had told him one night in winter, with Bob the terrier asleep at the bottom of his bed.

The robin sang of hope, of the beauty stirring anew in the cold earth.

Willie walked on quietly, thinking of the party that night. Jack's father had promised to show him his gun! A real gun it was, with double barrels that would kill two rabbits at once. If only he had a gun like that, not like his stupid catapult, he would never want another thing, not even a ferret.

A cry came from over the ploughed field, lonely and plaintive. Two male lapwings were flying above in erratic flight, then flinging themselves downwards toward the ground as though they would die with joy. He watched them, feeling sad and yet happy. He could see their broad wings as they turned, then 'see-o-weet', 'see-o-weet', calling to their mates walking on the damp furrows below. Behind, the sun was going down, and the sky was a lake of draining crimson and yellow.

For a long while the boy watched them, then he began singing to himself. It was not one of the songs or hymns that he knew and was wont to pipe as Biddy vamped on the piano when his father was out of the house, such as 'Won't you come home, Bill Bailey, won't you come home?' or 'On Richmond Hill there lives a lass'—all learnt under the same instruction—but an improvised chant in a minor key, sad and wistful as the lapwing's song. Quite unconscious of what he was singing, or why he was singing, yet his words were almost in the form of a prayer:

> 'Oh God, make me like a plover
> Calling in the rain,
> Oh God, let me sing like a skylark
> Up above in the sky
> So high
> Beautiful God!'

In this strain he sang for some minutes, until his eyes were brimming with tears. Suddenly he stopped, his beautiful misery all gone. From the spinney on the ridge of the field against the sky-line, half a mile over the wet furrows, a cry had floated, followed immediately by a sound as of something hard beaten on a piece of tin. 'Hull-oo-oa, hull-oo-oa,' with renewed bangings and metallic noises.

'It's Jim starving the crows,' shouted Willie to no one, as loudly as he could.

He jumped the ditch and set out across the field. But the loamy soil was full of moisture, and clung to his feet. After going for about fifty yards his enthusiasm diminished to such an extent that he decided to turn back. It would be a pity, of course, for the crowstarver was a fine fellow, and it was fine sport to twirl his rattle round and fine fun to bang on the cans to frighten the rooks and jackdaws away from plundering the grains. He would have to scrape his boots well, or get old Biddy to do it, before going to Jack's. Oh! ah! he was going to see the double-barrel, and eat roast chicken done on the spit before the fire, and baked potatoes—not the mashed ones that he had every day except Sundays—and lots of cream and apple pudding. Lemonade, too. And—best of all—he was going to sleep with Jack that night!

He kicked up his heels with glee, then started for his home. A hare watched him from its form among the dry grass, crouching low down. The same hare had seen him for many days, and knew that he was harmless, although sometimes stones and small rounded objects were flicked a few paces into the air.

'Well, my lamb,' said Biddy when he got home, 'you be in a mess. Where 'ave ee been?'

'Find out, then you'll know, suck your finger, bite your toe!' he chanted, dancing round the table.

'Naw, midear, doan't ee be rude. You'm a proper limmer sometimes, you be! Naughty boy, that's what ee be.'

'I've been fighting,' he said, sitting down and allowing her to pull off his muddy boots.

His imagination was in full flood.

'Naughty boy. Who've ee been a-fighting on?'

'A low little gipsy boy. He called me a oddmedodd, like Jim puts up to scare the rooks. I gave him a black eye, and tapped his claret. Feel my muscle!'

Frowning, and with lips compressed, he clenched his fist and slowly drew his forearm up. Biddy felt it gingerly, as she did

31

four or five times a day, with her finger and thumb. It was possibly the size of a half-grown bean pod.

'Not bad, eh? I gave him socks. Knocked him into a ditch. He ran like hell!'

'Hush, ye mustn't speak so!'

'Big Will'um du,' lapsing into the dialect of the labourers.

'That ee doan't!'

'That ee du!' mimicking her. Big Will'um, a widower, was rumoured to be courting Biddy, and had been for over ten years. It was not yet known to the village, ever untired of waiting for a bit of gossip and information, if he were accepted, or had yet to declare himself. The number of tarts and meat pies that he had consumed in that period was considerable.

'I'll tell ees feyther!'

'Pouff, not you. You wouldn't be such a bliddy sneak.'

'If ees a naughty boy ee'll be a-whipped.'

'I don't care for a whipping, ye ould booger, you!'

Biddy had pulled off the other boot when his father called him. He heard him walking down the passage. The next moment he was looking round the door.

'Hullo, Willie. Been for a walk?'

'Yes, Father.'

'When are you going to Jack's?'

'At five o'clock, Father.'

'Mind you're a good boy, and don't pester Mr. Temperley with questions. And give him my kind regards.'

'Yes, Father.'

'Come and see me before you go, won't you, old fellow?'

'Yes, Father.'

The reserved man went away, and his son immediately brightened. He stood up in his stockinged feet.

'Naw give us a kiss, my lamb.'

He went to her, kneeling on the ground, and threw his arms round her neck.

'Dear Biddy,' he whispered, 'I do love you, awfully.'

32

'Naw then, miboy, naw then,' crooned the apple-faced Biddy.

'Biddy!' excitedly.

' 'Es, midear?'

'I like Jim Holloman.'

'Ooh naw, ooh naw!' cried Biddy, jumping up in wrath, for she never failed to be roused to anger when that name was mentioned.

'Ooh, naw—ee be a proper vagrant, and a grawbey[1] that ee be. Let 'un come 'ere, I'll show ee!'

'He's a nice bloke,' persisted Willie.

Biddy bustled up to him as though she would box his ears, and he fled from the room. Upstairs, in his bedroom, he tore off his old clothes and proudly donned his new suit. A very swagger affair, this new suit, chosen by himself at the store at Rookhurst. Save for the fact that the sleeves were three inches too short for his long arms, and that it must have been designed for a boy with a barrel instead of a body, it was a very good fit. The pattern, Willie thought, was both distinguished and note-worthy, consisting as it did of broad gray herring-bones running in wide lines up and down the coat, each line being separated from its neighbour by alternate streaks of red and green. Willie, thinking of the sportsmen who went riding over Colonel Tetley's estate, had scorned trousers and insisted upon having breeches, with buttons and not a buckle, and these had been specially made, of a vivid check pattern. The tailor had cut them with an eye to the boy's eventual growth, for they would not have been too small for a lad of fourteen. Willie was very proud of them—they looked horsey. Perhaps people would think he was a famous jockey, for jockeys were small, as he had read in the *Thuddenblunder Series of Thrilling Stories for Boys!*

He fastened the buttons, pulled on stockings and shoes and ran downstairs. Outside his father's study he suddenly stopped.

[1] Sneakthief

It was such a gloomy place inside, and he always made him feel afraid. Then Biddy came along the passage to bring his father the letters that had just arrived, and he followed her timidly.

Mr. Maddison was writing at his desk, and called out to his son:

'Well, Willie, let's have a look at you. Lucky boy, going to a party!'

Willie crept out from behind the protection of the housekeeper, and stood before him.

The father stared, the son fidgeted one foot with the other in an endeavour to conceal his breeches. He felt that any minute they would fall to the ground in a great heap. His father still stared. At last he spoke, in a voice that his son realised to be favourable.

'Good Heavens, Biddy, where did you get those awful things?'

Biddy answered quickly, and in the tone that she always used when talking to him about the boy—slightly antagonistic:

'Wullie chose um, zur, and real proper I consider um to be. The wearing of um gives Wullie pleasure, Mr. Madd'zun, and I axe ye to 'member that ye axe me to tend to all of ees clout!'

'My dear Mrs. Crane, I don't want my child to get the reputation of being a bookmaker or a desperado at such an early period of his life. Just fancy a boy of his age with check breeches—with that wide cut, too! Don't you think yourself that it is absurd?'

'It pleases the little dear, zur.'

Willie was wondering, in misery, if he would have to take them off. All the joy that he had felt at the thought of the party had gone. His mouth began to tremble, and he blinked quickly, terrified lest his father should see his tears and call him a coward, and a weakling.

'Well, *I've* no objection to what he wears—it's your affair, not mine. Ruin the boy, only don't blame me when you've done it.'

34

Biddy answered, and then went out of the room in a huff. Willie was pulling the ears of Fidelis the spaniel, while Bob the terrier was rolling on his back and kicking his legs into the air.

'Now I expect you want to get along. Come and say good-night, and then be off.'

Willie went forward, and shyly held out his right hand as he had done every evening as long as he could remember. Very rarely had his father kissed him.

'Good-night, Father,' he said.

'Good-night, Willie,' said his father, looking at him and smiling. Willie smiled back, as shyly and nervously as his father had smiled at him. His father hesitated, as though about to caress his son, but something in his eyes, a shrinking almost, made him say quickly:

'Now toddle along, and be good. See you to-morrow. Good-night, old fellow.'

'Good-night, Father,' said Willie respectfully, and walked sedately to the door, which he opened eagerly, and closed with a bang, rushing away down the passage to dance in the kitchen because it was now time to leave and go to Jack's house.

Chapter 3

SKIRR FARM was a long, low building. It had been in the possession of the Temperley family for over two hundred years, and for more than half that period it was on record that a pair of barn owls had nested, every spring and summer, on the rafters under the thatch. Part of the original walls had been rebuilt, and more than a score of times the wheaten straw had been laid afresh over the roof. In spring the stares whistled and cluttered on the chimney stacks, or shivering their wings, called from the gables. Under the broad eaves they had their homes, using old nesting holes that had seen many generations of bronze-winged birds into the summer sunshine. The house was surrounded by a large garden on three sides, and by an orchard on the fourth. At the bottom of the orchard the brook ran, in whose light-burthened waters the roach and dace swam in shoals, often pursued by the pike that lived their lurking life behind the weed beds.

There were only two rooms on the ground floor, with the exception of the kitchen, which had been added comparatively recently by Jack's great-grandfather. The one room was rarely used, containing as it did all the best furniture of the house in crowded profusion, an age-worn spinet that tinkled hymn-tunes on Sundays, and dozens of portraits, faded photographs, whalebone hunting-whips and silver buttons, mounted foxes' masks and otter pads, stuffed birds in glass cases, china vases, bowls, pallid waxen flowers under glass domes, all the accumulated heirlooms of generations.

The living-room was the larger of the two, floored with red tiles, and having a wide open fireplace on which the pine logs blazed and crackled. There were wrought-iron fire-dogs at each corner. The walls were whitewashed, the ceiling crossed by oaken beams, black with age and smoke. Two old blunderbusses, clean and polished, hung on nails driven into the side of one of the beams, and these were objects much coveted by the two boys. Often had they planned to steal them, procure some gunpowder and shot, and lie in wait for the dab-chicks and moor-hens that came out of the reeds around the lake and fed like little black corks bobbling on the water.

Two casements were let into the walls facing east and west, with rusted hasps that creaked when the leaded panes were swung back. If the wind blew from the east, the trailing vines of jasmine tap-tapped gently on the glass, and when it swept the clouds from the west strongly the branches of the cherry-tree just touched the other window.

On the stone in front of the fireplace the figures 1427 had been recut, as the original date of the erection of the house had long since been swept away by the besoms of many housewives and their sturdy daughters.

In the far corner of the room stood a grandfather clock. It was said to be as old as the house, but no one knew; the lettering on the face of it had long ago been rubbed away by human hands correcting the wrought-iron hands of time. Its case was built of yew, blackened in maturity and bored in the sap-wood by insects; many times its face had been restored, often by the amateur attempts of its owners, but the works were the original ones. Opening the case, one saw the rudely-fashioned pendulum on its pitted iron swing, and by looking closely at the graven brass framework, dulled and covered with deposit, it was possible to discern the scratched figures 1798, which date denoted the last time it had been sent away to the clock-makers at Colham for an overhaul. Its tick was impressive and eternal; the clock rarely stopped. The reckoning was faulty, and liable to be an hour fast or an hour slow at any time during the day or the night, but it was the treasured possession of

Skirr. Every dawn for centuries it had seen the darkness paling before the flowing light, the room filled with spectral atoms not thrown in one direction, but moving in invisible silence everywhere. The sun had sent its broad beams through the elm-trees in the morning, casting instant shadows behind them, had swung through lucent space, and lacquered the room with gold, changing at sunset to a purpurate red. One by one the stars had crept into the profundity of night, brilliant in winter and dusky in summer; the moon swam over the old hills, swollen and hazed with lavender and yellow; the great herald of night changing her blazoned shield, with its battle scars showing so dimly, from *or* to *argent* as it was carried into the higher solitudes of heaven. Sometimes its ghost rose before the dawn, a pale feather floating upwards and followed by the morning star Eosphoros, the light-bringer; at other seasons it sank beyond the wheat plains of the west as the stars commenced their faint tremulous music with the wind in deepest space. The seasons had passed with invisible feet across the savannas of infinity: the wistfulness of spring, the gold and glory of summer, the fires and abandon of autumn, the snows and frosts of winter. Those who had turned the clock's rusty key had done so as youths, sturdy men, then as old and bent men, their years spent in wresting a livelihood from the stubborn and unaffectionate earth. Its tarnished hands had pointed the hour and the minute in joy and sorrow, merriment and quarrel; they had seen blood spilled in anger and lamented in remorse; gnarled and shrunken hands had pointed at its green dial; tiny creased hands, not long unfolded into life, touching the cheek of ecstatic mother, had waved in glee to hear its irregular 'tick-tock, tick-tackle, tock'. All the light and shade of the years, the bloom and scent of the seasons, the colour and contour of the meadows and trees had passed, to be renewed eternally, and still the old clock kept intermittent record.

Chapter 4

BEFORE THE fire two little boys were sitting, talking in rapturous whispers. Between them was a roaster, and two fowls were turning slowly on the spit. Now and again Dolly, the maid, would come in from the kitchen and baste with an iron spoon. The little boys looked on approvingly.

The flames of the wood browned the birds, the grease hissed faintly, falling into the dripping pan beneath. Pine logs, they were, and gave to the tender flesh the odours of summer and the scent of the mornings.

Willie sniffed joyously.

'Fine, eh, man?'

Jack wriggled.

'We must catty some wild duck by the lake, and bake 'em in an oven of clay, like the gipsies do, eh, man?'

'Or some of the carp!'

'We must lay night lines!'

'Creep out at night and bait them, too!'

'If we're copped there'll be a rumpus.'

'They won't cop us!'

The flames lit the room, and dark shadows played mysteriously on the beams of the ceiling. The two conspirators spoke in whispers, thrilling with the daring and wonder of it all.

'Feel hungry, man?'

'Not half, man.'

Willie leaned nearer his friend, his check breeches creaking at the knee. He felt that he wanted to dance with happiness. Then his face grew important with the great secret he was going to tell.

'I say, Jack.'

'Yes?'

'Jim Holloman is going to show me how to snare rabbits!'

He spoke slowly, to allow Jack to realise fully the importance of his words.

The effect was more than he had desired. Jack sprang up, nearly knocking the roaster over as he did so.

'I say, how ripping. When? Did he really promise? Won't it be ripping! Do you think he's kidding? Have you got the wire yet?'

They talked on, Jack listening with bright eyes to Willie's plans. They were going to be real poachers. Willie was to be chief poacher. Jack could be second in command, only he must obey without murmur. Charlie Cerr-Nore could join if he liked, and be a private soldier, but not Jack's sisters. Girls were no good. They were soppy.

Their stealthy talk was interrupted by Dolly, who came in to lay the table. She carried a paraffin hand-lamp, which she set on the broad window-ledge. A great lamp hung suspended from the central beam, and this she lit, first trimming the wick with care, for it required skill to prepare it so that a full and even flame burned at the base of the tall chimney. This done, she came to the fire and basted the fowls with the iron spoon, curved of handle. Her other hand stroked Willie's hair, while Jack looked on with faint hostility. Willie liked Dolly, and Jack disliked her, mostly for this reason. She also teased him whenever she could. Dolly stroked Willie's cheek, then kissed him; she was a pretty girl, with brown eyes, sometimes gentle like those of the little fellow she caressed, but usually with a roguish shine. Her voice was deep and liquid, with a suspicion of huskiness that always made men turn and look at her whenever she spoke. She often said that she couldn't abear young men, who were only fit to hop over the 'vores'[1] and gulp down

1 Furrows

ale at harvest time. She was unpopular with some of the village women, who called her a hussy.

'Get out, Dolly, we're talking. You're not wanted!' said Jack, snorting.

'Naw then, I'll box ees ears for um, saucy boy.'

'Beast and fool!'

'I'll lick ee!'

She went towards him, but he slipped under the table, and from that security jeered and taunted.

When she had gone from the room to fetch the knives and the silver, Jack came forth, moving rapidly on his hands and knees with a motion like a frog, and protested against his friend's soppiness.

But Willie would not listen to him, although inwardly he felt ashamed for being kissed. When Dolly kissed him he felt he was in love with her, and he would rather have died than any one should know it. He only felt himself to be in love when Dolly was actually near him; when she was out of the room he forgot all about her.

Soon the long heavy oaken table was laid, and the browned fowls taken from the spit and laid in a dish that had been warming near the fire. Jack's two sisters, Doris and Margaret, came downstairs with a rush, followed by their father and mother.

Mrs. Temperley kissed Willie, saying that she had not known that he was there.

'I crept in the window, and nearly choked Jack before he knew I was here.'

'You didn't,' protested his friend. 'I pretended not to hear.'

'Oh, you great liar!'

'You liar! Of course I heard you.'

'That you didn't. You were caught unawares.'

Mr. Temperley interrupted.

'Don't quarrel, you two boys. Come and sit up. Willie, you haven't said good-evening to my daughters.'

'Oh, how are you?' he hastened to say to them, holding out a frail paw. In their turn the two girls clasped the extremity of his third finger and murmured that they were quite well. With a sigh of relief the visitor left them, and sat down beside his friend. The girls were shy, feeling themselves to be insignificant in the company of one who wore such grown-up breeches.

There was another quarrel in a few minutes, because Jack had received only a wing instead of a luscious leg. His mother scolded him with her usual gentleness, but he continued to whine about it until his father stopped carving, and looked at him. Then he was quiet.

The family ate on. Permission being given, the boys picked the bones up in their fingers and sucked them, sighing with delight as they did so.

After supper, Dolly came in to clear the table, Mr. Temperley sat in his arm-chair and smoked, his wife sat opposite to him and watched her son's every movement, the boys sprawled before the fire, now sunken to a glowing mass of embers, Doris and Margaret linked arms and sat against their mother's chair.

Doris fidgeted for a while, as though eager to ask something, but feeling nervous of doing so. She nudged her sister, Peggy, then whispered to her mother, the watchful Jack immediately telling her with the dignity of his eighteen months' seniority, that it was rude to whisper. But her mother replied: 'If you like, dear,' in an encouraging tone, so she said in a quick, timid voice:

'Please, Willie, will you tell us a story?'

Willie breathed deeply. He had been waiting to be asked for a story. With a careless air he said:

'Oh, I don't know any. Besides, I can't tell stories.'

'Oh, you can, Willie, you know you can!' said the little girls together.

Willie was famous for his stories. His imagination led him into wild soarings, and often he gave them as his own personal reminiscences. If he was to be believed, in his short life he had fought a bandit in the woods one dark evening; stopped an express train from being wrecked by robbers by waving a red shirt on the line, the express pulling up six inches before himself heroically refusing to move from the track; discovered a cave in the woods where strange men were 'brewing' whisky and coining sovereigns with 'ally' (that was his term); and once he had achieved greatness by writing a letter to the local newspaper stating that he had seen a large bird, which he recognised as a South American condor, carry off a sheep on the downs.

After much persuasion, and repeated requests from the girls, he still wriggled and protested that he was no good at stories. So Jack suggested Tiddlywinks, and Willie immediately remembered a story.

'This is quite true,' he began, 'it was told to me last winter by a wandering gipsy——'

'What was?' asked Jack quickly.

'Oh, please don't interrupt,' pleaded Margaret.

Willie paused. Only when the girls had asked him three times did he condescend to continue.

'It was a curious sperience altogether. "Billo!" I said, and ducked my nut, as the report shattered the silence. I wondered who would be shooting at the gipsy, but luckily I had my catty with me. "Don't move," I said to the gipsy, who was quaking with fear. "I will soon have him out of his liar."

'Out of his *what*?' asked Mrs. Temperley.

'His liar. It is liar, isn't it? Anyhow, it means a hiding-place. It said liar in the bo——' He stopped just in time.

'But who was shooting, and why?' grumbled Jack. 'It's a silly story.'

'It isn't—it's thrilling,' said Doris, snuggling closer to her mother.

'Don't you see,' Willie went on, 'it would be obvious even to the biggest fool that the gipsy, who was wandering in the wood, was a royal prince, disguised. The shooter was tracking him, one of the band of the Bloody Hand!'

'The Bloody Hand,' he repeated, rolling the words out slowly and distinctly, and glancing at the girls to see the effect, 'for upon a piece of paper pinned to a tree was the mark of bloody fingers. The gipsy's cheeks blanched when he saw it. "I am undone," he gasped, frozen in horror to the ground "They have found me." But I had my catty, and taking careful aim at a figure I saw dimly in the green leaves——'

'It must have been winter if he was frozen,' interrupted Jack sourly. He could never think of a story himself, try as he might.

'All right, then,' said Willie. 'I won't tell you any more.'

'Oh, please, dear Willie,' urged the girls.

'All right then. Now I come to think of it, the figure wrapped in a long cloak, was crouching under the evergreens. I shot, and a howl of pain came from the bushes. There was a splash, and a blood-curdling shriek.'

His voice dropped. 'When we went over to the lake, we saw nothing. He had sunk into the mud. And,' he spoke in a whisper, 'there his bones lie at this moment.'

The little girls hugged each other, their mouths drooping in terror. Then something passed the window outside, a throaty 'skir-r-r' came from the darkness, and Doris shrieked.

'Willie, you bad boy,' scolded Mrs. Temperley, 'the girls won't sleep a wink. It's only the owl, my darlings,' to the shivering children, 'and don't believe the story.'

Jack was grinning delightedly. Willie leapt up and rushed to the window, his diabolical fiction forgotten. Beautiful phantom owls, crying so mysteriously: they made him shiver with excitement!

A few minutes later Jack used his new swear word 'damhell', and so displeased his father. Bellowing with mortification he was sent to bed. Willie felt ashamed, for Doris and her sister had said that they dared not go upstairs, for fear of a man there with a cloak and a dagger, Mrs. Temperley told her husband that she would put them to bed, and opening the door, called to Dolly to bring some more logs. But Dolly was nowhere to be found.

'Where is the girl, I wonder?' she said to him. 'That's the second time she has gone out without permission.'

Five minutes later Willie slunk behind her as she went up-stairs, thinking that he would go to bed with Jack rather than stay with Mr. Temperley, who spoke so seldom and whose light-blue eyes seemed to glare at him. In anticipation of his coming Jack had placed a can of water on the door, in such a position that the moment it was moved a cold sluice would descend on the unsuspecting entrant. Unfortunately for himself, the can fell on the wrong side, where he was crouching in readiness to taunt his victim. Alarmed by the noise his father came up-stairs, and saying that he would end his nonsense quickly, proceeded to whip him. The cries of the unhappy boy brought his mother in, followed by the little girls who sobbed unre-strainedly declaring that there was a man in their bedroom with a dagger and piercing eyes.

Snug in the same bed, Jack and Willie talked in whispers, seeing the new moon through the window, and hearing the cries of owls far away in the mysterious night.

Chapter 5

WHEN DOLLY had cleared the table, she returned to the kitchen and sat down on a wooden chair. Almost immediately she arose, and stared at the stone floor as though wanting to do something, but not daring to do it.

She thought that the family would not want her for another half-hour at least, and that she might safely go out for that period, not longer, as she had arranged that afternoon when returning from Rookhurst village by the footpath across the fifty-acre wheatfield.

Behind the kitchen door hung her coat, and this she lifted off the rail and put on. Then she went to the closed door and listened. She smiled as she stood there with her head on one side, for the funny little tacker with the brown eyes and high cheek bones—she was an observant girl—was telling the master and missus that Jim Holloman was a fine fellow, and knew all the birds and the stars, and was not a grawbey as Biddy said he was.

Dolly did not like Biddy, for Biddy hated her, and showed it whenever she saw her. Biddy's hate was the sole cause of Dolly's dislike. Her temperament was such that dislike was ready at any moment to be changed into liking, if only Biddy could cease talking about her and saying nasty things.

'She bean't no good—a loose 'un, her be,' was Biddy's summing up of Dolly's character, as the other women in the village had told her, making a point at the same time of assuring her that she should take no notice. Their kindly advice was possibly meant when it was said, but whenever Biddy held forth on the subject of Dolly invariably they agreed with her,

46

and were always ready to add any information they had garnered either first, second, third or fourth hand. But they could not understand the cause of Biddy's hate. She was jealous because Willie liked Dolly.

Dolly tiptoed away from the door, and then realising the necessity of making some noise, she moved several plates on the table. The next moment she had lifted the latch, which seemed to click very loudly, opened the door, closed it quietly, and passed away into the darkness towards the Big Wheatfield. This was a field originally owned by the Maddison family, who had built Fawley House in the fifteenth century after a migration from the Border country. It stretched behind Skirr Farm up to the sky-line half its length away, when its farther half dipped gradually into the valley beyond. A right of way went through the middle, passing on the ridge a small circular spinney honeycombed with rabbits' holes.

From a crowstarver's point of view, the spinney was situated in an ideal position. It commanded a view down the slopes of the field, and this was essential if the rooks, jackdaws, hoody crows, and occasional sea-gulls were to be prevented from uprooting and swallowing the winter-sown corn. Although the art of crowstarving dated from great antiquity, it was not one requiring much skill or tuition. The chief duty of the crowstarver was to give by his voice and clappers some suggestiveness of life to the oddmedodds placed in various parts of the field; these consisted of dummy figures leaning at all angles, tins containing stones and suspended on string, and swung potatoes with rook feathers stuck in them. Sometimes a rook or a daw was shot, in which case it was hung sweeing from a stick as a warning to its more fortunate and indifferent brethren.

The erection of oddmedodds was one of the lesser occupations of Jim Holloman. In the spinney he had several old zinc baths nailed to trees, and a short length of iron rail hanging from a low branch, upon which he thumped and banged from early dawn till sunset, whenever birds alighted on the field.

For this service he received the sum of seven shillings a week. The period of crowstarving lasted for three months, but he was rarely without work. Often he did the work of a hedger and ditcher, split wood for people, acted as gardener's casual help to some of the houses round about, joined the mowers in June, the reapers in August; then there was the picking of hops in September, followed by work among the root crops and potatoes, and crab-apples for jelly making; trapping rabbits in the winter for Mr. Temperley; a thousand and one jobs to be done. And always in the sweet open air, where the wind came free and strong, or gentle and laden with flower fragrance; the sun by day and the stars by night.

On the last evening of February, at eight o'clock, he was lying before the opening of his shelter in the spinney, hands supporting head, his large eyes staring into the fire. A pot lay on its side a few inches away from the edge of the fire, his sole cooking implement, while among the embers, blown bright and rapidly wasted by an intermittent wind, the remains of rabbit bones were slowly becoming red cinders. The shelter itself was a domed structure, covered with sods and overlaid with tree branches roughly pleached; it's floor lying about two feet below the surface. Within the shelter was a bed made of fir boughs, supported at each end by a crossbar laid on stakes driven into the ground. Potato sacks were flung over this springy mattress, used as blankets.

In appearance, the man who sprawled in the opening was very tall and thin. His hair and beard were auburn; his eyebrows drooped as though for ever he were meditating. His face had very little colour, except for the large and clear blue eyes which were so full that they ought to have been short-sighted, yet his sight was far as well as keen. He had great powers of endurance, but his physical strength was not great. In manner he was reserved, almost morose; he never visited the inn; the villagers said that he was mazed.

He had no friends among them, they treated him with

contemptuous indifference; the children shouted after him His only friend appeared to be Willie Maddison, who was reputed to be mazed as well, taking such an interest, as he did, in birds and animals. It was noticed, however, that the dogs never growled or barked at Jim Holloman, and this itself was argued by the shaggy, loud-mouthed labourers in the inn at night to be a sign that he was a witch—even the dogs were frightened to growl at him.

Jim Holloman's origin was a mystery. The little boy, his eyes red with weeping, had been found in the village one morning very early, when the sun sent its beams over the hills in the morning, and the mist of the valley still lay like the gathered ghosts of the yellow celandine and pale windflowers, whose life in the early spring was just ended. A label on his coat said 'Jimmy, c o Mr. Robert Lewis, Gamekeeper, Rookhurst.' Bob had taken care of him, whilst refusing to discuss the strange affair with anyone. As the boy grew up it was often remarked that he was like old Bob's dead son, both in looks and behaviour; he 'kept himself to himself', and seldom played with other boys in the village. Since he had often been seen peering in hedges, holding young birds in his hands, and doing other odd things, it was decided by some that he was a white witch. Once he was thrown in a horsepond by some drunken ploughboys; then he had run away from his home for over a week. At fourteen years of age he left school, and not liking gamekeeping, he went to work for Farmer Turney. Usually he felt the last of the whip, and often the dull thud of the butt, for he had ever been considered indolent, especially in the spring-time, lying by the brook, or wandering along the hedges, all alone.

When he reached the age of fifteen, he had left the village but had returned some years later, calling himself Jim Holloman. His return was met with guarded surprise and many questions, but all he would say was that he had been away. In reality he had been working in Southampton, as a dock labourer, but had pined for the downs above Rookhurst, the

49

beech wood when autumn spread its colour after the corn was shocked and gathered, and the brook with its sparkle and gurgle by the pebbled shallow where the red cows stood in summer.

For years he had worked at odd jobs, saying little to those he worked for; making no friends among the heavy-booted ones or their ever-toiling wives. Now he was about twenty-five, and recognised by the village as a moucher; and two people were particularly interested in him—Willie, and Dolly the house-maid at Skirr.

He lay before the fire in which the rabbit bones were slowly being reduced to feathery ash. Beyond the glow, he could see the new moon, like a gold curven goose-quill, floating west-wards between the fir-trees.

The brittle skeletons of the fallen beech leaves trembled as the mice hurried by them, their feet pattering like small drops of rain shaken from the trees. The shrill lisps of the little trav-ellers, intent upon their life-long quest for food, sounded sharp and yet inaudible if deliberately listened to—needle-notes of sound scarce piercing the darkness. Over the crisp curled leaves they sped, stopping to gnaw a shoot of young grass, split open a beech mast, or seize a morsel of bread or potato in fore-paws and perching on hind legs, to nibble uneasily. Their lives were one long shadow of terror. By day the kestrel hawk hung still above the fields, his talons ever ready to grasp, his notched and hooked beak to rend; the weasel, rippling sinu-ously and low on the ground, followed remorselessly once he had scented a victim—to drive his sharp teeth into the base of the vole's skull. Then at night the ghost owl with broad winnowing wings glided by the edge of the spinney, his large dark eyes directed downwards; within the spinney came its brothers the wood owl, who hooted so mournfully. Sometimes the long-eared owl paid a visit, a tawny creature with two feathers sticking out of his head like the devil's horns. By day and by night great creatures made relentless war on the little mice and voles, nor were the rascally rats left in peace, except by the weasel, who feared their chisel-like teeth.

Jim Holloman knew all about the wild beasts and birds. Once or twice he had been seen to pick up a dead bird or butterfly, holding it in his hand for a minute or so, and then laying it gently down. The wise villagers, whom no man could cheat of a farthing, held him in great contempt for this—it bore out their opinion that he was mazed.

Creeping out of his shelter, he threw some more sticks upon the fire, then walked to the edge of the spinney. His footfalls were nearly as silent as those of a fox as he went over the sandy soil, littered with pine spindles and tumuli of windrifted leaves. Kneeling down on the ground he listened intently.

He remained in this attitude for a few moments, then rose upright, his heart beating faster, and went behind a dwarfed beech, whose massy twisted bole completely hid him.

Someone was walking along the footpath, slowly and hesitatingly. Jim kept quite still, his hands pressed against the smooth bark of the tree. He heard the steps pause, go on again for a few yards, stop altogether. A voice called, soft and low:

'Jim Holloman.'

He did not answer. The needle squeaks of the field mice were shrill and insistent whenever the wind lifted its veil above the million tongues of the firs. Again the voice floated over, clear and beautiful.

He did not move. She called his name once more:

'Jim—Jim Holloman. Where be ee, Jim Holloman?'

Dolly came nearer. He could see her, an indistinct blur with a haziness of white that was an apron under her coat, about twenty yards away.

The blur became more indistinct, the sound of boots slipping on wet loamy soil came to him. A dull pain went into his heart. He started forward, as though to run after her, and speak tenderly to her—a thing he had often wanted to do, but never had done yet—but the inward voice that had bade his tongue be still when she had called his name so softly held him back.

The wind sighed in the fir-trees with a sound of music high in heaven, the dead beech-leaves spun and risped over the sand, and Dolly had gone away.

He swore at himself fiercely, yet hugging the dull pain in his heart, walking quickly back to his lonely shelter. Hardly caring where he went, he bumped into the suspended piece of track rail, which vibrated softly at the impact of his head. His hands went up to his forehead, and he sat beside the fire which was now burning brightly.

'Dem vool, you dem vool,' he groaned, grasping his hair savagely in his fit of self-hating.

Suddenly he looked up, his eyes wide open. A cry of despair had come from the night, followed by silence lasting but a moment; another scream, not so violent this time, but the piteous cry of some creature that knew its life was about to be crushed out.

Jim leapt to his feet and padded in the direction whence the scream had come. He knew exactly when to drop on his hands and knees, and beat the earth with his hands, and shout out to frighten the weasel that had caused the scream. His eyes, trained to see the slightest movement at night, saw it move not a yard from him, then ripple silently away.

He found the thing that had screamed. It was a brown field mouse. Carrying it in his hand, he went back to the fire. It looked at him with its black, brimming eyes, from which the brightness had already gone. Slowly the tiny head drooped to one side. He propped it up in the palm of his hand, it made no resistance or effort to escape. Behind its head there was a jagged bite, where the teeth of the weasel had nearly severed the spinal column. With his forefinger he stroked the soft head, and felt the transparent silk-like ears; its body was soft and warm.

'What's the good of life, eh, mousie? You've been made a

perfect little body, yet no one cares if you'm killed or not—you eat corn and peas, and others eat you.'

Then, realising that his ponderings about the indifference shown to all things on the earth led him only to despair, he threw the dead rodent in the fire, and crept into his hole to lie on his bed. But sleep did not come till long after the golden goose-quill had dipped into the vast ink of blackness beyond the western rim of the world, for he was thinking about Dolly the maid at Skirr Farm; wondering why he had longed for her to come and see him, and then, when she had come, why he had felt that he wanted to hurt her, and himself as well.

The fire went out. Over the leaves the mice pattered, and along the furrows; a fox barked at a distant hooting owl, hunters both; westward swept the stars, and the night went on.

Chapter 6

ONE MORNING Willie rushed down the stairs in a hurry, nearly killing old Fidelis, who had been standing at the bottom for two minutes without moving.

'Look out, Fidelis, you old fool,' he shouted, but Fidelis looked up at him with such a mournful expression in his filmy eyes that Willie knelt down beside him in remorse, and placed his arms around the dog. The tail of Fidelis moved slowly and wearily with a pendulum-like movement: he was immensely pleased. He had been waiting at the bottom of the stairway all the morning—waiting for this. Bob, the terrier, came along, and jumped around Willie, licking his face and ears indiscriminately. Fidelis growled, but Bob ignored him.

For a while the boy played with the dogs, giving most of his caresses to Fidelis, for he felt sorrow for his feebleness, but soon he leapt up and ran into the kitchen, followed by Bob the terrier.

Left alone, Fidelis stood on the mat, swaying slightly on his legs as though unable to grasp the fact that his young master had gone away from him.

'Biddy, give me some of that tart, please.'

Biddy, with flushed face, had just pulled a large treacle tart from the oven, and laid the tin upon some newspaper spread on the table.

'In a minute, my lamb,' crooned the cook. 'It be mortal hot now at present. Do ee like triccle-tart?'

Biddy knew he did, but nothing pleased her more than to hear her child say so.

'Um, rather, Biddy! I say, you are a sport, you know. Your tart's much better'n Dolly's at Mrs. Temperley's.'

'Hum, an' I should think so, naw! That there low 'ussy can't bake no tarts! All her be good for is to cheek the men and lead'n on!'

'She's lovely, Biddy, and I love her. And I know someone else who does, too!'

Biddy's face grew more flushed. For a moment she stood still and looked at him. Then she seized a dry dish-cloth and rushed at him, flicking at him with the cloth as though he were a black beetle or a spider.

'I'll tell ees feyther, that I wull! Naughty boy, ee'll be a-whipped.'

'Biddy's a devil, an old devil!' chanted the boy, dancing nimbly around the table.

'Bad boy. I'll a-whip ee, an' no tart shall ee 'ave!'

'Pooh, Dolly'll give me some. Old cat, bliddy old devilskin!'

Doubtless the dance and pursuit would have gone on till Biddy sat down and cried, to be met with remorse and endearments from the boy, had not Mr. Maddison suddenly come into the kitchen. He saw Biddy's red and angry face, his son with his spread fingers to his nose, his tongue out, and heard his calling her a devilskin.

At the sight of him both stopped. Biddy's face had assumed a look of hostility.

'Willie, come with me!'

The boy looked appealingly at Biddy, hesitated, then followed his father into the study.

Fidelis, who had just crept into the room in order to collapse easefully on the hearthrug, lifted his gray head and moved his tail, almost imperceptibly, once, in greeting.

'Sit down in that chair, Willie.'

His son sat down on the extreme edge, his palms moist, his throat suddenly dry. The seed of several excuses came instinctively to his mind, but would not blossom coherently.

'Willie,' said Mr. Maddison, leaning forward and resting his hands on his knees.

'Yes, Father?'

'Do you remember what I told you last time I caught you being rude to Biddy, and what I should do to you?'

Willie did not answer.

'Do you, Willie?' quietly and patiently.

'I don't know, Father.'

'Try to remember, Willie.'

He looked at his son, evidently trying to master his emotions. Those hands, with their long frail fingers, were twisting and rubbing—his mouth drooped at the corners—terror was in his eyes. Poor little fellow, he was terrified to death of his own father!

Then he realised that his own feelings had nearly mastered himself. He wanted to take him in his arms and nurse him as his mother would . . . his mother! Jenny was dead, gone for evermore: that child before him was a manifestation of Beauty, giving itself in death willingly by its sacrifice to achieve Life. That boy with Jenny's eyes was his son: his head was shaped like his own, though his eyes were that other's . . . his son did not love him—he was always unhappy in his presence. Never told him anything—and, that child, his only one, was frightened of him. Oh, the irony of parental endeavour, the un-understanding!

That damned woman Biddy was the cause of it all!

'I can't, Father.'

Suddenly he felt irritated, and hardness covered his emotion.

'I said I would thrash you if I caught you behaving in a rude manner to Biddy. Do you remember that?'

He rose from his chair. His son shrank back. Ignoring him, the father started to walk about the room. Fidelis looked up at him when he nearly trod on his outflung paw, as though saying: 'Master, why do you talk like that to your son? He was only playing when you came in. Is it that something went from your heart that evening when you sat here with your gun

56

loaded by your side, after She had passed into the night, although the window and the door were closed?'

'I beg your pardon, Father. I beg your pardon. I'm sorry, I'll never be rude any more. Please don't whip me, Father.'

The tears ran down his face, and his body shook. Fidelis rose up on shaky feet, and lurched wearily over to him, licking his hand.

Once more his tail resembled the pendulum of an exhausted clock. Mr. Maddison, his hands in his pockets, and looking on the ground, was about to tell him to go away: that he was a coward and not manly enough to bear punishment, or even a reprimand, when the door opened and Bob, the terrier, jumped into the room. In the doorway stood Biddy the cook.

'Well, Biddy?' he asked.

'A shame, I calls it, Mr. Maddyzun. Th' little dear were only funning. Doan't understan' chiller, you doan't, not nohow.'

Her eyes had lost their kindness; her hands clasping elbows, bare where the sleeves of the print blouse were rolled up; and although she felt bitterly incensed against him, she did not look angry. To appear so was beyond the good-hearted Biddy.

'You are impertinent, Mrs. Crane, and presume upon long association. You will pack your bags, and leave this afternoon.'

'That I woan't, Mr. Maddyzun. I'm here, and here I stays! Leastways, while th' little lamb be here.'

'Yes, I think that is a good name for him. Willie!' turning to his son, who was sitting quiet and shamed, in the chair. Fidelis was still standing there as though on duty.

'Yes, Father?'

'You will apologise to Biddy for your rudeness. Do you understand?'

'Yes, Father.'

'Now go, and try to be a man, not a whining puppy.'

Willie got up quickly and went out of the room. Biddy closed the door and followed.

'I beg your pardon for calling you rude names, Biddy,' he said, with head averted.

'That be all right, my lamb. Now give me a kiss.'

But Willie opened the door, and ran through the garden to the footpath beyond, which led to Jack's house. He hated his father.

He found Jack trying to cut with a rusty saw an ash branch into logs when he reached the farmhouse. All the morning Jack had been engaged upon this work, making but meagre progress. It was punishment for breaking a window. Again and again he had applied beef-dripping to the blade in an endeavour to ease his task, but it would not cut properly. It frequently stuck, and each time this happened, he said: 'It's bloody blunt you know, that's the trouble,' out loud, there being no one in the immediate vicinity. He felt rather magnificent as he did so.

Seeing Willie, he abandoned his purgatory, and ran towards him.

'I say, man, I'm so glad you've come. Let's go out in the woods!'

'Rather! We won't take the girls!'

'No jolly fear!'

'We'll build a fire.'

'And see Jim!'

'Oh, how fine, man.'

'Come on, man!'

Jack flung the saw into a ditch and kicked the beef-dripping violently in the same direction, but it shot diagonally from his line of propulsion, and a small piece stuck to the visitor's cheek. Willie clawed it from his face, and tore after Jack, who was racing towards the distant woods.

In the meadow the tame bees from skep and hive were crawling over the bright yellow flowers of the celandine. Their petals were bright as with gold-dust, varnished and gleaming, and stained at the hub whence radiated the petal-spokes. The spiders had come from their long winter sleep, and their airy prospecting lines, breathed along by the warm south wind, shone and glistened; busy in the short grass were the blackbirds; in the hedge a robin sang; above trilled a lark, striving with fluttering wings to lose itself in the blue vision of reawakened heaven.

The fresh smell of the stirring earth was borne with the wind; although the dog-violets raised on slender stems had no scent, yet they too gave forth an essence that spoke to the two children, for suddenly, without any reason or cause, they flung out their arms, kicked their legs into the air, and shouted.

The humble bee was stirring from her rest in the dry ditch, the sun had sent its message of life and work to her, deep among the moss. Far over the wastes of the sea the call had gone forth: even now, the birds of passage were restless and waiting for an inward urging to send them across that remorseless sea; soon the chiff-chaffs and willow warblers would arrive, with wings that looked weak and for short flight only, not capable of the sustained journey of thousands of miles; pied wheatear and the gray-black sand-martin, then the bluebacked swallow and later the whole joyous family of warblers, white-throats, swifts, cuckoos, and pipits would follow and fill the sweet air with one waterfall murmur of song. Soon, too, the windflowers would fleck the woods as with light fallen from the moon, white when the wind has burnished its shield among the stars. . . . From the sun came the unseen messages to still seed and sleeping butterfly-grub; the sap rose in the grasses and in the rugged oak-trees; bird and flower, tree and butterfly—so every year life came again from the gross earth—the return of fabled Proserpine with song and colour in her wake.

They passed through the hay meadow, crept under the stile in correct poacher fashion, ran across the water meadow and over a thrown willow that had been felled to form a bridge across the swift brook with its bubbled eddy of brown leaves and waving green grasses pressed flat by the current, and ran up the farther field to the beech wood.

The torch-like buds of the beech were still wrapped in their fibrous covers; their time was not yet, for the pheasants had not begun to lay. The boys did not go to the field which every year saw the yeaning of the lambs, but walked through the forest till they came to the preserve.

The preserve was a place of romance and mystery to them. The ancient guardian of Colonel Tetley's coverts was eighty years old, and had known the wood for seventy of them, as his father had been keeper before him, and during that time he had had many affrays with poachers. Then he remembered the time when man-traps were laid in the wood to catch trespassers; when they carried guns with sawn-off barrels to shoot pheasants, and if disturbed, keepers as well; when the ravens and buzzards built in the dark North Side pine forest.

They went along the footpath through the hazel wands, the soft earth imprinted many times and beaten flat by the hobnailed boots of Ned, the under-keeper. And they had not gone far when they saw him ambling along in front.

He turned and waved the stick that he always carried. He was a dark, lithe, short man with black eyes and hair, and a scanty black moustache. His complexion was sallow, owing to his gipsy strain—his teeth were strong, firm, and yellow, like old ivory—such teeth last a lifetime. He knew the two boys well, for last year the Colonel had given them permission to go anywhere on his estate, except during the critical period in April when the pheasants were laying and a search was made to collect their eggs to place them under brooding hens in the protected rearing field.

'Hullo, Ned,' they said in unison.

The smart under-keeper nodded. He was a silent man, and spoke usually in monosyllables. He only talked much after six pints of ale, when he was liable to be quarrelsome upon slight pretext.

'Old Bob about?'

'Ah.'

'Where?'

'Field,' and he pointed with the hazel wand in the direction they were going.

'Heard the chiff-chaff yet?'

'Um.' He shook his head and showed his splendid teeth.

'Trapped any more stoats?'

'Ah!' His eyes gleamed.

'Can we have 'em to skin?'

'Um stink,' and again he showed his teeth.

'Seen any squirrels about lately?'

It was Willie who asked. He had never found a squirrel's drey, and it was one of the ambitions of his life.

'Um.' He shook his head.

They found the head-keeper sitting beside his hut under the larch trees, which had put forth bright-green shoots, and here and there the tiny reddish cones glowed on the knotted twigs. A sweet little whispering call came from above, and a female long-tailed tit flitted to her mate seeking for spiders in a pollard oak near. Old Bob was listening to their rapturous twitterings. His cap was off, for he loved the sunshine, and laid across his knee; a few silvery hairs, like the silk threads of a dandelion 'clock', still remained on his head. He did not wear a beard, nor was ever noticed to be clean-shaven, but always a white thin stubble grew on his face. The exposure to winds and rain had tanned his cheeks till they were the colour of an acorn; under the tangled and drooping brows his pale blue eyes, misted by age, looked almost vacantly at the boys. But the brain behind was not vacant, but versed in the lore of flower and bird; none so learned as he. He knew when the early visitors would arrive; when the 'guckoo' would first call from the uplands, and the nightingale sing its early liquid notes as the damp warmness of an April evening hung over hazel bud and færie bluebell. Although so old, he worked at the rearing field in May and June, feeding the chicks himself, rising at half-past four to do so. He was always ready to talk about the wild things, and what was most remarkable for a keeper, he never shot kestrel hawks, jays, jackdaws, or owls, which the keepers on the neighbouring estates invariably did. They had neither the knowledge nor the heart of Bob Lewis.

A patch of ground in the churchyard, long since levelled by the years, was the resting place of his wife. Among the leaning stones in spring grew sweet-violet, primrose, celandine, and daffodil; in summer the crane's-bill, daisy, buttercup, speed-well, eye-bright—wild flowers so beautiful when seen with the eyes of love. The dead woman had been mother of one babe, who had grown into a tall auburn-haired youth, helping Old Bob in the coverts and rearing field; Harry had a passion for reading, and the Colonel's young wife used to lend him books, often bringing them herself to the keeper's cottage in the forest. She came to the rearing field as well, sometimes early in the morning, to watch the chicks running to the scattered feed. Old Bob remembered that once he had found her in tears by the boat-house; someone had left her as he approached. He told his wife about it, and she said that it was no business of Bob's. It was said the Colonel was as unhappy as she was; and when the Colonel went north to the grouse moors in August that year, she did not go with him, but went elsewhere. When she returned the pheasant shooting was over, and in the coverts the windflowers were trembling in the April wind. Many things were said among the low-voiced cottage women at their doors. Harry had left his home, and had gone—ah, and who with him? The Squire's young wife came no more to the cottage among the pine trees, and when another year's chicks were hatched in May her feet left no green tracks in the silver grasses of the dewy field. Years afterwards it was still being said that Harry had gone to London, to seek fame as a writer; some of his 'writin'' had been 'seen on th' papers'; and one day the rumour came that he had died there. Bob

Lewis never mentioned his dead son; nor did the Colonel.

'Good morning, Mr. Lewis,' said the boys.

'Eh, ooh?' replied the ancient, peering at them under his thatch-like eyebrows. 'Ah, it be young gennulmen! Marnin', midears.'

He leaned forward on his chair, putting his weight on a massive stick of oak, once a young sapling.

'Isn't the sunshine lovely, Mr. Lewis?'

'Eh, ooh? 'Zactly! Naw then, that little willow-bird'll be yurr soon. Saw a bumblehum s'marnin'. Oo ay!'

He gave the information about the humble bee with great satisfaction and in a cracked voice, wheezy as the mildewed leather bellows of the chapel harmonium that Big Will'um's feet worked clumsily while vamping with the raucous choir every Sunday afternoon.

Then he chanted softly:

> 'A swaam o' bees in May
> Be worth a field o' hay
> A swaam o' bees in Joo-un
> Be worth a zilver spoo-un,
> A swaam o' bees in Joo-lye
> Bean't worth a fly.'

'Eh, young gennulmun? What say, miboy? Bean't worth a vly, hey?'

And he shook his silvery head, clutched the stick firmly, and rose to his feet, saying, 'Noomye! Bean't worth a vly, they bant!'

Willie looked at his gaiters, which were made of thick cloth, fawn-coloured, and buttoned loosely. He wondered if he could manage to get a pair like that. Quickly he calculated. His weekly allowance of twopence was due on the morrow, and there was sevenpence in his drawer at home. If only he could persuade Jack to buy his rotten leather belt for two shillings, because it was so stiff that it made his hips sore and the swivels stuck into him whenever he crawled like an Indian, in a very short time he might be able to buy a pair of leggin's! Jack might be a decent man and buy the belt: it was almost new, and—jingo—what was . . . *that*?

Old Bob Lewis stiffened suddenly. Jack looked up, an alert expression in his eyes. Ned, the under-keeper, showed his yellow teeth in a grin, and nodded at Willie as though saying, 'I told you so,' when in reality what he tried to imply had never occurred to him. As for Willie, when his envious thoughts about the 'leggin's' had been interrupted by the 'chiff-chaff, chiff-chaff', piped thinly and monotonously by a small olive-brown bird upon a chestnut twig, his mouth had opened, and the next moment he was jumping and shouting.

'Hurray, hurray! Oh, Bob, he's here! Did you hear, Jack? the first chiff-chaff! Oh, Glory, Glory, Allelulia, my hat! He's come—ooh!' and he rolled on the beaten green of the path, joined immediately by a black retriever that hitherto had been dozing tranquilly in a bed of bracken near by. Old Bob Lewis was nodding his head, and smiling, his wan blue eyes peering at the tree.

'Aiy, aiy!' he said, 'li'l grass-bird be back, aiy, aiy!'

It was the first of the passage birds to be noticed in the covert. Across the great green dim sea it had travelled, with a million others, the forerunners of a joyous and ecstatic multitude soon to pass by way of the old Nile, as when Cleopatra dipped in its ancient waters; some falling into that dim uncaring sea, weary of wing, little fluttering things that they were; the survivors to arrive exhausted, yet soon refreshed to life and love in the sweet countryside whose beauty of dream-flax, though fail faith in friend and love of maid, is ever for those who would weave it.

Chapter 7

FROM THE wood across the meadow a continuous mellow call floated—*cuckoo, cuckoo, cuckoo*. The boys who had been sitting at the foot of a pollard ash in the corner of the field looked at one another. Then the smaller of the two jumped excitedly to his feet and said: 'Come on, Jack, there he is. Two days late this year. But I knew he'd come. By God, how lucky we didn't go to church, man!'

He started across the meadow, turning round repeatedly, and calling to his companion. But the man who was called Jack continued to sit still and finger his worm-jar.

'Wait for us, Willie; I must watch this worm.'

'Bah, you silly ass, if you don't come now it will be too late. I swear there will be an egg shortly, and I want to mark the place.'

Jack continued to gaze at a series of earth spirals that rose slowly out of the earth: in another moment, he felt sure, the worm itself would appear. And how could that fool Willie expect him to rush after a cuckoo, when at any second the worm might poke his head out of the moist earth!

'As I thought, it's a lob,' he said to himself, peering eagerly into the ground. A worm had thrust its pink head out among the green blades of grass. Jack tried to hold it with his finger and thumb, but it disappeared into the earth again. He sighed. It would have been a fine specimen, and just the kind he wanted for his bait-tub. Now where was that silly ass Willie?

His friend had walked quickly through the long green grass in the meadow, and entered the wood at the other side. He looked eagerly up into the trees, peering first one way, then

65

another, trying to distinguish the cuckoo. Suddenly he sat down under a tree and kept quite still.

In the wood he could see the primroses. The sight of all the flowers, and the warmth of the sun, filled him with a wild elation. He sprang up, and as he did so a largish bird, with a fan-shaped tail, for all the world like a hawk, flew out of an oak-tree where it had been perched, and went through the trees into the meadow. A few small birds uttered cries of alarm, and started in pursuit. They thought it was a hawk, and hawks are driven away frantically. The enemy flew straight on, and more joined in the futile chase, chirping, wheezing, and scolding. It was spring, and the cock-birds wished to show their respective mates that they scorned hawks —especially when they flew away, and there were many other birds about to join in as well.

Seeing his friend in the wood, he ran towards him. The feeling of happiness that had surged over him still remained, and when Jack had joined him he caught him by the arm, and gasped: 'Oh, Jack, isn't it all wonderful? Look, there's hundreds and thousands of primroses over there. Do let's come and get some. And I say, isn't it simply spiffing in this wood? We'll have such luck here later on, I'm sure. There's bound to be a hawk or two nesting here, and there may be a carrion crow! Oh, we'll make this the great egg season!'

'We must beat those Vicarage kids!' urged Jack.

Willie spat contemptuously. Charlie Cerr-Nore, old Pig-face! Of all the nerve, to try and emulate *him* in his knowledge of birds, and where to find their nests! Why, Jack and he alone knew more than any other boy in the village, and besides, didn't all the birds belong to them? Pouff, the Vicarage kids simply weren't in the same class as Maddison and Temperley.

Charlie was a funk, absolutely a blue funk, and hadn't climbed a rookery yet, and as for Bobbie!—the two just ragged nests, and pinched all the eggs, instead of taking one only, and watching the young ones grow up! Jack interrupted his thoughts by suddenly calling out in alarm: 'Oh, Willie, look there!'

Willie followed the direction of his pointed finger, and saw a rabbit squatting on its haunches under a beech-tree. It did not move as they ran forward to catch it, and something in its attitude made them stop quite still. Its head leaned slightly to one side; its fore-paws were raised as though in prayer, and over the wistful eyes a faint terror still lingered. Behind its neck the fur was wet, and as they looked they saw that it had been bitten and its blood drained.

'A beastly stoat did it, Jack.'

Jack knelt down, and picked up the animal. It took no notice of him, it was dying. Terror and exhaustion had paralysed all movement.

Willie took the rabbit, and stroked its soft head, and the long, gentle ears. The poor creature was so warm and its fur so soft. And its eyes looked so gentle, too. If he had only been able to kill the filthy stoat! The rabbit's head fell limply forward, and suddenly a mist formed over the boy's eyes. It seemed so cruel, that such a beautiful creature could be tortured like that. It was so happy, too, he was sure, that the spring was here. Almost as happy as he and Jack were. A tear fell on the rabbit's head. He brushed his eyes with his hand, and looked shame-facedly at Jack. 'Poor thing,' said Jack, stroking its fur, 'such a shame,' and his mouth quivered. 'Why were weasels invented?'

Two minutes later they were quarrelling over the possession of the 'game'. Jack wanted the fur to cure, so did Willie. But Willie wished to treat the skin with his own mixture: he had been the first to skin an animal, and had taught Jack all he knew about it. Jack, however, had been absorbing knowledge in taxidermy from someone else and this annoyed Willie. It also made him slightly jealous. However, possession was decided in favour of Willie, who promised that he would help his friend that evening catch lob-worms on the lawn with the aid of a lantern. The rabbit of course, was unquestionably Jack's, because he had seen it first. Willie wanted it very badly, so Jack gave way, as he did nearly always. He had a secret admiration for his friend (although he usually got a good hiding in a fight, being so thin) ever since Willie, in one of his silly moods, had thrown a plate of porridge at the Vicar from behind the hedge. The prestige acquired by him on that occasion had been enormous, and Jack had received quite a lot of the reflected glory. Willie, however, was thrashed.

Chapter 8

Sunday afternoon in the village of Rookhurst was like nearly every Sunday afternoon for many summers. In blue suits of serge some of the younger unmarried labourers lounged by the elm in the middle of the square, smoking, spitting, and watching the passers-by. The trunk of the elm was smooth, its bark having been bared by the teeth of a hundred horses, and polished by as many Sunday suits leaning against it.

The conversation of the idlers was as simple as the expressions on their faces. Wheat were coming on fine, it were; oats not so good, though; Varmer Turney had bought a new hat, he had, ay, and it cost him five shilling and sixpence, it did—according to Freddie Rendle, who was buying packet of fags same time, he were; Jim Holloman were selling watercress round about; Mr. Temperley sold bay gelding to John Fry, the priccher for dwenty pun', so 'twas rumoured; young Mas' Will'um and Mas' Temperley fell in brook last evening, catching frogs, ay, that was so, with mazed Jimmy.

Nothing happened in the village or its neighbourhood but was duly reported and discussed in every inn and cottage. Even after passing along the tongues of five or six villagers the gossip was rarely exaggerated or the original statement altered. The only thing likely to have the appearance of distortion to a balanced mind was the perspective of the onlooks.

Dolly at Skirr Farm was known to be keeping company with Jim Holloman. A dozen pairs of eyes had seen him walking near the farm at night, a dozen pairs of feet pursued him. Jim was known to be mazed—if only for the reason that he avoided themselves and preferred to lie by the brook or wander on the

69

downs, mooning about. As for Dolly—her were no good—ah, they knew a thing or two, did the women—what for did her want to go out with a common crowstarver and moucher!

Walking quickly, and dressed in coat and skirt of rough serge, black stockings, patent leather shoes, with a red tam-o'-shanter on her head, Dolly came down the road. She tried to hide a basket of food she was carrying. She looked straight ahead, her feet treading the roadway without falter; the heads of the idlers swung round in her direction and regarded her stolidly. She passed, head held slightly higher and footsteps more pronounced. When she had passed John Strong-i'-th'arm, the blacksmith, one of the men, a butcher's 'boy', spoke:

'Wisht I were mazed Jimmy!'

'Her be a pretty li'l maid,' he added, looking at her ankles.

'Takin' Jim some dinner,' said another.

'Going arter Jim 'Oll'mun, reckons!'

'A wouldn't want no dinner if I were mazed Jimmy!'

The last speaker, George Davidson, a prematurely wizened mason with a drooping, gnawn moustache stained with cigarette smoke and regular immersion into ale, laughed, the noise of his mirth resembling the sudden up-tipping of a cartload of bricks heard in miniature.

Dolly walked on quickly. She knew that the men were discussing her, and probably saying that she was going to meet mazed Jim Holloman. But she did not care, and gradually the thoughts of defiant wretchedness—for her apparent boldness only covered a sensitive tissue—gave place to pulsing happiness at the thought of the coming meeting.

Jim had suddenly appeared at the back door of Skirr, ostensibly to sell watercress, while the family, less Jack who was sulking in bed, was at supper the night before. Dolly had replied simply that she did not think that any was required, and he had made to go; and she had then asked him, her timidity overcome by sudden pain in her heart, if she would see him again.

She had not spoken to him for six weeks; nor indeed had she seen him, except at a distance, since she had stolen out during the supper. She had spoken less to people, and taken to brooding, moving and walking in the kitchen as though only by a great effort of will—there was a more subdued look in her eyes: almost a sadness.

Dolly was eighteen. Her mother was dead, and her father, an old man—he had married at the age of sixty—was a paralytic in the 'Grubber'—as the dreaded workhouse was called. He had been a quarryman, and used to burn the chalk in the kilns. So Dolly, like the moucher Jim, was alone in the world, which to her was bounded by the fields and forests around the village of Rookhurst.

She had first taken a personal interest in Jim when she was fourteen. Dolly and four other village maidens had gone to the Witch pool in the cool of the evening for a dip. She was splashing about, a slim white figure with brown sunburnt arms and legs, while the others were still undressing, when suddenly she cried out and crouched in the shallow with her hands wrapped round her and her child-woman's body bent low over the water. She had seen him sitting on the bank behind a bush about twenty yards away. But Jim had not even looked her way; he continued to gaze into the stream; then risen slowly, taking no heed, and ambled away. Seeing her two days later, he had smiled, and something inside her had seemed to melt; from the moment of that smile she had been sorry for him—he was so lonely and sad; she had championed him, and received jeers and taunts from the others, and in the years that followed she had come to care yearningly about him.

Now, with her patent leather shoes a-shine and scarlet hat on her dark head (it had taken six months to save up the price of those shoes and that scarlet tam-o'-shanter—six months to save up nine shillings and fourpence—but she wanted to look nice in the eyes of Jim), Dolly walked gaily a-down the road, opened the swing gate by Farmer Turney's field, half-ran, half-walked across the meadow, passed along the footpath through the small spinney of fir-trees behind Mr. Maddison's garden, and was hailed by a boy's voice. Willie was looking over the quick-set hedge.

'Hullo, Dolly!' he said, smiling with pleasure.

'Hullo, Willie. Up to mischief agen?'

'Um,' he spoke moodily. 'Got to stay in all the afternoon because I fell in the river yesterday'—(he always alluded to the brook as the river, having had a romantic conception of its singing mysteries since he was four)—'and got sopped through. How's Jack?'

'He was a-whipped yesternight.'

'Yell much?'

'Ah!'

'Where are you going? How's Jim? Ah, I know where you be a-going now!' as he saw her face crimson. She pretended to go.

'Oh, don't go, Dolly,' he cried, 'stop and talk to us. I won't give you away, straight I won't.'

He drew his finger across his throat, hollowed his hand, and spat through it as an earnest of good faith.

'I say, Dolly,' he whispered eagerly.

' 'Es?'

'Promise not to tell anyone?'

' 'Es.'

'Look!'

And triumphantly he held up the carcase of a half-skinned stoat, stolen that morning from Old Bob's vermin pole in the covert, while officially confined to the garden.

'Fine, eh?'

Dolly put her hand to her nose, and drew back.

'Nasty,' she reproved.

'Poo! Who cares? I'm going to make a fur coat, I am. I shall want two hundred more, though. Tell Jim, will you?'

'Must be a-going now, Willie. Gude-bye,' her soft voice

whispered. She held red lips up to be kissed. Willie looked round nervously, saw that no one was near, thrilled gloriously, and laid his own on hers. Oh, how he loved, *loved* beautiful, darling Dolly!

Then he was alone, feeling miserable and disconsolate. He decided that love was a bitter, heart-breaking thing. The next minute he was listening in ecstasy to a thrush that had mounted the topmost branch of one of the flame-shaped firs, and was singing to the beauty of flowing sunlight.

Chapter 9

IN THE reed-fringed mere swallows were dipping and singing a plashy song the old rippling brook had taught their ancestors ages before. The lake was shut in by beech-trees, whose branches were flecked with gentle leaf-foam. An island, the home of water-fowl, stood in its far middle. Within the glooms of the water, deep and sullen everywhere, brown carp drifted lazily; the barred perch, with their spiky back fin like the crest of a Roman helmet, lurked in the deep 'holes', preying on minnows and fry; red-finned roach swam in shoals, ever in terror of the dread pike which lay like sunken, time-greened logs in the shadow of the weed-beds.

Jim Holloman, a rusty hat on his head, leaned against a beech-tree. He had not moved for over half an hour, so interested was he in a little tree creeper that brought a withered stick or a dead grass stalk every minute or so to a crack in one of the low-hanging branches of the tree. Sometimes her mate came with her, and perching above, a trickle of song fell from his curved beak. A very feeble trickle it was, for he was scarcely larger than a mouse. And watching the pair, lost in their happiness, Jim was oblivious of time—he forgot all about the coming of Dolly.

A twig cracked, the empty cover of a beech-mast was crunched—he turned round, and saw her coming along the mossy path.

Before any conscious thought had time to form in his mind he had an almost uncontrollable desire to run away. His heart thumped in his ribs, seeming to choke his breath. Languid with emotion, he rose upright, removed his old hat, and went towards her. He saw that her cheeks were the colour of the apple blossom that had just been spilled by the winds of April —the loveliest colour tinted her skin, glowing as the first light glows in the eastern heaven at dawn—he thought that the red hat on her dark hair made her most beautiful; yet when he greeted her nothing of this showed in her face, for he felt humbled with a sense of utter unworthiness. His eyes were downcast. The shine went from Dolly's eyes, and they became mournful. She thought that he was not pleased to see her, especially when he said, looking away from her:

'Nice day, Dolly.'

'Fine, Jim.'

'Mas' Tem'ly all right?'

' 'Es, Jim.'

'Go for a walk, wull ee?'

' 'Es, Jim.'

They were both nervous.

By the great smooth beeches they went, under the clangouring colony of rooks; passed round the other side of the lake—it was nearly a mile across—and came to a rotting boat-house, deserted save for spiders and wrens who searched for them.

The lake belonged to Colonel Tetley—a retired commander of Yeomanry—and the boat-house had been built by his grandfather. The Colonel's wife had been found drowned there on the morning that the little boy Jim Holloman had been discovered wandering and crying in the village street. The night before there had been, it was said, a terrible scene 'up to Big House', between the Colonel's sister, the Colonel, and his young wife. Ever afterwards the Colonel had avoided the lake; the boat-house had fallen into ruin.

Jim suggested, hesitating lest she might be afraid of him, that they should sit down in the boat-house. Dolly said she would like a rest.

Inside, it was damp and forlorn. Mildew clung to the rotten wooden walls, and the timbered pillars; they sat on one seat

75

and it crumbled with a moist creak. She laughed. Jim laughed too, and they became less shy.

'Oh, Dolly,' said Jim, sitting beside her on the remaining seat, which might slither into ruin at any moment. 'Oh, Dolly, but you be kind to come out to see me.'

'For why, Jim?' she must needs ask, turning her face to his, very near. He saw that the apple blossom had stolen back into her cheeks.

' 'Cause they say I be no gude. Oh, see——'

A silvery whistle has come from the lake in front; a blue line drawn across it, disappearing into the edge. It was a kingfisher, gone like a sapphire and rufous arrowhead into the leaves of the thorn trees.

'They be beautiful things, they kingfishers,' said Dolly.

'Shall us go outside,' suggested Jim, 'an' hear wood doves a-singing?'

They left the damp boat-house. Two wood-pigeons were crooning in a holly bush, a blackbird was singing on the island; a moorhen croaked across the lake. Down came the sunlight, gleaming in the rippled hollows of the water, thrown upwards on the stained green leaves of the hazels along the bank, shadow and light alternately slipping through their veined fragility. The wind cradled the branches of the beech-trees, a shadow maze was formed on the ground below, dancing and ever changing.

They walked close together, shoulders sometimes touching. Once the tips of their fingers brushed; moved away; brushed again. Then Dolly's warm soft hand stole to Jim's large and harder one; he wound his fingers round hers, and pressed gently.

On a thrown oak they sat down, half an hour later. Dolly pulled the red hat off her head and threw it on the ground. Jim did the same with his.

'They be grand shoon,' he said, looking at her feet. She felt very happy.

For the time being Jim's moodiness was gone. He stole a look at Dolly, whose hair was beginning to loosen in the knot at the back of her head; the same feeling that came to him when he watched the dawn or the sunset, or the brilliant stars above the downs at night came to him now—a feeling of sadness, as though realising that however much he might love it, it was not for him.

Again he looked at her, at her maid's beauty, at her eyes, brown like a rusted leaf in an autumn wood-pool. Something seemed to squeeze in his breast till the pain nearly made him cry out. All the loneliness, the misery and despair of his life seemed to be torn from him: in that instant he wanted to die, to keep the feeling forever.

Dolly turned and looked at him; her eyes were loving and untaught. She felt that nothing she could give or do would be sufficient for Jim. Jim was so gentle with her.

Then a sound came from his mouth; the misery of past years in that sound, as though fearing that he was wandering in a dream.

'Oh, Dolly. You'm so pretty.'

She leaned towards him, drawn uncontrollably. Her hand stroked his cheek, his auburn beard; passed around his neck and drew his head towards her.

Like a mother she wanted to cherish him; like a child he loved the cherishing. Like a girl she wanted to be admired, and her eyes regarded yearningly; as a poet (though all unknown) he wanted to worship. As a woman she desired to be protected, and made to feel weak, to be merged into his strength; but Jim did not kiss her.

In the soft shadow they sat, while the doves fluttered in the domed greeneries above, and the bees went down on the south wind to the wild flowers, singing their tune of coming summer, but the loneliness was still upon Jim.

So happy were they that neither time nor place had any

77

care for them, and at evening they came to the coverts. The pheasants had crowed as the pools of sunshine ebbed from the stilly trees; blackbirds scurried down the drives and in the hazel bushes, shrilling their metallic 'spink, spink' of alarm; jays taking up the chase of a soft, flapping wood owl with harsh, querulous screams.

Jim picked a skeleton leaf, and showed it to Dolly: the brittle web, the filigree pattern. She had not noticed such things before. But she was eager to listen and learn, and he loved her for it.

Lower in the west sank the sun, shining through the slender wands like a great round cocoon with its silk-spinnings pregnant with the living gold of pure flame. In the air played a fountain of song; wrens, robins, blackbirds, thrushes, and warblers singing of the joy that had been the day, and the joy that would be the morrow. A late hawk dashing down the drive knocked a wood dove off an oak bough, clutched at its torn body, and bore it away to his favourite plucking stump. A few feathers danced and fluttered in the half-light, a red drop lay on the bough, and the other birds went on singing. The vision of death's terror lasted as long as the hawk was seen.

A bee burred past—they could hear it flicking into the leaves; a mouse ran swiftly by their feet, heeding them not as they sat still.

The woodland was hushed, the last pool of sunshine drained from the tall trees; no sound except the squeaks of mice and the risping of a bat's leathern wing as it flittered above their heads.

In the deepest concave the blue was most profound. One by one the stars glimmered: the night drew its cloak over the dying day.

Jim leaned nearer to Dolly, the dusky riot of her unbinded hair had bewitched him; he ran his fingers through its tangle, crow-black in the moonlight, touching its silkiness with his lips. She drew away from him.

In a low voice he asked her why she had done so. She did not answer, but kept her face averted. He bent over her, and suddenly she leaned to him and kissed him with shy maiden haste, drew back as though ashamed, and then a murmur of words came from her lips. Her eyes closed: she loved him.

And now through the glowing darkness of night came a low, liquid note. It wavered to a higher key, like the sound of wind crooning in the lonely tree-tops. Followed a subdued trilling, and the shadowy spirit of beauty trembled in the air. In tones of silver it fluted, bubbling and rippling, a spring of song-water in whose brimming purity untarnished light was held in thrall. The wind sighed through the hazel wands, sighed in the darkness, and the nightingale sang its reverie of flower and green leaf, of light coming in the east when the morning star rose, of all wild longings and ancient sunshine.

Dolly felt that Jim was lost to her; he had flung away from her and lay with his face on the dead leaves.

One great faerie cobweb was the sky, glittering with the dew of stars, and bearing a halved moon like the wing of a gold moth ravished and torn. It showed through the trees, a stain of light behind black branches.

The genius of the woodland was expressed in the bird's song; and like genius in this too, it told the illiterate dreamer of sad beauty, of the drifted sorrow of centuries in spite of the willingness of earth to give all that man required . . . the little obscure bird sang, and Jim listened: his face on the dead leaves, his feelings choking him.

The broken wing of a moon swept upwards; a ghostly owl winnowed silently overhead, heeding not the two so still on the leaves of last autumn, in the sanctities of the nightingale and the loneliness of their pain.

79

MRS. TEMPERLEY had waited up for Dolly. Her husband had to rise at four o'clock in the early summer, and had gone already to bed.

Slowly the clock in the corner moved its green hands; sometimes the jasmine tap-tapped against the eastern window; the pendulum swung, the clock ticked off the slow minutes.

At half-past eleven came Dolly.

Mrs. Temperley, looking at her face as she blinked in the lamp-light, knew that something had happened to the girl. Her face was changed—it appeared subduedly radiant and softened.

Her eyes were shy.

And there she stood looking at her mistress.

Mrs. Temperley was a kind-hearted woman, yet in some things she was hard. Being a woman, her sympathies extended further in the toleration of a man's doing than a woman's. At the moment she was tired, and worried—for she liked Dolly.

She told her that she would have to leave. Dolly looked defiant, and then, to her mistress's astonishment, tears ran down her face.

'Oh, no, missus, not for that,' she sobbed, 'he were so lonely, and I love him.'

'Who?' asked Mrs. Temperley.

But Dolly would not say at first. Only after Mrs. Temperley had asked in a kinder tone did she tell her.

'If ee please, missus, it be Jim Holloman.'

The elder woman was not astonished. In her own heart was

a fair amount of romanticism. Also, with her husband, she liked Jim.

But it was hard to break down the inherited custom of centuries. She was a yeoman farmer's daughter, and, like her husband, her ancestry dated back many centuries on one farm. And this close and narrow life on the land, with its work and labour, neither tends towards sympathy for the labourers—the descendants of freed serfs—nor broadness of outlook in affairs of life generally.

She looked at Dolly's face—the girl was very beautiful. It was the face of a good girl. If she and Jim loved each other—surely there was no harm in it. Jim was quite a superior sort of labourer, too, although he was obviously unbalanced. . . . Dolly *was* pretty!

'But I won't have you staying out late again, mind,' she said, 'and if Jim Holloman wants to come and see you here, I have no objection.'

'Oh, thank ee, missus,' Dolly smiled, through her tears.

'Now go to bed, and be a good girl. We've got to be up early to-morrow. It's washing day. All right, you go upstairs first—I'll see to the lamp.'

Dolly went up the creaking staircase to her room, there to lie in an ecstasy and dream of the wonder that was love. As she passed Jack's door she heard him crying out in his sleep, a thing he often did. He was dreaming that he had hooked a great carp in the lake, and it was pulling him into the depths. Just as he was sinking for the third time he awoke, and burst into tears of relief. Five seconds later his mother was kneeling by the bed, holding him in her arms. For all his bold swear words and contempt of women, he was only a little boy, like most men when they are unhappy and the arms of a loving woman would soothe them.

EIGHT YEARS OLD

Chapter 11

THE ORDER for the mowing had been given, and at dawn a little group had gone down to the meadow called Hangman's Mash. Big Will'um was there, the sleeve of his gray and blue striped shirt rolled up, showing the brown hairy arms: an old straw hat on his head; heavy booted and trousers of fawn corduroy. He was the master hay-maker: none to equal him in the long sure sweep of scythe or endurance. Under him worked John Fry, who preached crudely in the tin chapel every Sunday about sin and repentance before the time of descent among flames should arrive, and who desired Dolly; Bill Adams, the local atheist, reputed to be capable of drinking twenty pints of ale in an evening, the bitter political rival of John Fry; George Davidson, a wizened mason who was out of a regular job; and Jim Holloman.

The scythes swung rhythmically, the grasses fell in cool sweet swathes. Sometimes a greenfinch flew to a flattened wave, calling a long and tender 'see-eep' to his mate in the hedge. The keen curved blades, sharpened every few minutes by the rasping stones, bit into the long stems. All the forest of the grasses, and those tall strangers, the flowers, so beautiful with colour and form, fell before the hissing shear of the knives. Scarlet poppies mingled with rich yellow dandelion and white corn feverfew: fallen forms of beauty coming from sunlight and cold dark earth to attract the dreuling bee who would sip, plunder and spill, yet ensure the future of another summer's loveliness of petal. 'Whit-what-whet', sang the rolled stone on sap-blurred metal, 'swish sweethe'—the grasses fell; the June air was one vast fullness of light and fragrance, while under the lacustrine wistfulness of sky sang the larks.

In the far corner of the meadow a man sat before an easel, painting. His name was Norman, a name famous for land-scapes and portraits of children. He was a member of the Royal Academy, and a great many people liked his pictures immensely; but the critics said they were no good.

He was short and sturdily built; the head large but finely modelled; eyes gray and thoughtful. The thick curved eye-brows denoted a sense of humour and power of graphic description—two qualities that often combine in the tempera-ment of an artist.

Yet his sense of humour was not foremost among his emo-tions when something zipped through his canvas, leaving a small ragged hole exactly in the middle.

'Well, I'm damned,' he said, leaping up.

Across the meadow the line of mowers was swinging slowly forward. No one else was in sight. Behind him, at a distance of about fifty yards was a barred gate showing the green sap-ling corn in the farther field.

He sat down again, puzzled. It occurred to him that perhaps someone had fired a rifle into the air a mile or so away, and the spent bullet gone through his canvas. The possible danger alarmed him when he thought of his daughter lying on her back in the middle of the field with Blackberry, the cocker spaniel.

He was about to call her when something hissed into the grass behind him. Looking round sharply he observed nothing. He was about to search the place where the missile had fallen, when his easel groaned and collapsed. A great blob of sticky clay was sprawled in one corner.

Sounds of restrained glee came from behind the hedge near the gateway, and he ran to it. Climbing over the gate, he saw two small boys about to disappear through a gap in the hedge. Realising that pursuit was useless, he shouted out that he would break their blasted necks when he caught them, and walked back to his easel. Meanwhile, Blackberry, hearing his voice had bounded over the long, slender grasses and was fawning around him in genuine glee. His daughter, Elsie, ran after the dog.

'I saw them, Daddy!' she cried. 'Willie Maddison and the farmer's son.'

'I have been outraged, Kitten,' he answered, 'two small and utterly insignificant boys, doubtless with nihilistic tendencies towards Art'—here he swung his arm with sudden despairing and circular motion around his head, causing Blackberry to bark in fatuous anticipation of a released stone. 'Those two animals have been hurling mud at me from long whippy sticks. As you observed, one of them was that Maddison imp.'

And he chuckled, remembering the time when he himself had possessed considerable skill in projecting clay bullets.

'Will you tell a copper, Daddy?' inquired the little girl.

Mr. Norman looked at her, thinking how the sunlight, burnishing her hair, made her very beautiful. Something stirred in him; he picked her up and kissed her.

'No, my masterpiece,' he answered, 'why add to the miseries of two utterly insignificant little boys by informing Bluebottle Bill? In the first place, he would pull out that dog-eared notebook of his, sharpen his pencil with his teeth, and pester me with archaic legal queries. Eventually I should be summoned for poaching, I expect. Such is Bluebottle Bill.'

'The Maddison imp stared at me,' said the girl, 'with his big eyes he looked like a gollywog.'

Meanwhile Jack and Willie were lighting a small fire by the hedgeside half a mile away.

'Some raid, eh man?' said Willie.

'Did you see how I knocked his old muck over?' queried Jack.

'My catty bullet hit it first,' recounted his friend, glorying in reminiscent prowess.

'I told you I could hit him easily enough,' chanted Jack.

'I reckon I am a jolly fine shot with a catty——'

'It all depends upon the kind of stick you use. It isn't every one who——'

'I've practised awfully hard, I reckon that I could——'

'Anyhow, I knocked it over with my——'

After a while Willie grew silent as he stared into the fire; and Jack noticed, and asked what was the matter.

'Nothing,' replied Willie, and for the first time in his friendship with Jack he wanted to be alone.

Chapter 12

THE WIND of evening sighed through the small triangle of uncut grasses, stirred the flowers, sighed onwards to the yellowing wheat.

Golden rivet-heads of buttercups, driven deep among the waving grasses, the scarlet poppies, the purple vetches, the tawny sorrel standing raggedly with them, the vagabond among the flowers; green beetles and coloured flies soaring and clinging to their feathery heads; the music of the wind as it trembled the dust-pollen of their jags and awns. As the wind came they drooped their plumes in wistful beauty, timorous and bending with love at its sigh, whispering to the wind banished of olden time to bear their seeds, for the mowers would come shortly. Mystery in the green sap, mystery in the shapeless seed that raises stained petal and glorious blazon of colour from all the dead life that has sunk into the earth. The seeds formed and fallen, borne with the wind, and the year's work is ended; among the wild, silent things colour and form, radiance and imagery, are but for the future of the species, as though the giving of all in death will assure some immortality henceforward . . . a lark sang soaring into the evening sky, having no knowledge of the mowers that would come shortly, leaving the swathes of wilting grasses behind, raked when sun-dried by the girls into wakes, the tumuli of the little larks.

Big Will'um, John Fry, Bill Adams, and Jim Holloman were resting by the hedge. Two wooden ale firkins were empty beside them. No one spoke.

Jack and Willie were gathering whole armfuls of flowers from the new swathes. At the far end of the field Dolly was

89

turning the sun-dried hay with two other women. Now and again she looked in the direction of the men, but Jim did not look at her. With downcast head he was absorbed by some thought. He had not drunk much beer. Big Will'um was content. The weather showed no sign of changing, the south wind came with a clear and open sky.

The women ceased raking, and walked over to the men. Dolly asked Willie to save her some flowers. Jim did not look up. He did not see her often nowadays, they did not agree.

'All right Dolly,' Willie said.

'I will kiss ee for a-doing it,' she whispered.

He looked round anxiously.

'Oh, be careful,' he said, his eyes shining. But Jack was engaged in trying to sharpen a scythe and had not heard. Big Will'um jumped up and took it away from him, saying that he would 'cuttyself' with it.

Dolly looked at him; at the light in his face that always stirred her so, and filled her with unknown longings. Occasionally he was a fierce, rude little boy, but with her he was gentle, speaking to her in a confiding, frank way—his voice was soft. She felt often that she must pick him up; especially had she wanted to when he was smaller—an elf-like, fantastic figure, wandering about alone—feeling yearningly towards his loneliness. She knew that his mother, whom she remembered in girlish fancy as a lovely, kind lady, had died soon after he was born. Dolly often wished she was his mother.

The men rose from the ditch, and continued with their mowing. Several of the villagers sauntered into the field, and other children came to tumble and romp in the hay. Willie and Jack wrestled and bombarded each other with wisps of sappy stalks. Suddenly Willie suggested a battle.

Jack called for volunteers, and clutched the arms of three smaller boys.

'You're in my army,' he cried, 'to fight against Willie.'

'Pouff, what a lot of rot,' scoffed Willie. 'I won't fight such a band of oddmedodds.'

Jack made an attempt to drive the boys before him, urging them on from behind, but the battle was a failure.

'These soppy kids are no good,' he said plaintively.

'Soppy kid 'eeself,' interrupted Dolly, who was looking on.

Jack snorted, 'Yah, orphan girl!'

'I'll tell your mother, you rude little beast!'

And now Jim came lumbering up, his beard made browner by the swimming light of gold, the mellow clarity of summer evening. His sleeves were rolled up, showing a skin more delicate than that of Big Will'um or the others, and his arms were thinner. Dolly's eyes seemed larger in a white face; she looked on the ground, unhappy because he would not look at her.

John Fry watched her all the time, jealous yet never speaking.

'Hullo, Jim,' his two friends said, while the other children were silent. In the presence of gentry they dared not to cheek Jim: moreover, since Mr. Norman and his reverence the parson had been seen in open and interested conversation with him, and he had been observed many times to be sitting in the kitchen at Skirr Farm, public opinion had been somewhat less intolerant.

'Well, miboy,' said Jim, addressing Willie, 'bin finding on any more a-birds' nests?'

'Rather. We found a buzzard's over at North Side, didn't we, Jack?'

'Rather. I say, Jim, can we come up to your hut to-morrow?'

'Go when you like, miboy. Only I shall be a-mowing, to-morrer.'

'Come on, Jim 'Olloman,' growled Big Will'um.

Without a word to Dolly he took his place in the line of mowers and worked steadily. The girls exchanged jokes with the lookers-on, but Dolly drew apart. She was hurt, because Jim had not spoken to her. Otherwise she might have cheeked them.

They hid the rakes among the tall nettles in the dry ditch, disturbing many small rabbits. One of them, scarcely eight inches long, attempted to run away, and in a moment the children were pursuing it. A red-headed boy of eight caught it, and was about to twist and pull its neck, when Willie rushed up, demanding that it should be released.

'I say, just you put it back. It's so small. Do you hear?' he said, his voice high with anxiety and emotion.

'What fur should ee put un back?'

'Damhell to you, you rotten cad,' added Jack.

But the boy refused to release it. Willie was nearly tearful: he feared that the little rabbit would die with fright. He caught hold of the boy's shoulder, and pulled his ragged coat, the rabbit fell and Willie clutched it.

The would-be murderer (as Willie's black rage designated him) dropped the rabbit, turned round, and kicked him hard on the shins.

Willie collapsed, howling. The pain was awful.

'Give it 'un,' said the red-headed one to his mate who held the rabbit.

'Damhell,' cried Jack fervently.

'I'll show ee,' shrieked Willie, jumping up and punching the murderer in the face, who burst into tears and clenched his nose. But tears gave place to rage, and the next moment they were fighting.

They not only fought, but wrestled, danced, swore, and tried alternately to scalp and throttle each other. Jack discovered one of the red-headed boy's mates, a wicked little devil called Bill Nye, in the act of biting the calf of Willie's leg, and promptly bashed him. He was bashed in his turn by someone else whom he then attempted to punch in the stomach.

And in the meanwhile the rabbit escaped back into the ditch, and obeying the agitated thumpings of its mother's legs, dived into a hole, which perhaps was all that really mattered.

As suddenly as the brawl had begun it subsided. The parties

drew apart. Willie had a torn ear, a bruised knuckle, a bruised eye and a broken collar. Jack had a cut lip, a tear in the trousers, and was nearly choked by his tie. The thumb of his right hand was sprained. The red-headed bully had several more rents in his coat, but this if anything added to his picturesque appearance; his collar had not suffered, for he never wore one, his father apparently being unable to find one attached to the oddmedodd from which he had pilfered the coat; nor were his trousers badly damaged, although they had no seat to them, since for the past two months the red-headed boy had not troubled about such a mark of civilisation and culture. Besides, his mother was busy. Except for the first accidental nose-bleeder, however, he was unharmed.

The women had been looking on during the fight with amusement, knowing that the boys would not hurt themselves. The men were laughing and making many grimaces and guffaws.

Willie and Jack, scorning to reply to the yaa-boos of the retreating urchins, were licking their hurts, actually with their tongues, and metaphorically by gloating on the wounds of their late antagonists.

'Did you see me punch his nose, Jack?' asked Willie, struggling with his collar.

'Not half, man. But did you hear his teeth rattle when I upper-cut him?' replied his ally.

In reality his upper-cut had resembled the swinging of the arm of a tottery windmill, urged with such blind rage that on meeting with no resistance he had fallen to earth with the momentum.

'He's blind for life,' chanted Willie ecstatically, if untruthfully.

'I cracked four of his ribs with a punch. Like this,' Jack said, approaching his friend and attempting to demonstrate, hitting Willie, who snarled at him to shut up. Reminiscence, however, was as oil to the temporary rage.

'My jingo, he won't forget William Maddison,' he urged fervently. And so they continued. If the red-headed one had received one quarter of what was mentioned, it would be certitude to imagine that he was crippled for life, if he had not already died of his injuries.

They had not noticed the presence of Dolly, who had followed them. The other girls had gone home another way.

'Comin' fur a dip in the brook, Willie?' she asked.

'Shall we, Jack?' anxiously. He felt suddenly abashed.

'Not with her,' snorted his friend.

'Do ees hurt a-good, Jackie,' said Dolly.

'I must go home.'

'And me,' said Willie.

'Oh, no, do ee come, now,' mocked Dolly. Her eyes were smiling and her mouth was red. Under a faded and shapeless straw hat her dark hair was coiled, carelessly, yet in contrast with the locks of the other village maidens it was silky and rich with life. Dolly loved brushing her own hair at night.

Willie glanced shyly at her. Yes, he thought, sadly, he loved Dolly.

'Good-bye, Dolly,' he said.

'Good-bye, Li'l Will'um.'

Dolly went to the brook, laughing. She was a great tease. As soon as she had gone, the boys commenced to reconstruct the incidents of their glorious victory, while Willie's eye grew red and blue, and it began to feel twice as big—much to his delight.

Chapter 13

DOLLY REACHED the dipping place and after making sure that no one was near commenced hurriedly to undress.

In the wind-rustled sedges beside the brook a reed warbler was chattering as it perched near its young. Upstream the water drippled and sang over the pebbles, and the murmur of shattered bubbles came softly. By the banks yellow flowers of the iris held their languorous blooms on the crest of the green stems and small white water-buttercups floated, like miniature lilies, at the edge of the dark pool. Here the brook curved in another of its meanderings, and the water of centuries had formed a deep 'hole'. After a winter flood broken pieces of pottery and tiles were sometimes left sticking from the bank, where the swirl and rush of muddy waters had exposed Roman remains hidden since Cæsar's legions came to Britain.

Although a fair swimmer, Dolly had never entirely overcome the fear of water. The pool had been used by rustic bathers for years and had drowned more than one. She still remembered what her father had told her about Old Troll, who was supposed to haunt the pool.

Dolly looked round again, but no one was in sight. The quiet seclusion of the pool was for herself alone, save for a garrulous flight of swallows skimming low over the water and anon dipping with their breasts.

In the sunshine her skin was faintly brown, and glowing with the beauty of her young body. She sat on the sward at the edge of the pool, clasping her arms round her legs, and resting her chin on her knees. The very joy of her own body caused her heart to brim with happiness. She stroked her own knees, they

95

were round and smooth. She stretched out a leg and wondered if it were beautiful.

Startled at a sound, she gazed round, but it was only a cow that had moved slowly near her, looking upon the unfamiliar human with curious and liquid stare. Its dewlap brushed the grasses, and was gold-dusty from touching many buttercups. Dolly told it to be off, feeling a slight alarm.

As she sat there in the clear summer light there stirred from the deep darkness of sex a thought that thrilled, growing till she saw a naked and gurgling child rolling on the grass beside her. With a sensuous delight she could almost feel its wet mouth groping for her breast. Somewhere into the shadowy mystery of her mind came the vision of Jim, who would be part of the little one . . . if only Jim—dear Jim—would not moon around so, but would get regular work with Mas' Temperley . . . he could wed with her.

Then a thought came suddenly. She would *make* him want her, and then persuade him to get regular work.

Rising swiftly she poised, and plunged into the pool. Her dark hair streamed behind her, she shook the water from her eyes and swam across, but fear of the rushes entangling her feet, if she attempted to climb out, made her turn and swim back.

Something touched her foot, and her heart thumped in fear. Momentarily she imagined that it was the hand of the Troll, who was in league with the corn-spirit and required a victim twice a year: at the mowing and the reaping, so Granfer Will'um had told her. She struck out wildly, swallowing water, which made her choke and added to her terror.

The thing was still clinging to her ankle. She screamed and swallowed more water.

Someone heard the cry, and with equal terror sprang up from behind an alder-stole, and ran forward. His pace was swift, although little energy seemed to be put into the long loose strides, the feet placed flat on the ground and padding along with bent knee. Coming to the edge of the pool, and waiting only to throw his coat off, he flopped into the water and swam rapidly toward her.

Dolly was about to sink when he reached her. Her eyes stared with horror, her mouth was open. Seizing her by the hair he turned on his back and kicked out towards the bank.

She was half-unconscious when he reached the clayey slope, and made piteous moans with her lips. In matted clusters her hair covered her face and lay on her smooth back. Her eyes were still fixed with fear, and her lips had lost their red fullness.

With difficulty he carried her up the bank, for its sides were steep and smoother by the scramblings of many boys' feet. But once on the sward it was an easy matter to pick her up in his arms (where she tried to crouch up in shame) and to bear her to her clothes. Laying her down, he picked up his coat and covered her shoulders and body with it, placing the skirt over her legs.

'Oh, Dolly, li'l Dolly,' his voice trembled, 'oh, li'l sweet Dolly. Thought ee were drownded, my li'l crackey bird.'

She was more frightened than hurt. Rapidly her colour came into her face; her lips stained red again. Under long lashes, wet and dark, she glanced at him. His eyes were gentle, and seeing the look in them she felt no shame.

'I thought it were thiccy Troll coming after me,' she complained.

'Mebbe 'twas floatin' water-weed,' he suggested. looking down at her. ' 'Tes just lies about the Troll,' he added, scornfully.

'But oh, Jim, love, thank God ee were nigh.'

She shook her head to release the hair from her shoulders, and made as if to achieve some neatness with it, but the coat slipped off one smooth shoulder, and she huddled it closer around her maidenliness.

But with a cry she remembered that his clothes were sobbled.

97

'Oh, Jim, love, take ees coat,' and made as if to give it to him, but remembered just in time her maidenliness.

'I be all right,' said Jim, 'reckon I shall get dry quick enough.'

Turning round, he started to lollop along the bank of the brook, and left alone, Dolly burst into tears at the memory of the recent horror. But she was not much of a weeper; the joy of being alive returned, mingling with the warmth in her heart. Jim loved her!

She was soon dressed, and ran to meet him, carrying shoes and much darned stockings in her hand. She dropped them when she came to him, and flung her arms around his neck, regardless of his sobbled clothes.

'Come and a-dry ee afore the fire, Jim 'Olloman,' she coaxed. 'Missus Temp'ly won't a-mind ee.'

Mrs. Temperley being told about Jim went and got an old suit of her husband's (ancient, threadbare, and quite worn out) which she gave to him. Dolly got some cold beef and pickles from the larder and a quart of 'Goliath' XXX ale from the cellar.

Jim quickly changed in an outhouse, and returned to Dolly.

Left alone in the kitchen the two ate, speaking little. Once Jim looked at her full in the eyes, and looked away again, for her eyes were filled with love for him. Then Jack came in, his right hand hidden with a superfluous mass of bandages. He was in genial mood, and told them about his overwhelming victory. Dolly was so nice to him that he became desperately polite, even suggesting that he should clean Jim's boots which were steaming near the fire.

His mother, however, called out that supper was ready in the other room, so he immediately left them in order to consume a steaming bowl of bread and milk in the intervals of telling his father about the five boys he had bashed in the meadow, while standing over Willie's unconscious body.

He grew quite hilarious in the telling of it. He had told a good story at last, and interested Doris and Peggy!

Dolly did not hear the noise in the other room. With a warm, happy heart she watched Jim eating the beef and pickles. She was overjoyed when he thanked Mrs. Temperley so politely, and that night, as she watched the red speckle of his fire in the spinney, she prayed for his happiness, kneeling by the open casement.

The night was witched with the light of the moon in its third quarter, riding on high and shedding its light among the wheat flags. Jim lay on his back in the spinney, beside the fire, watching the brilliant stars.

Capella shone in the northern sky, high overhead serene white Lyra with its star-chord trembled faintly. He saw Arcturus, and wondered at its mystery; Aquila, the plunging eagle, and Draco the dragon snorting fire, and Antares the star of summer glowing low down.

Lying there in the warm night, alone, he was content. No one else cared about the stars, whose names he had learned from an old book, or wanted to watch them at night . . . and then insistently came the vision of Dolly, with her hair darkened by the water, lying so soft in his arms. She had been frightened, and he had saved her. And he had seen her maidenliness. Remembering the way in which she had tried to hide herself with her arms, while he, Jim, was carrying her, he forgot the stars. Thinking of what had happened, and seeing the persistent vision of his lovely dear, he wished that he had held her longer. But at the time he had felt cold. Now he felt warm. As he lay there, he yearned toward her wet lips and soft cheeks. His heart ached as he thought of her.

A star was flashing red and then green above the shadowy outline of the downs: he knew it of old, and to himself called it the Kingfisher of Heaven. He wished that Dolly were there beside him to see it. And yet whenever she came he felt only that he would like to kiss her, and crush her; he didn't want to

99

think about the stars. Perhaps, after all, he was mazed. The stars drew him at night, but they did not care. They cared neither for man nor for mouse.

Insistently came the thought of the maid against his body, her naked body hidden by her long hair. With the piercing sweetness of the thought came jealousy, and fear. Perhaps some one else might love Dolly.

The stars had lost their interest. He went into his hut, to think of Dolly, with her little pink ears and black silky hair, lying in his arms, her eyes shining like those stars, yielding herself.

Chapter 14

THE REARING field was a level rectangular piece of ground surrounded with coverts, consisting of ash, alder, hazel, oak, and elderberry trees. In the early spring the leaf-littered floor of the woods was one lambent flame of flower when the blue-bells pealed their chimes of fragrance to call the dusky bees from nettle and apple blossom; the sunlight stained the leaf-sprays with splash of light when the wind came suddenly, while below the shadows slipped and shuffled their silent patterns.

Then Bob and his assistants would go cautiously through the woods, their eyes alert for hummocks of apparent dead leaves, for the plumage of the hen pheasants resembled the earth and bracken. A nest found, the place would be marked and watched with care till the full clutch were laid, when the eggs would be removed and placed under affectionate hens cooped at intervals in the rearing field itself. Many nests were missed every season, the eggs remaining a prey to rats, hedgehogs, and crows, while the mother-bird was away; the sitting bird a prey to wandering fox, although at this period of the year she gave out no scent. But the chief danger was to the chicks themselves. Everything pursued them, the rat, stoat, weasel, hawk, and fox, so in order to ensure a greater 'head' of birds for the first of October, the eggs were gathered and the chicks reared in the 'aviary' in the wood, its sides marked off with wire netting to keep away animals of prey.

One morning, Bob the keeper sat on a log in one corner of the field, a gun lying across his knees. He had been about since four o'clock, wandering from coop to coop, throwing a

few handfuls of feed before each, to be greeted by shy chicks
running towards him from the cover of tree branches laid con-
veniently near and the clucking of the imprisoned foster-
mothers. Sometimes he would turn a clod of earth over with
his heavy boot, disclosing a disturbed ant's nest. The little
pheasant would leave the food and run towards the ants,
pecking eagerly, especially if they were red ants.

It was ten o'clock, and he was dozing. Now during the years
he had lived in the wood the keeper had collected the seeds of
many wild flowers, and scattered them over the rearing field.
All colours mingled together; the palette of summer. Pure was
the air around the aviary, as though sweet-breathed. Proserpine lingered lovingly in the azure above, dropping scent and
colour from the immortal sky; those idealists, the bees—tame
from hive and wild from hedge-bank—hummed happily as the
sunlight crisped their iridescent vanes. From flower to flower
they passed, gathering the golden pollen and trading it for
nectar, working ceaselessly, going to the flowers as the light
flowed over the rim of the world, and resting only when its
pools ebbed westward at evening, labouring all day for those
unborn in the cells.

Bob had breathed the soul of the flowers during all the years,
heard the slumbrous hum of the bees, in harmony with the
trickle and plash of birdsong afar and near, until his mind had
their simplicity and sweetness. And now, in his lonely years,
with his wife lying under the waving grasses of the churchyard,
and his son Harry a dim memory, the essence of the beauty
absorbed since boyhood gave him happiness. Sitting on the
log, his cap off and the wind just stirring his dandelion-down
hairs, the sun warm, he was not conscious of living; the reverie
of song and flower took him beyond the care and fret of life.

He looked up. No hawk, to swoop, clutch and flash away,
was in sight. A kestrel had paid several calls to one coop during
the past week, but Bob had not seen it. His rheumy eyes could
not see very well.

Someone was coming through the wood, he could hear a twig crack. A small figure emerged, hailing him with subdued joy.

'Morning, Bob.'

'Oo, ah! Young gennulmum, surelye! Fine day, eh, miboy?' he said, his voice high and uncertain.

'Lovely, Mr. Lewis. Your flowers are fine.'

And sitting down suddenly, the boy peered at a bunch of ragged robin, stroking the flowers with his forefingers. The action was an unconscious one—often when walking through the wood he touched leaves gently in passing, especially when the claw-like buds of the hazel were unfolding to the croon of the pigeons and tap-tap of the woodpeckers. It was in greeting that he touched them, the leaves he loved, this queer child.

He watched a dark bee, half of its body the colour of dull copper, filling the pollen bags on its hind legs in a frenzy of labour. He stroked its back with a grass, but it did not fly away or sting. It was too earnest and busy.

'What 'ave ee got on ees 'ed?' queried Bob, looking at him intently.

'Oh, I made this,' replied Willie, carelessly, and pulling off a moleskin cap. He had cured the skins himself—with salt—and sewn them together. A more disreputable thing it would have been difficult to discover. It bulged and gaped, sat down low over his ears; the flies pursued it. Recently he had read *Dick o' the Fens*, and immediately desired a fur hat.

'Not bad, eh, Bob?'

'A good un, that!'

'Made it myself.'

'Ah!' said Bob, vacantly.

'How are the chicks, Mr. Lewis?'

'Mustn't grumble, miboy.'

Willie threw his cap on the ground before him. A black retriever dog crawled out from where he had been sleeping somewhere behind his master, and licked his face. Then he sniffed suspiciously at the cap; continued to sniff; barked delightedly, and commenced to roll on it.

'Hey, come off it, I say,' cried Willie.

The keeper began to laugh.

'Dog rare 'un fur a-rolling on a dead rat, mister,' he chuckled. 'Dog'll always roll on dead bird or rat, miboy.'

'But my hat isn't a rat,' protested Willie.

'Ah!' said Bob vacantly.

Then Bob told him that he had something to show him. Rising slowly, he shouldered his gun, and walked to one corner of the field, where blackberry bushes grew low. Willie peered in, but could see nothing. Bob chuckled and told him to look again. Looking intently he saw a heap of broken shells.

'Molly's doin',' said Bob.

'Molly?'

'Yaller fessant.'

He chuckled.

'Molly'll lay eggs here every spring, just inside t'wire nettin'. Fur eight years I've seen her. Let me stroke her back, she will: no one else, though. She'll send chicks forrard fur food when I'm feedin'.'

'When us be a-shootin' on um in t'season, Molly allus lighter in colour than t'others, woan't rise and fly, but runs all the time, dodgin' past t'beaters. Us doan't try to shoot her, anyhow.'

Willie had read a great deal about birds, and found this interesting. He knew that it was an exceptional case of reasoning over instinct, and determined to write to the *Colham and District Times* about it. Perhaps he would have another letter from the British Museum, as he had when he wrote about a South American condor carrying away a sheep off the downs, only this was true!

And now the time for feeding arrived. Domestic hens clucked, and poked flurried, perky faces through the bars of their coops. Bob scattered the feed from a tin box he carried, and the drab chicks darted, from nowhere it seemed, to pick it up. From a dense mass of cover, branches of trees and ferns, a dozen or so miniature pheasants came forward, all the colour of dead wood and leaves, Molly remaining in the background.

Willie went closer to her, and she called in alarm. Immediately the dozen or so miniature pheasants seemed to sink into the earth—by crouching and remaining still they became invisible. Meanwhile the fawn-coloured bird continued her agonised cries, and ran just in front of his eager hands outstretched to catch her, trailing a wing on the ground as though it were broken. She eluded him for two hundred yards or so, then flew up with a whirring of wings and swung round behind him, alighting with spread tail among the brambles.

Meanwhile Bob had kicked the clods from off some ants' nests, and whistled. Immediately the crouching birds ran forward to pick up the swarming ants.

'Good-bye, Bob,' said Willie, coming back, 'I promised to meet Jack at the lake. We've got a plan on. Good-bye,' and he ran off, leaving the old man standing among the sun-stained flowers, and the hum of bees, and the sweet air of young summer's glory.

The way to the lake lay through two adjoining coverts, and across a cornfield where the young flags of wheat rustled softly as the wind rippled them like sea-waves seen in a dream.

With the green wheat stood the poppies, spilt blood-drops of flower, hated by the farmer; *argemone*, the slothful, the sleeper; the born wanton, petulantly beautiful, the broad silky leaves unfurled by the ardour of sunlight; taking, wanton-like, slight root and draining the nourishment from the earth which should go to the civilised wheat; and ancient as the wanton in this too, ever condemned but ever existing; and beautiful. . . .

A brown kestrel, leaning on the wind with chestnut bosom, bared tail and streaked quivering pinions, was waiting for a mouse to stir in the young wheat below. Willie watched it, pausing half-way across the field. The hawk dropped, slanting downwards, the boy shouted, saddened at the thought—which occurred to him for the first time—of such death in the sunshine, death to maintain life.

His shout availed nothing, for as soon as gripped by the talons the mouse had died.

A girl sitting on the stile looked up at the shout, and immediately became interested.

Willie walked on, a small figure with an untidy mass of dark hair, a thin face, high-cheekboned, a wide mouth slightly drooping at the corners, snubnosed, and two large and earnest, inquiring brown eyes casting the whole expression into wistfulness. He had not seen the girl on the stile, who was looking at him with blue eyes wide open, frankly and ready to smile if only he smiled at her first. Then she saw his rather browny-white face get pink, and thought he looked a nice boy.

Willie came to the stile, coughed hollowly, making a profuse action of shielding his mouth with his hand to show that he knew all the best manners. He did this because Charlie Cerr-Nore had told him that the girl's mother had said he was ill-mannered and swore. Then gracefully and easily he mounted the stile, as far away from the girl as possible, in order to show her that he was polite. Unfortunately for himself, however, his nimble grace was partly marred by a twig of the may-tree hooking his poaching hat, and trying to save it from falling off his head while mounted on the top bar, he lost his balance and fell, legs and arms, sprawling awkwardly, into a mass of wild parsnip. Humbled, he snatched at his hat and walked rapidly away, feeling that his legs were like a tomtit's (which indeed they resembled).

When he had passed over the hill and was out of sight, he sat down and wondered if his face were bloodstained. Supposing it to be so, he saw himself telling Jack that he saved a runaway horse—yes! with a pretty girl on it crying for help; and he was dragged through a hedge, still clinging to the bridle—but his face appeared to be all right. Well, it was a good thing, for he had only just got rid of a black eye.

In his mind he saw the girl again. Her face, with the steady blue eyes and smiling red lips and plait of thick golden-brown hair, filled the sky; and his heart began to ache with the steady gaze of those eyes.

Perhaps he might offer her his rare birds' eggs, or his new fishing rod. If only his legs were not so thin. . . . Charlie Cerr-Nore had been to tea there, but he never got invited anywhere like that. Ah! and he had thrown a clay bullet at her father! He hurried away, lest she should see him. He longed for Jack, dear, dear Jack. Never again would he speak unkindly to dear Jack!

Chapter 15

NEXT MORNING in the sunshine the girl was again sitting on the stile, reading a book called *Ever Heavenward*. Her legs swung idly to and fro; she wore black stockings. As she perched there, her gaze frequently wandered from her book, and she would look leisurely along the footpath that divided the cornfield in front of her. She was wondering where the Maddison boy, who had been coming along the path a few minutes ago, had suddenly vanished to.

The Maddison boy was resting in long grass at the base of the hawthorn hedge, which ran at right-angles to the footpath, after a rapid and exciting run and crawl of nearly three hundred yards along the lower hedge.

He pulled a long bennet out of its green sheath, and thrust it between his teeth. Meanwhile, his intent expression of watchfulness was maintained. He was wondering if he dared go up to her and speak, or would she be annoyed? The very thought of such boldness caused a sickly smile of fear to come over his face, and his heart to beat even faster than it was. But why not? Oh, but whatever would she think! He was sure she would really want to read her book, and not speak to him without hair-oil on his head, and with coat torn by many brambles. How he wished he had taken some of his father's hair oil: he would have risked any possible consequences. Last time he had taken some to dubbin his poaching boots, there had been a row. As though he had known that the bottle filled up with paraffin would make much difference! However, there it was; his hair was undoubtedly untidy. Hands filthy, too. But the traps had been responsible for that: perhaps he could explain to her that he had nearly caught seventy moldiwarps that year, only all except one had escaped. Yes, that would be bound to impress her! He might even offer her a cap made of moleskin. She would refuse, of course. Girls didn't understand that all real trappers wore such things. His father had had the cheek to laugh at his own, so that now he only wore it in his bedroom at night, when furtively making a new catapult, or gloating over his collection of birds' eggs. Sometimes when it was hot and he wore it out of doors, it attracted so many bluebottles that he was forced to take it off and hide it in his pocket. Certainly, it did smell a little, but then it was only the natural smell of a moldiwarp, and not, as had been suggested, because he didn't know how to cure the skins!

A lark was singing in the sky above him, and he turned on his back still chewing the grass stem, and watched it. Just a little black speck in the blueness above, climbing, climbing. One long ripple of song came down with the sunshine. How sweet was its song! Very much like the singing of the brook over the stones, where the cattle went down to drink. Its wings were beating so quickly, and its song never ceased. As he followed its flight, trills of happiness shivered over his body, and he felt suddenly that he must shout. Everything was beautiful, beautiful, in the summer, the swallows glided above the corn, then the wind came, and swayed the sprays and stems, with such a gentle, whispering sound. And the wild things were so happy: all the birds sang, and the butterflies fluttered by in the sunshine. And how the bees loved the thyme on the downs, and all the flowers! And all loved the sun—oh, the sun, and its glory! He shut his eyes, and held his face directly in the warmth of its rays. And again he had the impulse to shout out aloud, to rush into the corn, and laugh into the blue sky.

A series of sweet sounds, *chee-chee—chee-chee*, oft repeated, and answered in the distance, and he was looking at a tiny titmouse hanging head downwards on a twig in the hedge above. He could see the blue and yellow of its feathers, and its fragile legs, slender as grass stalks, with delicate little claws. It watched him for a moment with bright, beady eyes, and then continued its search for caterpillars. *Chee-chee* ever so loving and tender, and his mate had joined him. The two flitted rapidly from twig to twig, and passed away down the hedge.

Meanwhile the girl got down from the stile, and walked down the hedge on her way home. She was feeling hungry, and was thinking about her friend Mary Ogilvie who was coming to stay with her soon. She had gone half-way to the lane when her spaniel in front started barking, and she saw the boy look up out of the grass. She called out: 'Come to heel, Blackberry!' and the dog came to her with wagging tail, half whining and half growling. The boy was looking down at the grass. What a funny boy he was, and what funny hair, like Shock-headed Peter! Much nicer than hair swarmed down with hair-oil, like Charlie Cerr-Nore's! Calmly she walked on.

But he behind, who was conscious that he looked ugly and thin, stood there with growing unhappiness. She didn't want to see him. He'd seen her glance at him out of the corner of her eye, but it was just a casual look, that was all. And now she was going home, and had never once looked back. What a fool he had been to lie there! She might think he was spying on her. He thought of her face again, of that sweet look of hers, and his heart ached. No use, of course. Glory, she had turned round just before turning the corner by the hedge. Should he whistle? Run after her? No, of course not. She might think he was following to be rude to her. The beating in his ribs died down again, and settled heavily.

He walked to the stile, and vaulted over, hoping that, if she were peering through the hedge, she would see how easily he could do it. Then he felt very lonely, and began singing to himself in a minor key.

Half an hour later, he met his friend Jack, who had spent the greater part of the morning in the boat-house, filling the chinks in the sides of the catamaran-floats with tow. Jack's other occupations, after he had breakfasted, had consisted of firstly, going into the pantry and cutting himself a slice of cake. At the time, he was not hungry; in fact, the sight of food did not really interest him, but he knew that towards eleven o'clock he would be feeling 'peckish', so with foresight he obtained permission to cut a small slice of cake for himself. Accordingly, the weight of the cake decreased about three-quarters of a pound. Secondly, he required some tow. He had a sudden idea. There was a stag's head in the hall that had gazed down on him ever since he could remember. He knew that there was a vast quantity of tow hidden inside that head. To get at it he would have to remove it, and this could hardly be done without ripping the whole thing up. He took it down from the wall, and ran up with it into his bedroom, which was also his work-shop. Beginning with a large screw-driver, he wrenched the head from the piece of oak to which it was attached. There inside lay the tow, tightly packed. He pulled it out, and with it the left eye, which fell to the floor and rolled under the bed.

With a sinking feeling in the stomach, he tried to put back the eye into its socket. After many attempts he fixed it, but no longer was the stare of the erstwhile forest monarch straight and true. It was now boss-eyed. Father would be sure to notice it, and then there would be a terrible shindy. It would mean a thrashing, of course. Still, it couldn't be helped: his father would not see his point of view, naturally; that it would save his son's life, for if he went out on a leaking old boat it would most certainly be sunk. Well, the great thing for the moment was not to be found out. He fixed the head on the wood again, but the result appalled him, so he carried the quivering thing downstairs and hung it on the nail. The head leaned drunkenly forward, and the eye leered down the passage. Jack slipped out of the house.

As he left the farm on his way to the lake, he had a sudden

desire to ride the Vicar's pony that was grazing in a field. He succeeded in catching it, and improvised a rough bit and bridle out of a piece of rope. The pony, however, resenting what he knew to be an illicit performance, threw him gracefully and easily to the ground. Jack, still on his way to the lake, passed a cottage, and saw a small boy playing by the door. He paused, entered by the gate, went into the living-room, which was empty, and seized a bowler hat that was the pride of its owner. This he wedged over the smaller boy's ears, who ran yelling to his mother. Meanwhile Jack had vanished up the road.

After this he had talked a little with the blacksmith, and borrowed a small pot of tar from him; gazed for the thousandth time in the window of the gunsmith; blown the horn of the doctor's car standing outside a cottage; hit a pig in a sty over the back because it had such greedy, insolent eyes, and punched the Vicar's son, Charlie, on the nose because he called him a bully. Then, on reaching the lake, he had commenced work on the boat, which he wanted for fishing, and eaten up the cake, all but the bottom piece, which was slightly burnt and had baked paper adhering to it. This he threw into the lake, not feeling hungry. Then he went homewards, and came across Willie, who seemed rather silent. Soon, however, they were laughing and happy together, as usual.

Chapter 16

THE SHADOWY spirit of summer's light and glory still loitered in the air; the moon was not risen above the hills. Mr. Norman was waiting in the lane for the moon-rise, leaning on the gate leading to a meadow where the hay had been dried and raked into wakes. An indistinct whiteness passed slowly over the field in front. He watched its phantomesque quartering, its sudden disappearance as it dropped to the ground, it rose again, and beat with broad silent wings down the hedge bordering the roadway, passing within two feet of his head, feathery legs dependent, dark eyes directed downward. The winnowing of its wings sent a wind against his face, but came no rustle of feather.

Passing onwards over the hedge towards Skirr went the barn owl. He heard a throaty, weird cry, and knew that it had gone to its young on the rafters.

Burr-r, a chafer went past, clumsily, hitting the hedge and whirring among the leaves. Like spun silver coins little white moths hovered and drifted over the fallen grasses, finding the night-opening flowers under the hedgerow where the curved scythes had not swept.

He wanted to remain there all night, one with the glowing darkness and its mystery, but there—he was no longer young, alas. A corncrake in a distant wheatfield began its jarring continuity of song, the afterglow still lighted in the west where the sun had dipped. The moon was a long time in coming, but he would wait for it to rise before going home.

A faint halo, a honey-pale sheen appeared over the beechen wood before the moon swimming slowly up the sky. For awhile he watched it, big and swollen, casting ghostly shadows from the trees, and storing its light in the dew upon the hawthorn leaves. He made mental notes about colour as he watched it.

Through the stillness came the sound of voices. He imagined that it was a 'couple' sitting by the hedge near the gate, unconscious of him standing there.

He would have gone had he not heard his own name mentioned by a deep voice which he recognised as belonging to the man who had asked him for work the other morning.

'Oh, I mustn't stop more'n a moment,' a woman's voice requested. The tone of the voice was so pure and sweet that he instantly conceived her to be beautiful. His imagination was interrupted by the man's answer.

'I asked Mas' Norman for job o' work as reg'lar gard'ner, and told him that I would a-get his garden the best round about. Mas' Norman, he said he would let me know. Nice chap, I reckon.'

'Oh, Jim dear, do ee be a-careful if ee gets the work. Don't go a-mooning and standing about when ee should be a-workin', do ee promise now, Jim.'

The solitude of the night was interrupted only by the needle-like notes of field mice and the distant cry of a curlew. Then the man's voice spoke again.

'Li'l Dolly,' he said, so softly that the listener, who dared not move away for fear of detection, wished that he had not stopped by the gate. 'Li'l Dolly, shall us wed if I get work reg'lar? Ah'll be kind to ee, like you be kind to me, Dolly.'

'Jim, ee knows I love ee,' came the passionate declaration of the woman, and silence.

Moving very quietly over the grass, though unable to prevent the soft sighing of the dew-weighted stems under his feet, Mr. Norman crept away. The moon had swung clear of the earth, and was moving into deeper heaven, leaving its tarnish about the pale summer vapour.

As he thought of the two by the hedge-side he felt quite joyful at the prospect of helping them. He would employ the man as a gardener and with his help start chickens, a thing he had always desired to do. There was no reason why Dolly—what a lovely voice the girl had!—no reason why she should not be employed in the house as well: he believed that his wife wanted a new parlour-maid!

Chapter 17

Waves of sunlight plangent on the domed oaks, and rushing with golden swell over cornfield and meadow bronzed the grain and dried the grasses. The sappy stalks of June were bleached and hardened; the wild roses raped long since by the wind and fallen into the earth, the green seeds yellowing. Gradually the colours of Summer's flowers took on the hues of her maturity—purple and yellow. Devil's bit scabious grew with golden ragwort and spiky teasle in the keeper's field, whence the pheasants had departed for the coverts; tall willow-herb sent its seeds from the sun-split pods with the wind, swung under ephemeral down.

July turned to August, when the wheat hissed under the wind, and the farmers went often to the fields and pondered on the advisability of reaping.

Jim had been with Mr. Norman for nearly a month. At first he had worked with enormous energy, and his employer had prided himself upon his judgment. Often he had made attempts to draw him out in conversation, but always to be met with but scanty success. Jim was polite, but seemed disinclined to talk, except upon one subject that both men had in common—flowers.

He was an early riser, but not for the purposes of working. Many times he rose with the dawn, returning for breakfast which he had in the kitchen with one immature housemaid and the cook (the latter contemptuous of him and resenting the idea of such a man associating with herself) when the sun had been surveying the freshness of the morning for hours. On such occasions he walked many miles, going up to the

Roman encampment, lying in the fosse, and watching the plain beneath goldening to high summer, or followed the brook, pausing to watch birds and flowers.

Gradually his interest seemed to wane. He did not like living inside a house. For so long had he been able to see the stars, and hear the tunes of wind and leaf at night that a bedroom, although the topmost one of the house, seemed oppressive and stifling. At least that was the idea of Mr. Norman. Elsie did not like him, being afraid of him. His wife thought that he was mentally deficient.

The occasion of his appointment raised considerable comment at the time in the ale-houses and under the elm-tree of Rookhurst. The general opinion of the inhabitants was that a mazed workman had gone to a mazed master, who would wake up one morning and find his 'vallables took'. Mr. Norman had not long moved into the district, having built his house in a style known as 'modern antique'.

One afternoon Mr. Temperley and Big Will'um, his foreman, went to the fifty-acre wheatfield. Big Will'um carried an ancient fagging hook and sickle. For a while he slashed at the tough stalks until enough had been cut to form one stook.

'Good enough,' said the farmer.

His foreman grunted.

Early the next day four men with scythes cut lanes round the field, 'opening of it up' for the machine. Until the sun went down in fire behind the beech clump on the ridge, the scythes ripped through the hard stems. Mr. Temperley from time to time rubbed some ears out between his palms, letting the hard berries trickle from one hand to another, blowing meanwhile to winnow the glumes or husks away. He nodded with satisfaction: it was consistently excellent. 'Rust' was almost absent, the ears full, the berries rich and ripe.

The next day the reaping machine arrived. The heads of the horses moved up and down as it was drawn down one side of the field, their tails swished; the red arms whirled rhythmically;

the sheaves lay behind, neatly tied. All the morning the machine passed round the immense field, where the poppies bloomed sultrily, and the oddmedodds were hidden in the wheat.

Mr. Norman was spraying the Austrian copper briers with soapy water, in order to discourage greenfly, when the distant whirring of the reaper-and-binder floated with the hum of insects and life of the summer day. He immediately called the attention of his wife to it. Deep in the nature of every man is the reverence for the harvesting of corn. Through all the centuries wheat has grown in his service, and though not consciously recognised the time of garnering causes a still echo of happiness to sound in the heart. It is not so very long ago that to the majority of country-dwellers the signal for the reaping to begin was the most desired event in their lives. Richard Jefferies tells how the labourers went into the cornfields and tore with sickles at the stems, in danger of sunstroke and collapse, gleaning scanty gold from the wheat. All the winter they lived on dry bones and bread, with perhaps a little lard. Few pounds at the most they could make by this continuous toil: 'The breast-bone was burned black and their arms, tough as ash, seemed cased in leather.' With the sadness of a great man he tells the beauty of the wheat; grown for man, the highest creature, the lord of earth; and the misery of the olden time tillers and reapers; hanging round the filled barns during the time of Corn Law troubles, their children dying. . . .

Jim, who was weeding in another part of the garden, heard the whirring of the machine. For a long time he stood still, as though pondering. Then he dropped the hoe and went to Mr. Norman.

'Beg pardon, zur, but can't abide here while they be a-cutting. Do ee mind, now, if I go down?'

The other man looked at him, and intuitively realised why he wanted to go to the reaping. The corn was calling him. He spoke in broader dialect.

'All right, Jim,' he said.

'Thank ee, Mas' Norman,' replied Jim, touching his cap.

Arriving at the scene of reaping he went up to the foreman and asked for work.

That taciturn person tilted his broad-brimmed straw hat and scratched his head. Jim explained that he no longer worked for Mas' Norman.

'Get on wi' it,' said Big Will'um.

He went back in the evening, and asked his employer for release. Mr. Norman spoke to him, saying that he had no fault to find with him—had he any complaint against himself?

Jim said that he hadn't, but didn't feel up to the work—was queer perhaps, but would rather be by himself.

Mr. Norman did not mention Dolly. He wondered what she would say to him when she heard. The man certainly was queer: he no longer thought as he had at first, that there was anything deep in his nature. Either that, or it was so deep as to be unplumbable—a form of genius which, if expressed, would ennoble his life, but which, finding no expression, would probably destroy its holder . . . madness. He pondered on this peculiarity, which he lacked himself, and decided that he himself was not a genius after all. He was glad. Ill-balance resulted from no expression, and the consequent thoughts of suicide in a genius. . . .

'I'm sorry, Jim,' he said aloud. 'Do you want to go altogether?'

Jim seemed ashamed and awkward, so he added:

'I quite understand, Holloman. You mean that you feel you must live out in the open—live unhindered?'

'Yes, Mas' Norman,' replied the man, looking on the ground.

'All right, Jim. I'll always be pleased to give you jobs if you come up at any time. There was the cottage . . . we hoped——'

Jim had turned away. Surly fellow, thought the artist.

In the azure the swifts were wheeling, screaming in mystic language, for the time approached when the Voice would come from the stars and bid them wander once more across sea and land.

Chapter 18

SUMMER LINGERED on the hills and in the fields till one day a heavy white mist hung above the meadows near the beech wood. The sun beat this away towards noon, but it was the beginning of the end. The cuckoo's voice had long cracked into silence, and the singer departed. In the sky the swallows still sped twittering, but the swifts had gone just after the harvest had commenced. Nearly every song-bird had finished for the season; every moment they had lived joyously, filling each one with crowded happy life, till one day love was forgotten. And no bird lamented the wane of summer for itself—only Willie lamented for them. 'Do not be sad because summer is gone,' he would say, to a swallow, perhaps on the roof of the stable building, 'the spring will come again'; and his eyes would fill with tears at the memory of the past springtimes. 'Gone, gone, forever,' and then he would wander away, singing a song without words which seemed to sing itself without tune, and yet, somehow, be part of the past years and also of the present.

He could no longer lie among the grasses, and gaze at the white clouds drifting, drifting ever so slowly across the blue. The feeling inside him amounted almost to despair; the spring had passed almost before he had ceased to tell himself that it had arrived, and with it the feeling of utter joy that he had felt on looking into a nest with its fragile eggs, or little naked young ones. He remembered how he had watched these young birds grow up, and how he had fed them; the nest of robins in particular, hidden in the thick ivy that was slowly killing a mighty elm. After a very few days he had

121

been able to stroke the back of the mother bird as she sat brooding over her babies, that seemed all soft skin and gaping yellow beak, without causing her any anxiety. But these had very soon grown up, and left the nest. How terribly sad was an empty nest! And now it was almost the end of summer.

One day he was walking in the beech wood, singing to himself, then he saw in front a figure that caused his heart to drum suddenly against his ribs. He was in agony. She might have heard him singing! She was coming towards him, walking rather quickly. When she came to him she smiled; immediately he pulled his moleskin cap off his head and held it behind him. He smiled nervously, while he tried not to breathe loudly.

'You're Willie, aren't you? My father knows yours.'

'Yes,' he managed to say.

'Are you going for a walk?'

'Yes.'

'Are those your dogs over there?'

'Yes, that's Fidelis. He's very old and fat, the other's Bob.'

'Fidelis is fat, isn't he? Still, it's better to be fat than thin, isn't it, like some of the half-starved mongrels in the village?'

'Yes, rather,' he said, wondering if she had meant the comparison to apply to himself. He dared not look at her frank eyes.

Among the crisp brown leaves under a tree, a blackbird had been searching. He had taken no notice of the two children, for in the mould were small insects, luscious earth-worms, and all kinds of food, and, being hungry, he was intent on his work. Certainly he did not see the chestnut-barred streak that flashed low under the trees. When he did, he opened his yellow bill and raised the alarm, loud-ringing and urgent. The next moment something hit him; he screamed, and little dusky feathers fluttered into the air. As the talons sank into his breast, Willie turned, and shouted at the sparrow-hawk. The hawk rose on narrow wings and sped into the forest.

He picked up the wounded bird, and carried it back to the

girl, who looked at him with a frightened face. Half the breast feathers had been torn away. Slowly the crimson blood welled from the jagged tears. Its claws were clenched as though in pain. He could just feel the feeble throb of its heart. Suddenly the girl cried out, and clung to his arm, peering at the little bundle of warm feathers that lay so limp and broken.

'Can't we . . . can't . . . can't we bandage him up with a hanky?'

It was lying, still and warm and bleeding in his hand. Suddenly the bird's breast fluttered, it turned its head, and lay still again. In its eyes came an alert look, its bill opened; it shuddered, and died.

'It's dead,' said Willie. 'Look, its neck's loose,' and he raised its head, with the closing eyes, and it fell back limply.

He wanted to put it in his pocket, and take it home for Biddy to cook in a pie; but it was nicer to think of the poor bird in a solitary grave in the forest.

'Shall we bury it?'

'Yes. Just here?'

'Yes.'

With some sticks they scratched a hole in the ground, and buried the dead bird. Elsie tried to make a cross for the small mound, but Willie had no string, so they put twigs on it instead.

After this enjoyable act, which somehow made him feel good, and quietly happy, Willie said: 'Will you come for a walk? We might see a squirrel.'

She looked at him, and thought how nicely he smiled, and what white teeth he had, and in what a nice way his nose wrinkled when he laughed. He was a nice boy and not a bit rude, as Mrs. Cerr-Nore had said.

'I've seen you a lot of times when you haven't seen me,' said Willie, suddenly, not daring to look at her.

'I saw you once in Hangman's Mash, do you remember? Daddy was painting a picture.'

Willie went hot with shame and anguish. He remembered how he and Jack had got some clay, and a thin, whippy stick each, and thrown balls of clay at an old man who was sketching in the meadow. He had chased them, and it had been great fun. To hide his shame, he said: 'How old are you? I'm nearly nine.'

'I'm nearly eight,' said Elsie, and Willie was glad, for their ages were all right—suddenly he ran to a tree, and turned himself 'inside out' on a low branch. That would answer for his red face perhaps.

Chapter 19

THE DAYS went on. The last stook was pitch-forked into the wain and borne away to the last stack in the south-west corner of the field. It was great fun to ride on the leader's back and to be rocked on the piled wagon. Came the gleaners, crushing the stubble with heavy boots; the partridges whirred in coveys to the field, running up wind, calling 'cher-wick, cher-wick', at evening when a thin mist lay over the brook. The birds ceased to sing, except the robin, in whose heart was always hope.

On the First, Colonel Tetley and the 'guns', including Mr. Maddison, went across the stubble, turning up the little brown birds themselves, shooting over dogs. Willie and Jack followed behind, lamenting the lack of a gun—even an air gun—with which to shoot. They decided that to be boys was rotten. In the afternoon they found a dead partridge that had somehow been left, or had perhaps flown a long way after being mortally hit, suddenly dying in flight. That was great luck! They took it to the spinney, once more the home of Jim, and cooked it over a fire, stringing it through a green stick. In their impatience they omitted to pluck it properly, so singed feather mingled with the odour of burnt flesh when they divided it with Willie's enormous single-bladed knife and tore it with their teeth, voting it a tremendous adventure.

They explored Jim's shelter—a domed dug-out, rendered rain-tight by a great pile of branches, earth, and turf, on which grew a cluster of pink willow flowers, founded by a single seed drifting there years ago. They lay on his bed of sprung fir branches, and wished that they could live there too. There was a niche in a wall with a candlestick in it, and grease had run down the earthy wall. It was a lovely place!

October days came, spent in loneliness by Willie, while Jack was at Colham Grammar School, except for the Wednesday afternoons and the week-ends when they went together on expeditions, sometimes scrumping apples.

One day, when the fire of autumn was kindled and the yawning flames spread to the trees of the forest, Mr. Maddison decided that his son's education was neglected, and forthwith spent a whole morning in explaining the multiplication tables and some history. One thing that lingered in the boy's mind from the morning's agony—which ended in juvenile tears and adult irritation and contempt—was that a nasty man called Norman Conquest stuck an arrow in the eye of an English hero named Harold. Nor did he ever cease to forget that eight rods, poles, or perches made a furlong. That one morning was enough for Mr. Maddison: his son would have to go to school. Willie had attended a dame-school in the village for six months about two years before, but after scarlet fever he had not returned. Biddy was supposed to be teaching him arithmetic; he had taught himself to read, and he could write—just.

Over the long pond in those autumnal mornings a heavy mist lay, and every passing of the wind beckoned from the trees a drear following of leaves; buff and spotted from the oak, flakes of gold from the elm, yellow from the ash. The rust of decay tinged the leaves of the hawthorn, leaving the red berries lonesome in the weak sunshine, or dripping with mist on windless, sunless days. The swallows gathered on the telegraph wires, round the oast-houses, and by the rustling, sapless reeds of the mere, sweeping suddenly into the air, rising, falling, wheeling all ways, disturbed and twittering for no reason. Old Granfer Will'um, sadly pained with rheumatism and lamenting the cold that rendered impossible his sitting in front of the inn all day, held the opinion that they dived into the lake during the winter and lay up beside the frogs and carp.

But by the lake the swallows were having a final banquet before leaving for distant lands. As the hour of departure drew nigh, they grew more and more excited. Every afternoon Willie went to watch them, sadly. His beautiful swallows were going to leave him. One day he went there with his father, resenting his presence, to bid them farewell, but he was too late. The lake was deserted.

At night the Voice had spoken: in a vast cloud they had fled towards the southern stars.

Willie was inconsolable. All that afternoon and evening he wandered about, singing softly to himself. Once his father, coming upon him suddenly, said, 'What's the matter now? You sound as though you've got the belly-ache.'

Father's voice sounded so friendly that Willie, in an outburst of gratitude, said: 'The swallows aren't here any more.'

'Well, they'll come back again, I expect.'

'Yes, but it won't be the same, Father.'

'Of course it won't be the same. Nothing is ever the same. That's life, my boy. I notice, however, that your hands are usually the same drab colour. I wish it wasn't necessary to be constantly reminding you of those things. You've been asked out to a tea, by the way, to some people called Norman, next Wednesday. I said I'd pass on the invitation to you. Would you like to go?'

'Yes, please, Father!'

On the Wednesday afternoon, he scrubbed his face until the torture resultant from a desire to look handsome forced him to desist. He cleaned his teeth three times, consecutively, and in his anxiety cut his finger-nails almost to the quick. A vague doubt troubled him about the wearing of his breeches, for once John Fry had guffawed after him: a momentary but nevertheless agonising thought had come to him that perhaps they emphasised the skinniness of his legs. Eventually he decided to wear his Eton suit and gray trousers (made from an old pair of his father's) which Biddy, with misplaced zeal, creased at the side. The trousers had been fashioned two years ago by her in that atrocious shape known as 'bell-bottoms' and ended very soon down his legs.

Nevertheless he felt distinguished as he walked down the road, where he met Jack.

'Hullo, man,' said Jack.

'Good-afternoon,' replied Willie, primly: the effect of the very stiff white Eton collar.

'I say, man,' Jack said in alarm, a moment later, 'where are you going?'

'Oh, to visit some friends.'

'Where to, man?'

'Mr. Norman's.'

Jack's face fell.

'I thought we were going after rabbits, man,' he cried in dismay.

'Well, you see, I've promised to go to tea to Mr. Norman's.'

'Norman's, you said? Right-o. Me, too!'

For a dreadful moment Willie felt a piercing jealousy. But upon reflection he decided that his fears were foolish, as Jack's face was awfully ugly.

So they both went to tea with Mr. Norman. The Cerr-Nores were there, two boys and their sister. Willie was shy at first, and in his desire to get rid of his feeling of utter nonentity, he made several startling statements: one of them being that he was going to sea as an apprentice in a month's time.

'But Willie, you never told me!' exclaimed Jack.

'I've only just known.'

'But how?'

'I'm not supposed to say,' said Willie, awkwardly, and started a fit of coughing. After he had made several trumpet-like noises with one of his father's handkerchiefs (taken without permission) Elsie brought another girl forward, and said:

'Let me introduce you to my friend Mary, who is spending

a week with me. This is Willie, I told you of him,' she added to her friend.

'Hullo, Willie,' said Mary, shyly. She was dressed in a brown frock, with a very high skirt, and a shiny red belt was round her waist. Her hands were tiny, and warm; her mouth rather big, her eyes brown and large, with long lashes.

'We'll leave you to play, dear,' said Mrs. Norman to her daughter.

The afternoon began awkwardly. At first they sat down and made stilted conversation. Jack sulked. Then Elsie proposed a game, and they brightened. Jack was disgusted to hear the suggestion of 'Mothers and Fathers' (the girls' faces brightened at the idea) and advanced, as a proposition only, Jack explained, an alternative game of 'Pirates'. The girls' faces glowed less perceptibly until Willie, with tact, told them that they would be pirate queens and bind up the wounds of their valiant captains.

'But are we supposed to be married?' asked Mary, and she gave a quick glance at Willie.

'Oh, no,' he answered promptly. Had Elsie made the suggestion he would probably have hesitated and referred to Jack for the answer. A suspicion entered his head that he might find himself married to Mary.

'Pirates' was not a success, chiefly because Mrs. Norman refused to allow them to rig the tablecloth to the lamp for a sail, and to strut upon the table as a quarter-deck. Without some sort of vessel the game was rather silly, declared Willie.

Time for tea arrived, with a temporary suppression of spirits on account of the attendance of Elsie's parents. Mr. Norman joked as usual, addressing most of his humour to Willie, who grinned feebly at his sallies, but could not see any point in them. Contrary to his expectations, he did not see any signs of subduedness in the boy, although he was certainly quiet.

He spoke about birds, wanting to make the boy reveal himself, and he was at once successful; the boy's face lit, and he talked vivaciously. What bird did he like best? The nightingale, oh yes, it was a fine singer, but didn't he think the blackbird was a better singer? Now if the blackbird sang at night, what would be the general opinion then?

'Nightingales don't come to the Burrows where I live,' said Mary.

'There was one in our garden this year,' said Willie, to Mr. Norman, 'it used to sing in the pear-tree outside my window.'

'Hoo, I'd'v set a trap for it,' cried Charlie Cerr-Nore, across the table. 'Beastly noise they make all night.'

'Unheard melodies are sweeter, what?' said Mr. Norman, and Charlie grinned, not sure that he wasn't being made a fool of.

'What did you do, Willie? Shoot it?'

'No, Mr. Norman.'

'Did you like to hear it?'

The boy nodded.

Mr. Norman was made curious by the expression on the boy's face: obviously an emotional memory of some power or significance. His mother? no, he hadn't known her, so he had been told. Tears had come into the boy's eyes which he had tried to conceal by looking on his plate.

Then Mr. Norman noticed the face of Mary. She too was in a dream, staring at the Maddison boy's face.

'Have some of this cake, Mary,' said Elsie, but Mary was lost.

Although he had not looked at her, Willie could see that she was staring at him; he felt uneasy and humiliated, disliking the silly little creature opposite to him who wanted to marry him at 'Pirates'. Mr. Norman was watching, and saw the different emotions expressed in his face. But he was puzzled by the sudden tear.

'Mary,' said Mrs. Norman, 'wake up, dreamy eyes. Elsie's offering you some cake.'

'Thank you,' replied Mary, taking some, and her cheeks going red.

'Willie?'

He took the smallest piece he could find, although plum and cherry cake was never to be found in his own house.

After tea they played 'Tiddlywinks'; tiring of this 'Snakes and Ladders', which interested them for thirty seconds. A fight with cushions occupied the attention of the boys and the interest of the girls till exhaustion compelled them to stop. Willie's collar flapped around his ears, and his dicky shirt-front was torn. Elsie immediately offered to sew it up.

She produced her new needlework box and said: 'Come here, and please stand quite still, or I'll prick you.'

'Yes.'

He stood before her: her fingers lightly touched his throat— 'It would be easier if Willie took his collar off,' said Mrs. Norman.

Ah, Mrs. Norman didn't like Elsie to come near him, because he was a rude boy, and swore.

'Please don't bother,' he muttered, and tearing off his collar, he threw it into the fire.

'Bravo!' said Mr. Norman, who was watching the boy's face. 'Down with convention!' and he threw his own collar into the fire.

'No, no! Really, Percy, you mustn't do such things!' exclaimed Mrs. Norman, seeing that Jack and Charlie were about to follow suit. They did not heed her; and the flames of four collars roared up the chimney.

Willie saw Mary smiling at him; he smiled back at her. The rest of the party was noisy: all the young ones were sorry when it was time for the guests to go home.

Chapter 20

The flames of autumn yawned through the woods and hedgerows in glorious fire of colour, till only the burnt-out framework of bare branches and twigs was outlined against the winter sky.

Fieldfares and redwings clucked among the hips and haws on the may-trees; duck and widgeon flighted to the lake; gray hoody crows from Scandinavia grawbeyed the farmyards and pillaged the eyes of dying rabbits caught in traps set along the hedges.

Willie seldom went into the meadows or woods, feeling no desire now that his friends (as he secretly called them) were gone. Once he went to the lake, and peered into its murky depths. The sodden leaves lay on the mud at its edge, black and rotting. There was a mist over its surface; the bright things were no more—the crystal-winged dragonflies, the blue kingfisher, the floating waterlilies. Somewhere on its oozy bottom were the sleeping carp, hibernating till springtime.

The shedding of the leaves from a hawthorn disclosed a nest, which he knew by its structure to be that of a blackcap warbler. Rain and wind had roughed its appearance: decayed notched hawthorn leaves lay in its minute cup. He pulled the nest from the tree, and picked out the leaves. It was damp and mildewed. Looking carefully, he saw that the bones and skulls of four little birds were collected in the middle, with three mouse-gnawn berries. They had gone—the mother bird who had toiled at the nest with such passionate desire for the eggs to be laid and the blind and naked young to come forth from their shells: the male who had sung as she toiled, who had helped to hatch the eggs, singing as he did so for joy of sunshine, the driven snow of may bloom, with the happy bees humming, and his mate—they had gone. Only the rain-darkled and frail structure of the cradle remained, with the bones thinner than the grasses of the nest, to tell of that song; only the decayed notched leaves to speak of that sunshine, the snow of bee-flecked blossom. Maybe a stoat had killed the mother bird on the nest, or a hawk swooped and struck as she searched for insects in the bushes. Bird-catchers sometimes came into the woods at the springtide, and took away the sweetest singers. Perhaps in some cage the bird now languished, near to death—pining for the sands of the south, whither its brethren had migrated—with an unknowing child weeping over its listlessness.

But a redbreast piped his tremulous notes in a tree near, and Willie forgot to think about the nest. Under some beech leaves—veined and curled as no cunning of sculptor in copper or bronze could fashion—he buried the tragic cradle, and went home.

Big Will'um was eating a meat pasty in the kitchen, and greeted him his usual, ' 'Ullo, miboy!'

'Look at ees clout,' exclaimed Biddy, 'all muddy. Where 'ave ee been now?'

'Been round the lake. The duck are there.'

'Ah,' said Big Will'um.

'Will ee 'ave piece o' pasty?' coaxed Biddy, apple-cheeked as ever.

'Thank you, Biddy,' he said, taking a piece. It was like an ordinary turnover, but the contents made it a thing of glory. Partridge and hare it contained, minced up, with potato, carrot, and egg, and all savoured with a special kind of onion, thyme, and sage. Big Will'um was the only man tolerated in her kitchen, and never once had he abused that privilege by mudding the floor, smoking his cutty, or presuming in any way. Often when work was done Biddy would sit on one side of the fire, clasping the elbows of her folded arms, and staring into the glow, Big Will'um against the wall in his special chair, stolidly eating pasty. The village, tired of waiting to hear the result of his courtship, had decided long ago that there was no such thing at all. But even Big Will'um's reputation and mighty fist had not saved him from being the subject of desultory and crapulous conversation at eventide.

'Saw Jim this morning,' Willie said, munching.

Biddy immediately abused him.

'Jim bean't no good. Jilted Dolly, so they be telling.'

'Poof!'

'Us be going shooting s'afternoon, Little Will'um,' said Big Will'um.

'Oh, Big Will'um, let me come.'

'Ee'll be a-shot. Mustn't go.' This from old Biddy.

'Poof, I'm not a child. Of course I'm going. Mayn't I, Will'um?'

'It bant my business if ee goes a-shutin',' expostulated the bailiff, drawing his iron-shod boots over the tiled floor in preparation to leave.

'Must ask Feyther,' said Biddy.

'Oh, no, it isn't necessary, he won't mind, I'm sure. Is Jack going, Big Will'um?'

'Ay, young máster.'

'Well, I can go.'

'Ask Feyther first, you must, midear.'

But Willie dreaded the demanding of any favour from his father. His father did not care whether he were shot or not, so why should he ask him at all. Besides, he would probably refuse.

When he did ask him at lunch time his father said, as he expected, that he was too young to go shooting.

'You'll only interfere with the others,' he said.

'But Jack's going, Father,' replied his son.

'I can't help that. If Mr. Temperley chooses to let his boy

go out with men carrying rusty firearms that their for-
bears picked off the battlefields of the Civil War, that is
his look out. Personally, I have no desire to see you
carried home on a hurdle because some wretched flintlock
has burst.'

'I promise to stand a long way away, Father.'

'And probably get peppered by some blear-eyed sportsman,
and blinded,' declared Mr. Maddison in a dry voice. How
could Willie know that it was his father's idea of humour, and
that he regretted greatly his son's inability to stand up to chaff
like a man. 'And then I should have a hopeless cripple on my
hands for the rest of my life.'

Willie did not answer. Disappointment had loosened the
controls of his voice, and he could only just swallow his food.
He wished passionately that he were dead. Father always——

'You're going to school after Christmas. It is time you were
licked into shape.'

For a terrible moment he thought he meant boarding-school,
where he would never see Biddy, Jack, or Big Will'um, or
Jacob or . . . Elsie . . . and there would be a Slogger Williams
who would toss him in a blanket, and a fat boy . . . and perhaps
they would force him to be a drunkard like Eric in *Little by
Little*.

'What, boarding-school, Father?'

'Lord no. You'd be killed if I sent you there. No, you're
going to Colham Grammar School, to play football and learn
to be a man.'

Willie wished miserably that he were a man, then he would
answer him back. But that state would never be reached by
himself—how *could* it? Cold mutton and potatoes dragged into
semolina pudding and prunes, and at last dinner time was
over. Willie went upstairs, where he could wear his poaching
hat, and shoot through the window at wheezy starlings upon
the chimney pots with his catapult. As an alternative he would
classify his birds' eggs once more and re-read *Bevis*, the best

boys' book ever written. If only Father were like Bevis's guv'nor! He let them wander all over the New Sea, visit the island Serendib in a boat, and have Roman battles and shoot with a matchlock—oh, lovely, glorious!... Father was calling him.

'You can go if you want to,' said Mr. Maddison, standing at the bottom of the stairs with Fidelis. 'Only be careful, there's a good lad.'

'Yes, Father.'

'Promise to take care of yourself?' gruffly.

'Yes, Father.'

'All right.'

The gratitude in Willie's heart made him call shyly downstairs.

'I say, Father!'

'Yes, my boy?'

'Thank you *very* much.'

Confused, and afraid that father would think him soppy, he retired behind the banisters and crept away to *Tierra del Fuego*—*Private* as a small inconspicuous notice pinned on the door announced to be the apparent location and nature of his bedroom.

Downstairs Mr. Maddison felt the same unwillingness to betray the feelings of his heart; he wished that he had not been thanked, especially as he felt that he had been rather mean over the whole business.

Willie was glad enough to leave the house. He did not dare to wait more than a minute after father had given permission lest it should be cancelled. He only stopped to get his catapult and bullets from the secret hiding-place under the floor, and then rushed out of the house.

The dog Fidelis made an attempt to follow him, having caught the word 'shooting' at dinner time, but he did not go farther than the gate. He was nearly blind, as well as doddering, and eventually decided to lie down beside the kitchen fire and tolerate the cat sleeping on his back, as was its parasitic and irresistable habit.

Jack hailed his friend with great delight. Willie saw Dolly for a moment in the scullery as she was washing up the dinner plates. He noticed that her face was thinner, and remembered that Jack had told him that she had sent Jim about his business. But he thought no more about it, as it was something to do with grown-ups and therefore not very important. Jack was excited about his friend going to school with him.

'I say, how ripping, man!' he cried.

The two boys went down to the village to meet the rabbiting party who were due to leave the King's Arms at three o'clock. They hung about, talking to several people, including Miss Nicholson, accompanied as usual by a slobbering bulldog called 'Mac', so named because when a puppy it had eaten half a rubber raincoat. At least she had told them so nearly a hundred times.

'Good-afternoon, boys,' she said primly.

Jack pulled his school cap—shapeless as the lining of an antiquated trouser pocket—from his head, while Willie saluted, a habit he had lately developed when wearing his fly-blown moleskin, owing to difficulty in readjusting it.

'Going for a walk?' she beamed.

'No thank you, Miss Nicholson, we're going shooting,' they replied together.

'How brutal. Children like you delighting in the prospect of torment and bloodshed. Why don't you attend Sunday school?' she demanded. 'You would enjoy it. One hour on Sunday afternoon. Ask Pa!' and she beamed at Willie.

'I don't think he would let me,' he said, as though saddened by the thought.

'Come now, that's all wrong,' rejoined the lady, while her dog nuzzled Jack's legs. 'Stop it, Mac, naughty old thing! You are Mr. Maddison's poor little boy, aren't you? I will write to Pa. How will that do? Or shall I get the Vicar to write?'

Willie mumbled something and felt depressed by the thoughts of his father as 'Pa' and the possibility of enforced collect and psalm learning.

Miss Nicholson beamed through her gold spectacles, and with her bulldog shuffled away as the sportsmen emerged from the King's Arms. 'Soppy old fool,' said Willie. 'Stuck up idiot!' said Jack. The sportsmen looked at the sky. Bill Adams was there, with his wizened crony George Davidson, Big Will'um and John Strong-i'-th'arm, the blacksmith, who carried a small sack wherein wriggled a ferret; in his other hand a crowbar for digging out the animal when it 'lay-up'.

Big Will'um and Bill Adams carried guns, and George Davidson had his lurcher, Polly.

They set out towards the foot of the downs, where were numerous rabbit buries in the hedgerow banks. Willie carried the ferret, and Jack slung Big Will'um's 12-bore over his shoulder. Its stock was drilled by insects, and the barrel and ironwork pitted and rufoused with rust. A spider peeped from the choke barrel, disturbed from his winter's sleep inside the clock case, where the gun was usually hidden in Granfer Will'um's cottage.

'This'n'll do,' growled Big Will'um, when they came to the beginning of a long bank. 'Bury bean't deep.' Willie's knowledge was sufficient to enable him to understand that a deep bury would mean much work should the ferret lay up.

The blacksmith opened the sack, and immediately a pink-nosed, pink-eyed ferret slipped out, sniffing every way. It half drew back into the sack, but he caught it between finger and thumb round the neck, and put it into a hole. Meanwhile Big Will'um got through the hedge to cover the retreat of any rabbits, and Bill Adams loaded on their side.

The ferret did not enter the hole—there was no scent. John the blacksmith, a sombre, dark-moustached, black-eyed dwarf, knotted like a pollard oak, put it in another. Immediately it disappeared.

A dull thumping came from the bury—the warning was sent along by the conies banging their hind legs on the ground. Almost at once a terrified rabbit rushed from a hole. 'Oh—ah,' cried the men, the dog quivered but was too well trained to bark or follow. Willie and Jack shouted, guns were raised, but it darted into another hole.

The excitement of the boys had hardly gone when another rushed forth, ears laid back in terror; it hared across the field— bang!—a flash, it rolled over, kicking. Polly, lithe, long of leg and tail—a cross between greyhound and bulldog, which strain produces the best lurchers—had it in a moment, and brought it back.

It was already dead. Naturally the boys must admire it, stroke the long gentle ears, look at the eyes, big and mournful, over which a film had come. Its soft body was limp and warm; the teeth slender, unlike the ferret's.

Jack looked at Willie, and Willie at Jack.

' 'Member the one we found last spring, man?'

'A stoat had bitten it.'

'No chance against a ferret, man.'

'Isn't fair, is it, man?'

'Hush, don't let 'em hear us. They'll think us soppy.'

Miserably they agreed that they were soppy; and immediately afterwards desired greatly to be allowed to shoot.

Another rabbit came out, and raced away; Big Will'um gave it the right barrel, and missed. The choke blazed forth, blowing the fly-swelled spider to hibernating continuity and killing the rabbit clean as a whistle.

'Good sport, man,' cried Willie.

'Lovely,' echoed his friend.

Two more were secured—the boys carrying them with pride, their sentiment fled—when the ferret lay up.

'Dang 'un,' growled Big Will'um from across the hedge.

The blacksmith put his ear to a hole and listened. The boys listened too.

They heard a sound as of something sighing, sighing . . . a flutter as of breath coming quickly, and in soft tumult—from the hole came a weak cry of abandoned despair. Through the earth came the thumping of rabbits' legs; they had heard that cry, and could not help, only warn the others. The sighing came again. Willie heaved inside, and nearly burst into tears. John stoically plunged the crowbar into the soft earth, removed some clods, and buried his thick arm up to the shoulder.

'Got 'un,' his deep voice grunted.

By the hind legs the rabbit was pulled out, kicking feebly. Behind its neck the ferret hung grimly, sinuous and its muzzle carmined. To demonstrate its courage, John swung it up and down; it wriggled and snarled with rage, but hung on. Skilfully he pressed the base of its throat, it pushed with its forepaws against the encircling thumb and finger, and being dropped to the ground, shook itself and glided towards the bury. John snapped the rabbit's neck, and threw it on the grass.

Sport continued, calling forth alternate joy and misery to the boys.

The weak November sun ceased to reflect on the downs, clouds came up; wind moaned through the hedge. The curved immensity of the hills became less defined against the skyline; silent rooks fled overhead to the rookery in the beech wood.

They counted up the spoil—fourteen and a half couple. John bagged the ferret, while they all agreed that it was a beauty. Willie and Jack felt regular sportsmen. The former was in high spirits because John said that his hat was a 'rare 'un', and Jack, who had not cared much for it before, made a secret determination to make one out of rabbit skin.

The plover were calling in the freezing watermeadows as the little band passed by—head to wind an immense flock crouched on the grass.

'Snow be a-coming,' prophesied Bill Adams, the village postman. 'Bliddy good job the potato crop were gude this year. Us be in fur a hard winter, shouldn't wonder.'

They made for the King's Arms, Big Will'um giving them a rabbit each, for which they thanked him tremendously.

'Gie my bes' respects to Missus Biddy, miboy,' he growled.

'Yes, Will'um,' said Willie.

Walking, they discussed the sport.

'We must get a gun.'

'How about the blunderbusses, man?'

'Oh, daren't!'

'Why not?'

'Guv'nor'd wallop me. Remember the stag's head.'

An understanding and sympathetic silence.

They parted by the footpath, just as the first flake swirled over the stiffening grasses, and a thin tinkling came from the hedge as the rising wind scattered a flurry of snow among the twigs. The wind lisped across the field, chilling; a lapwing soughed past, calling forlornly, knowing of the bitter weather sweeping from the north-east.

As Willie went along the lane a dark tall figure loomed out of the duskiness; hat pulled down over his eyes, collar up, hands in pockets. It was Jim Holloman, and he did not answer his greeting. Perhaps he did not see him. Willie felt sorry that he had no overcoat.

He was pushing back the white gate—Mr. Maddison had recently been painting about the house and buildings by day and by night—when two other people passed him, coming from another direction. One was the man whom Willie hated— John Fry, the primitive preacher in the chapel. The other called out, in a low soft voice: 'Gude-night, Willie.'

'Good-night. It is going to snow, Dolly. I've got some rabbits.'

'Have ee now!' They passed on, and Willie ran up the grassy drive, a rabbit hidden under his coat.

Chapter 21

ALL NIGHT the snow fell, covering the fields and hills with whiteness, and drifting against the hedges till they faded into nothingness. Nor did the storm cease that day, but continued for over seventy hours. To Willie it was a superb adventure, but both Biddy and Mr. Maddison knew that disaster would follow. On the morning of the fourth day snow ceased falling, although sullen clouds hung above, graying with an almost supernatural light the landscape. Willie, wrapped up and protesting the brown paper tied round his legs as gaiters, went out with his father. No newspapers had been delivered at the house, and no milk. The baker had called bringing with him tales of sheep lost on the hills, and a stoppage on the railway. Most of the telegraph lines were down, broken by the gale that had roared over the countryside at the commencement of the storm. Passing carts and horses had beaten solid the snow on the roadway, stained brown by their pounding; frost kept it from becoming slush.

The main street of Rookhurst was full of people. Little groups of men and women talked, stamping feet, blowing through mittened hands, and swinging arms till the blood glowed and pulsed. Already small boys had knocked together different sorts of sledges, and were pulling each other along on the road. They met the Vicar and Miss Nicholson chatting outside the general store, and stopped to speak to them. Hardly had conversation started when the Vicar was struck by a snowball which sploshed over the back of his head and knocked his wide black hat upon the pavement. As an intermittent bombardment between various small boys was pro-

142

ceeding at the time, the Rev. Odo Cerr-Nore, who held the living from his cousin, the Earl of Slepe, was constrained to accept it as a joke, and his organist remarked that boys would be boys when a miniature avalanche from the roof of the shop slithered over the party, causing hidden joy among the small boys and Willie to wonder if Miss Nicholson would exclaim that roofs would be roofs and snow snow.

'Thawin', I do hope,' gasped the Vicar, his nose blue.

'Rather unfortunate. Are you very wet?' said Mr. Maddison to Miss Nicholson, who was shaking her head vigorously.

'It's gone down my back,' she said, wriggling.

'Yes—I think it will thaw,' reiterated the Vicar, looking at the sullen sky.

Willie could hardly refrain from laughing, as he thought of the snow down old Nicky's back! After a few more futilities in conversation they passed on, going towards the butcher's, for a leg of mutton.

'Sorry, Sir,' said the butcher, a fat, short man with soot-coloured hair, protruding ranine eyes and a blue-black chin, 'but us haven't got much. Tse-tse,' and he blew through his teeth.

'Any beef?' mumbled Mr. Maddison, bored with shopping.

'Sold out, sir. Trains from Colham suspended. Don't think you'll get any in Rookhurst, nowhere. Tse-tse.'

They tried the other butcher's shop, and found he had nothing except tripe, which made Mr. Maddison shudder, although Willie wanted to try it. As Biddy had told him that provisions, except for hams, were rather low in the house, it appeared as though they would have to live on ham, at any rate for the duration of the bad weather.

'Let us go to Skirr Farm,' suggested Willie, 'and see how they are.'

To his surprise his father consented.

So to Skirr they went. It was warm in the parlour, the flames of a wood fire licked and flapped up the broad chimney. Doris and Peggy were delighted at the sight of Willie, and Jack showed a sledge he was making. While the young ones were talking by the fire, Mrs. Temperley told Mr. Maddison that her husband was out with Big Will'um, and all the men he could get, trying to locate the sheep on the Downs.

'It has been a terrible time,' she said. 'They've been out all night, but so far have had no luck. The shepherd is still out too.'

Dolly brought in a big tray of steaming cups of cocoa, which she placed on the table. Willie looked at her and smiled, and wanly she smiled back. He noticed the shadow under her eyes, and wondered why. Suddenly the reason occurred to him, and impetuously he exclaimed:

'Oh, Mrs. Temperley—Jack—I wonder how Jim is?'

The cup that Dolly was handing to Mr. Maddison rattled in the saucer.

'Oh, he's all right,' said Jack's mother. 'I expect he's snug somewhere or other.'

Dolly took the tray, and closed the door quietly behind her.

'I wonder if he is snowed up in his hut,' suggested Jack. The four children ceased talking, and stared at each other. Doris and Peggy looked frightened.

'Is that the fellow who won't work, whom my housekeeper so dislikes?' Mrs. Temperley was asked.

'Oh, he works all right. He's different from the others, that's all.'

Jim was soon forgotten, except by Willie. Jack began hammering at his sledge, and was told to cease doing so by his mother. His petulant protestation was cut short by interest when a thrush, puffed out and toad-like, flew to the sill and looked in at the window.

'It's hungry,' cried Willie.

'Poor thing,' cried Peggy.

'The birds will suffer,' said Mr. Maddison. 'The berries won't last for ever.' Willie looked at him gratefully.

They drank the cocoa, and prepared to leave, Willie to his great disappointment not being allowed to stay to dinner.

On their return Biddy was eager to hear the gossip from Rookhurst, and listened with horror to the tale of the avalanche upon the Vicar and Miss Nicholson, which Willie told her in the kitchen. She declared it was a sign from heaven, and was very indignant when Willie burst into laughter. She was a devout church-goer.

Day succeeded day, and still the frost bound the earth. Willie was allowed to go to Jack's whenever he liked, much to his delight. When the snow had lain a fortnight, Mr. Temperley found a small flock of the sheep, huddled together and very feeble, under the lee side of a hedge. They had been living chiefly on twigs. Big Will'um and his helpers, the bailiff tireless and working stolidly, carried them in couples on hurdles or 'flakes', as they were called, to the orchard where mangel wurzels were thrown for them. Big Will'um slung one across his shoulders with the greatest ease, holding its feet in his hands, and worked all day and far into the night upon the rescue. The farmer feared anxiously for Jacob, who should have been at his hut—composed of turves and sarsen stones— on the Downs, for a rescue party, taking a whole day to travel there, had discovered it empty, except for dying finches. There was a possibility, however, that he had gone to one of the scattered cottages on the plains away over the hills, his sheep with him, led by the bell-wether.

The lambing ewes were secure in the yeaning field behind the beech forest, with enough rootcrops to keep them for months, if need be.

When after another week the frost still held, the older inhabitants shook their heads, and Old Granfer Will'um held the opinion—and expressed it to everyone within earshot, whether they had heard it an hour previously or not—that the tarrible winter of '81 had come on them agen, and that Jacob were buried, as George had been in '81.

No more snow fell, and skating began on the big lake. Thousands of duck and geese, widgeon, teal, and plover thronged the brook which, being swift running, was not frozen entirely. Wisps of snipe haunted the stream, flying away when approached with their peculiar zigzag flight; herons were observed to kill small birds that came within reach of their dagger-like beaks. Rooks and jackdaws, sometimes accompanied by the gray hoody crow, searched in the village streets for food, their shyness overcome by hunger and desperation. Some even preyed upon the starlings, pursuing the sickly ones and eating them. In the weak daylight—for the sun was hidden continually by plumbean vapour suspended above—the white owl hunted openly, looking like a ghost risen from the spirit of the snow; the brown wood owl called mournfully from the woods, where nothing stirred, no sound save for the creaking of rimed branches. Hares limped slowly and weakly to the outskirts of cottages, or with floppy ears drooping with exhaustion, lolloped along the lanes, an easy prey to dogs and children. It had been a good berry year, especially for hawthorn and yew, but all disappeared during the first few days.

In silent misty whiteness the snow shrouded the downs, and no news of Jacob or the flock came to Skirr Farm. Again and again search parties went out, braving the vast drifts at the foot of the hills and in the hollows. They returned as many times without result. It was thought that he had started to lead the flock into the valley beyond, and wandered about till he had lost direction.

One morning Jim Holloman appeared in the village, clad in a coat made of rabbit skins, laid two-fold and uncured. A great cap of similar material covered his ears and neck. The natives looked at the skins, and mentioned the word 'poaching'. There were many rabbits in the spinney, and from the coat it was obvious how he had fared.

A month after Guy Fawkes' Day Willie and Jack bought up at half-price hundreds of Chinese crackers, which they exploded on all possible occasions and in all positions, throwing them over hedges at passers-by, dropping them in letter-boxes, and shops. Searching for some new thrill one evening Willie fired some in *Tierra del Fuego—Private*, thus justifying its name and his father's punitive wrath and confiscation of the remainder.

The feeling of anticlimax and the tearing down of his notice by his father left him moody and feeling miserable. Gray days and star-cloaked nights drifted slowly; and still no change. A black frost bound the earth. As the advent of Christmas drew nearer, so the general excitement at 'The Firs'—the home of the Normans—and at Skirr Farm among the children developed. Willie no longer believed in Father Christmas, any more than he credited the fables of the Snake and the Apple, and the Menagerie of Noah. In like manner Jack's vigilance three years since had detected the inaccuracy of his mother's account of chimney visitation, resulting at the time in remorse at his self-encompassed disillusion and lacerated fingers when he sprung unwittingly the gin set in the grate overnight to catch the annual visitant and ensure more acceptable presents—he was tired of soldiers and rubber balls.

At Willie's home Christmas Day was a solemn affair. In the morning Mr. Maddison took his son to church, while Biddy cooked the dinner. Willie still suffered disappointment over his presents—his uncle in London, whom he had seen on one occasion only, sent him an undersized and anaemic-looking football. Biddy gave him a pigskin purse; his father a new tweed suit and a pair of brown boots, almost canary coloured. Jack gave him a small French-English dictionary, obviously second-hand, but the most cherished gift of all was a hand-painted card inscribed: 'Poacher Maddison, Esquire, from Elsie.' He cherished it, and put it away, and took it out again a dozen times in as many minutes.

Willie had eaten no supper on Christmas Eve and no breakfast that morning, as turkey, sausages, bread sauce, bacon, brussels sprouts, and baked potatoes, all together, were unique in the year. With red face, Biddy brought the huge dish into the dining-room unrelieved by holly, mistletoe, or Chinese lanterns, and his father solemnly carved the bird. Plum pudding, flaring with brandy, followed with mince pies; and after an hour's feeding Willie rose from the table wondering quakily whether the reaction to his piggishness would be instantaneous or deferred. Such doubts, however, were dispelled after half an hour's meditative quiet, when he inquired with a boldness that astonished him (not all the brandy on the pudding had gone into flame) whether he might go to Jack's house for tea and supper as he had been invited.

Permission being given, off he went, and Mr. Maddison was left with Fidelis and Bob before the fire, and his own thoughts.

Both dogs were sleeping—old Fidelis snoring. He stared into the fire while the empyreal flames of pine logs licked and fluttered up the chimney in hues of lilac, gold, and red. Twilight filled the room: outside a frosted mist obscured the trees at the end of the garden. How bare the room was—no holly, or mistletoe—why hadn't Willie put some up? Perhaps he himself ought to have done it—O, well, but what was Christmas to him?

He thought of his isolation: of that evening years ago when Jenny had passed—whither? He brooded backwards to the time when he had first met her; their stolen meetings in London when she was stopping with her grandmother, the visits to the Opera . . . in the gallery, he had not much money in those days, waiting for briefs. They had held each other's hands, thrilling with the warmth: how her sweet eyes had shone in the dimness while Jean de Reszke's golden voice floated into the domed loftiness of the building—all that was ended. Had it ever happened . . . if the spirit after death did not go out like one of those flames in front, she would be near. And perhaps she would understand that he wanted to be proud of his boy when he grew up—that his habit of lying must be checked—

she would be near, and watching her baby, from whom he had estranged himself for ever—no, *he* was not estranged—it was too late now. Queer little fellow Willie was! Old Fidelis was stirring: she had loved Fidelis, had nursed him through distemper . . . sentimental rubbish: life was just a blind waste, a marking-time on the way to Death.

Willie was glad to be leaving his father, and he ran till he was puffed. Once only he stopped to watch a starving rook chasing a starling in the air, the pirate silent and the pursued screaming harshly in fear.

The frost caught his toes, and the tips of his ears. How dark it was getting. Elsie would be there, and her friend Mary Ogilvie, worse luck.

He was pleased by the cries of joy with which he was greeted.

'Here's old Willie!' yelled Jack.

They pulled him into the house, and removed his coat and muffler.

'How's Willie?' said Jack's mother, kissing him. 'How cold his face is!'

Willie, pushed into the room, shook hands with Mr. Temperley and the others, who asked him if his father were coming. Willie said hopefully that he didn't think so.

The great problem to solve was the choice of game, whether 'Indians', 'Cowboys', 'Pirates', 'Blind Man's Buff', 'Mothers and Fathers', or 'Thump'im'. This last was the invention of Willie's, and consisted of drumming the ribs of a victim selected till he could endure the tickling no longer, the one who stood it the longest being the winner.

They agreed to play 'Thump'im', and Willie was chosen to withstand the first onslaught, so he said it was a poor sort of game after all. He feared that Elsie might feel how thin were his arms and ribs if permitted a too intimate propinquity.

'I'll tell you a tale, if you like.'

'Do, Willie, there's a dear,' urged the girls. Elsie looked upon him with a proud air of possession—was he not going to speak while the others listened? Her friend Mary, who sat cross-legged beside her, linked her arm with hers and smiled happily to herself.

'Go on,' they whispered, snuggling round the fire.

'More gipsies, I suppose,' came from Mr. Temperey, deep in his arm-chair.

'Hush, daddy,' said little Doris, squatting beside Peggy.

Willie did not know what to say. In a mental flurry he tried to recall one of the *Thuddenblunder* thrillers, but could not remember anything. Suddenly a fine theme suggested itself—knights and ladies!

'Once upon a time,' he began, 'there was a deep black forest. Curious to relate, there was a lake in this forest, full of carp, perch, pike——' Here Jack's eyes began to brighten—'in fact,' —Willie was wishful of pleasing his friend, 'in fact, there was a pike of sixty pun in its depths.'

'Rats,' said Jack, unappreciatively. 'Why, even the Trent Otter in his book says that one has rarely been known to exceed——'

'Oh, be quiet, Jack,' said Peggy.

'Go on, Willie,' the girls coaxed.

'Sixty pun pike,' reiterated Willie, feeling a true sportsman because he had not said 'pounds'—'however, since Jack objects to its weight, we will leave it out,' he added magnanimously.

'Out on the bank, so to speak?' interrupted Mr. Norman.

The girls groaned, and Jack sitting apart from the others in a dark corner laughed hollowly to himself for several moments.

'Yes, out on the bank,' shouted Willie, waving his arms at his friend. 'It had been caught at last! And what bait was used on the hook? Shall I tell you? Right. It was Jack disguised as a tiddler!'

They all laughed except Jack, who muttered his swear word.

'To continue,' chirruped Willie, pleased with his joke, like a sparrow that has successfully hatched an egg hitherto supposed to be addled, 'the lake was in the wood. One day a party of horsemen rode up. Two of them. "Sir William", said the other, who was his squire, "here is the place where the foul deed was perpetrated."

'A cross marks the spot where the body was found,' interrupted Mr. Norman, 'as a reporter upon a Sunday newspaper would write.'

'I don't read them,' continued Willie, with excessive politeness. 'The squire said: "Is that so, Sir William?" No, it wasn't the squire, but Sir William who said that. Anyhow, while they were speaking, a lady, terribly beautiful, looked from behind a beech-tree, where she had been waiting for her swee— husband,' he concluded nervously.

A sigh went up from the girls. Willie heard it, and with the instinct of a raconteur realised that he had blundered. Yet sweetheart had seemed too daring and intimate a word, somehow.

'As a matter of fact, they weren't married—although the Baronet, her father, was putting pressure upon her to marry a neighbouring earl.'

'What was the Baronet's name?' inquired Peggy.

'Sir Grawbey de Oddmedodd!' jeered Jack.

Willie scoffed. 'He was putting pressure on her——'

'What's that, Willie?' lisped Mary.

'The Baronet was up the tree, dropping weights upon her head, I suppose,' chuckled Mr. Norman.

Willie decided to ignore such futile humour.

'The princess was very pretty.'

'What was she dressed in?' whispered Mrs. Norman, winking at her hostess.

'Oh, a green hat, with purple feathers on it, and a long silky gown—bright pink, oh, such a lovely colour. Just like a rose! Her hair hung down her back in a long plait, the colour of corn'—he spoke nervously, and avoided looking at anyone, especially Elsie. 'Her eyes were—the colour—of—er——' He looked away, flushing.

'Gray eyes greedy, gobble all the world up,' said Jack, 'brown eyes beauty, do a mother's duty.' There was silence when he stopped.

'What colour were they, Willie?' asked Mrs. Norman.

'Blue,' he replied shyly, not daring to look at Elsie's face.

'It's Elsie,' whispered Mary, hugging her friend's arm.

The tale floundered on to a rather tragic and morbid conclusion. The princess, Willie told them, scorned Sir William and married the earl after all, breaking Sir William's heart, and driving him to suicide in the lake. At this part a sympathetic tear shone in his own eye, and Mary, still absorbed in her gaze, wished dumbly that she might marry Sir William instead.

'What happened to the princess?' asked Elsie. There was silence, broken by Jack shouting from the corner:

'The pike swallowed Sir William, who was Willie himself, the swanker, mistaking him for a FROG!'

Laughter produced the distressing feeling of anticlimax in Willie, so he declined to play 'Indians'.

'Soppy game,' he mumbled, retiring to Jack's vacated corner in order to mope, driven there by the same reason that drives an old actor to drink.

His spirits were restored by the prospect of tea. First Dolly came in from the kitchen bearing a tray laden with plates, knives, spoons, cups and saucers, and a great teapot. The round copper kettle on the hearth stirred its waters into a frail song, and a thin wisp of steam joined the flames in their exploration of the chimney mazes. Dolly laid the cloth, smiling at the children in spite of the desolation in her heart. Jim had never come back since the quarrel—she had taunted him for his weakness in giving up such a good job for the miserable common labourer's work of harvesting. Most of her misery was for him: not hearing about him was terrible: and John Fry—who had long desired marriage with her—was poor consolation, regarded impatiently now that Jim had not got jealous.

Tea was a wonderful glory of iced almond cake, practically no bread and butter, sugared biscuits, gingerbread—not much in demand—Carlsbad plums, figs, preserved fruits, dates, the stones used with surreptitious glee as missiles—and crackers.

Only too soon the tea ended.

Games were played when the table had been cleared; after but a moment it seemed came supper, a riotous meal, and then ... time to go home ... and Christmas Day gone, gone! Eyes nearly brimmed with tears, lumps rose in slender throats—the joy had gone out of life.

Perhaps reminiscence had lighted some dark archives in the memory of the elder folk, for they too were silent when the time came for the visitors to go out into the moon-cold night.

When they had gone, and the children put tearfully to bed, Mrs. Temperley helped Dolly to clear away and wash up. She felt sorry for the girl, although she could not help thinking that, after all, it was for the best.

'Help yourself to anything you want, Dolly,' she said kindly, when the work was done.

'Thank ee, mum,' replied Dolly, almost listlessly.

She ate a piece of cake, sitting by the fire, but did not really want it. Feeling that the darkness would be more comforting, she turned the lamp low. What was Christmas to her—where was Jim—cold, perhaps ill ... dying ... if only she knew.

And her heart in a tumult of self-hating, thwarted desire and misery, she wept softly, head on hands, and staring into the draught-champed flames.

A mouse ran swiftly across the floor, unseen and small, seeking the means of life.

Outside in the night the burnished shield of the moon, its battle-scars showing so dimly, shone through the elms, forming a pleached pattern of black branches: slowly it swept higher: obeying its wan radiance the pallid shade of the trees slipped from the path: the snow freed from umbral thrall sparkled once more.

A long shadow passed over the grass swiftly; appeared to run up the wall and then rise and fall softly as the man walked across the snow. Coming to the pathway, he went on tiptoe, keeping well into the wall, reached the window and looked through into the kitchen.

For a long time he looked, making out the figure sitting by the fire, then tapped gently upon the pane.

Dolly looked up, and saw the silhouette. Her hand went to her mouth to stifle a scream. The window became clear.

She waited, not daring to move. For a moment her terror lasted, and then with a feeling of faintness she realised who had looked in.

Came a tapping at the door.

She turned the milled screw of the lamp in the wrong direction, the flame died; again the faintness swept over her, and she clung to the table to prevent herself falling.

The tapping came again. In the cold Jim waited. He heard no sound.

Her heart thumped, causing a sensation of nausea; she wondered if she were going off. The spluttering lamp rose slowly towards the ceiling, showing a bluish flame: it would hit the ceiling——

Her heart had stopped thumping, she was lying on the floor, and feeling queer—she must have gone off—of course—Jim was at the door.

Shakily she went across the room, a happiness coming with the warmth of blood; she opened the door, but only the apple-trees framed in light and shade were in front, with the Plough uptilted in the northern sky—and silence, except for the creak of branches and the gaggle of geese, flighting high up under the moon.

Chapter 22

THAT WINTER was a miserable time for the labourers. Children went out with sacks, gathering firewood; a few knowing ones walked to the pine woods for cones. Seeing a party return thence one day, Willie suggested to his father that he should go there and gather some. So he and Jack set out, mufflers round their throats, half-running, half-walking to keep warm. It was a two hours' walk, and by the time they reached it their cheeks were rosy and they were singing and shouting.

'Do you think your father would buy the cones from us?' asked Willie. 'It would be a good idea to get some money.'

'Oh, I don't expect so,' replied his friend, 'but I think yours might.'

'Yes, but why not yours?'

'Oh, no, yours.'

The argument continued, neither seeing why his own father should be swindled unduly, until it nearly precipitated into a quarrel. Eventually it was decided to sell an equal portion to each parent.

The pine forest was on the northern slope of the downs, bordered along its lower side by the main road. Jumping over the fence, they entered its edge, and were immediately in semi-darkness. The branches bore the frozen snow, and light shone through gaps where it had slidden down. Soon their eyes became used to the dim filtration of light, but the silence gave a feeling of awe.

'Let's explore, man,' whispered Willie.

'Think it's safe?'

'Let's risk it!'

They went on, pausing to gather small cones lying on the fallen spindles. A great owl flapped away from a tree in front, and they clutched each other in sudden fear. The sombre apparition disappeared into the murk, but the feeling of fear remained. From old time the owl has been the symbol of death, coming as mysteriously, solitary and silent, a thing of omen. The fear in the boys' hearts arose from the depths of olden time—they knew the tradition that the country people held: Willie knew what Biddy fearsomely believed, that they awaited the souls who should wander forth at death . . . she had told him how they had made moan at his own birth.

Once they turned back, afraid to penetrate deeper into the wood, but with a fearsome persistency they walked onwards. They might have been in an ice cave, so still and dead was everything, the light so spectral.

'We're lost,' yelled Willie, suddenly.

They looked at one another in terror, then commenced to run, the twigs whipping their faces. Exhaustion brought them to a standstill. Holding hands, they climbed up the slope, agreeing that it would be nearer to daylight in that direction. It grew steeper after half an hour's frenzied scrambling; they reached its edge, and commenced to tunnel through the immense drift of snow against its western border.

A silver sun was shining weakly when they emerged, almost blinded by the whiteness everywhere. The air was sweet and cold to breathe. Their hands were trembling, black sootiness from the trees smeared their faces, furrowed where tears had run down.

A flock of hoody and carrion crows flew up as they shouted, wheeling and croaking near the summit. Willie sat down on the snow—it was nearly three feet thick, but so frozen that their feet made but a thin impression, while Jack held out a tattered packet of cigarettes.

'This will steady us, man,' he said, with an air of shaky bravado.

His friend took one, and blackened its end with seven matches, finally causing it to smoulder satisfactorily.

Everywhere the hushed country was in serfdom to the snow. On the plain beneath they could see plumes of smoke cirrose and drifting from the chimneys of cottages and farmhouses; the new weathercock on the church spire gleamed in the sun; somewhere beyond the dazzling whiteness was the sea. The rounded hump of the hill was on their right hand, topped by a barrow anciently raised before Cæsar's time.

The surface seemed to be rippled unevenly up the gentle slope. Crunching over the snow, wishing to stand as high as possible, they wondered what had caused it.

The sombre crows still circled over their heads.

'Wonder what they want,' said Willie.

'Isn't it funny,' replied Jack, 'all wavy.'

They stood and stared, their faces going white. Willie began to choke, and put his arm around Jack's neck. Both boys started to cry, then turning round, they rushed away, often falling over. They ran in terror from what they had seen.

Under the solid snow, scarce covered by it, close together as though gathered in last companionship, were the lost sheep. Where the uneven and hummocky surface became smooth at the head of the frozen flock, crested with snow yet scarce rising above the level of the sheep, a cap stuck out, motionless as death and the torn face below it whence the eyes had been picked . . . with his sheep in the barrow of snow, and near to that anciently raised, was the lost shepherd.

In the air above the crows wheeled, croaking rude requiems.

NINE YEARS OLD

'So beset, the child fled into the tower of his own soul, and raised the drawbridge.'
— FRANCIS THOMPSON in the *Shelley* essay.

Chapter 23

Colham Grammar School, founded in the sixteenth century by a beneficent merchant, was one of those old institutions that had never assumed the appellation of public school, possibly on account of the fact that no one outside the county whose lesser sons it prepared for the conflict of mature life professed to have heard of its existence. None of its sons had risen to the rank of Cabinet Minister or achieved any equivalent notoriety. To be sure, a pupil with the reputation of being the worst boy of his generation had been expelled, and taking his wretchedness overseas had eventually become famous in three continents as an empire builder, which fame in no wise equalled his pristine record of releasing a dozen rats in the head master's study half a century before. Even to this day boys point with wonder at the portrait of a toad-like gentleman hanging above the model steamship in its glass case in Little Hall, and marvel at his temerity with the rats. It was agreed, of course, that the Head of those days, the Rev. Dr. Bullnote D.D., could not have equalled in ferocity Mr. Rore, or his eyes possessed of such terrifying and serbonian glare.

As the majority of its scholars were drawn from those classes for whom a strictly classical education was waived in favour of one more utilitarian, atypic youths leaving at the age of sixteen or seventeen in no way varied from other members of the class of commercial folk, estate agents, lesser impoverished gentry, smaller solicitors and doctors, poor clergymen, to which they belonged. No distinct 'tone' was acquired: the types were too diverse, consequently the soft dialect of the yeoman farmer's son was not alchemised into the clearer speech of the doctor's boy; nor was the enunciation of the doctor's son perverted to that drawling articulation so much coveted by illiterate snobs who desire so fervently that their sons should be varnished with the Oxford manner. Every type maintained its own peculiarities and characteristics, nor was the new boy ostracised, because his father was a tradesman. No standards of gentility were enforced among its population; the term *It is not done* had never stained its vocal escutcheon; heterogeneous as its pupilage was, Colham Grammar School, crowning the hill above Colham town, and adjoining the London road, had a reputation locally as permanent as it was good: both masters and old boys cherished its traditions, however obscure in the world outside they might be. At least, they would have understood it to be so; they never thought at all about it.

The opening of the Spring Term was an event of general excitement. The faces of pupils and masters beamed; even the face of Porter Samuel Crinkle took on a less unpleasant vacuity; Mrs. Duffe the matron, beamed; only the silent line of boys, enduring the continued criticisms of those already privileged to wear the Colham cap, standing and gazing at the portrait above the steamship, the ship itself, the ceiling, the floor, anywhere and everywhere, did not beam.

All the morning they had occupied a class-room, sitting at brown-stained desks, scratched and cut: biting pens, writing furiously, or staring at the gowned man with the heavy moustaches who sat on the raised dais before them. Some considered the questions in the general knowledge examination ridiculously easy; others found them puzzling; one fat boy attempted to plagiarise from the paper of a thin boy at his side, and was disgusted to find that the thin boy in question had only written a single sentence in answer to the dozen questions.

The chief exports of Africa are diamonds, gold, wool, ichiargo nuts and momentoes, he had written in a spidery hand below his name, W. Maddison. The fat boy thought that it would be too risky to duplicate ichiargo nuts on his own paper, so substituted the word argichigo instead, wondering the while what it meant, as from its very abstruseness it was obviously correct, momentoes suggested no suitable paraphrase, so he decided to ignore it, which perhaps was for the best.

At half-past twelve o'clock their sheaves of papers had been collected, and another master, tall, gaunt, with a drooping black moustache and weary eyes, and wearing an antiquated mortar-board, dull green from age, with a gown that looked as though it might sigh to pieces at a puff of wind, led them, silent and insignificant, to the Hall, where at long dining-tables sat fifty or so other boys, awaiting the serving of luncheon. The fat boy with a freckled face sat next to Willie, and in a squeaky but lowered voice said that he had done awfully badly.

'My name's Slater,' he said. 'I say, what's yours?'

'Mine's Maddison.'

'Don't like the look of this place, do you?'

'Not much.'

'Do you know anyone here?'

'Yes.'

'I don't. Let's be friends, shall we?'

Maddison hesitated. He was not sure whether he liked red hair, and besides he had one friend at the school already.

'Yes, let's,' he assented without enthusiasm.

The fat boy, who volunteered again among other things that his name was Slater—'Charles Montifiore Slater', seemed to think that the jointure of their two lives in friendship carried with it the necessity of unburdening a case of dog-eared photographs, which he told his friend were portraits, taken by himself, of his seven sisters, his aunts, uncles, and parents. By the time that Willie had looked at them all with a pretence of interest, the faces of the boys were turning towards the other end of Big Hall, where emerging from Little Hall was a groaning wagon, pulled in by the red-coated and scowling porter, bearing several steaming joints, tureens of green vegetables and snowy piles of mashed potatoes. He was helped by the maidservants and the housekeeper. The carving of the joints and portioning of the vegetables took at least ten minutes, when plates swimming with a brown gravy that smelt suspiciously like coffee, Willie thought, were handed round with their burden of meat and vegetables. Mr. Worth, the master on duty, called the attention of the boys by rapping on the side of a convenient water jug, and in a throaty voice of attenuated pitch, ordered them to stand up, which they did after considerable coughing and shuffling; and some semblance of quietude being obtained, Mr. Worth mumbled a few sentences composed in Latin by the late Dr. Bullnote, which implied grace. Sitting down when he had finished the boys devoted the next half-hour to consuming their meat, relieved by a fungous-looking tart besmirched with jam that formed the second and final course.

'There aren't many boys in the school, are there?' said Slater, with an air that held the feeling of having been cheated.

'Oh, only a few board here or stay to lunch,' Willie informed him. 'See that fellow with fair hair and a brown tie on? That's my friend Temperley. He's an old boy here. He told me there are three hundred and fifty altogether.'

The fat boy blew wind through his teeth at the mention of such a vast number.

Lunch finished, they had been free to wander about in Hall or the playground. Jack had joined Willie and the fat boy—who had sworn eternal allegiance to both of them not only during school time but throughout life afterwards—and conducted them round the playground, swept of snow, where a motley rabble of big and little boys were rushing about kicking an old tennis ball, shouting the while 'on the pill, boys, on the pill'. Some fairly large youths were playing fives in the court, while four smaller boys standing some distance away were bleating threats on having been 'turfed out' of the court, and suffered the additional indignity of having their pill 'rooted' on to the school roof. Coming away from the lower playground the trio walked round the upper playground, which surrounded two sides of the school buildings; the southern side being a favourite haunt owing to its somewhat irregular style of architecture, many indentations and buttresses being left by the designer years ago when the school had been enlarged, but not to the extent originally anticipated. Willie had been alarmed by the sight of two large boys whacking two smaller ones, hidden behind one of the jutting-out stacks. Jack informed him wrathfully that they were two bullies, one an overgrown, red-faced, stolid-looking boy and the other his crony, an extremely tall youth with a melancholy expression, pimply face, eyes resembling glass-filled gimlet holes, and mouse-coloured hair standing straight up from his head like a brush.

'They give the whack to most of the kids,' explained Jack, 'with that strap. That rotten cad Chapman and that filthy lout Dennis, whose father keeps the bacon shop in Colham, are always getting the whack from the Old Bird, so they take it out of the kids. It doesn't hurt very much, but some kids blub through sheer funk.'

His explanation had reached this point when the two victims ran past, pursued by the gruff shouts of Chapman and Dennis. An emaciated, sallow-complexioned boy slunk by Jack and the two new boys almost immediately afterwards.

'That's Evans,' Jack whispered. 'He's their spy. His headquarters are in The Bog, because that's where the kids go and hide, locking themselves in when they think those cads are after them.'

Fearing that the spy in question might report upon them, Jack took his friend away and went into the Hall again. Mr. Worth sat on the platform at the far end, correcting exercises and oblivious of the clatter and noise arising from the other end of the room. Here gymnastic apparatus was erected, ladders, parallel and horizontal bars, rings, and a vaulting horse. Gymnasium except at specified hours was forbidden, especially after meals, but when Mr. Worth, the drawing master, was on lunch duty the rule was seldom kept. Deviation from discipline would begin gradually. A boy would swing on the horizontal bar; another would pull himself up one of the ladders by his arms for a short distance: a third sit on the horse, until in time the ropes would be unwound from the ladders, the rings freed, and a swarm of boys swing, slide vault, and climb with simian movements. After twenty minutes or so of license Mr. Worth would realise the cause of the noise that had been disturbing him vaguely and bellow forth, in a voice, that threatened to become inarticulate with rage, an order to put back the apparatus.

The fat boy still clung to their company as they wandered round the Hall, looking at the notices on the Football Board, the selection of teams, announcements for the Harriers', Natural History, Debating and Literary Societies (the three last being in a permanent state of member-bankruptcy), glancing at the pictures from *The Illustrated London News*, *The Graphic* and *The Sphere* tacked on brown paper by drawing pins. Suddenly a miniature and high-pitched thunder had loosened from behind the green-baize table; a tall, gaunt figure flapped from the platform as the boys scurried away out of sight. Mr. Worth rushed up to Willie, and demanded ferociously what he meant by it. The fat boy looked as though he might burst into tears, and said that it wasn't him. Temperley inferred, when the thunder was, metaphorically speaking, reverberating in the far distance, that the thought of breaking a rule gave him intense anguish. Mr. Worth prepared to take their names, Jack digging his friend's ribs violently and whispering 'Maddison', fearing lest he should say 'Willie Maddison', but Willie mistook his meaning and gave his name as 'Middleton', wondering miserably what his father would think when he returned home that night having been expelled on his first day.

'It's all right, man,' Jack reassured him when the drawing master had drifted back to the green-baize table and his exercises. 'Old Useless won't report you. He never does. But I say, man, fancy having the nerve to give a wrong name! I say, Clemow, just you listen to this,' and he told a small dark boy, standing near, of the new man's prowess. Willie glowed with pride, and determined to keep the fact that his apparent nerve was due to misunderstanding and funk, and when Clemow told two of his friends, Hoys and Macarthy, and they whistled softly at his temerity, he felt quite a hero.

Shortly afterwards the first 'bell' in the turret was rung, and steady trickles of boys meandered into various class-rooms. The new boys were taken into Little Hall to await inspection by the Head. While standing there many faces had peered at them from the open doorway leading into Big Hall. Willie smiled as Jack came with some others to talk with him, and felt that the eyes of the whole school were contemptuously upon him. There was no cause for his misery, however, for rumour had already travelled far that a new boy had bluffed Useless with great coolness and cheek. The red face of Chapman looked at him, the melancholy Dennis directing his gimlet gaze over the shoulder of his crony; they had heard of his deed and decided to put his courage to the test of the 'whack' at the earliest occasion—that would decide if he had any guts! Dennis heard Jack call him Willie, and immediately his mouth opened and he emitted a solemn 'ho-ho'.

'Willie,' he ho-ho'd. 'Weary Willie, is he? Doesn't he look weary too, eh, man?' 'Is the boy ill?' he enquired, in a different, sharper voice.

'I don't think the brat is more than four feet high,' said Chapman. 'That's a good name, Spotty. Weary Willie! And look at Mummy's carroty-nut there—pudden face! My aunt, what a riff-raff of new bugs, Spotty. We'll show 'em, what?'

'We will,' ho-ho'd Spotty, glaring sinisterly down his long nose.

At this moment the second 'bell' throbbed from the turret—it was driven by electricity—announcing the time to be one

minute short of two o'clock. The crowd at the doorway
scampered away; a minute afterwards the porter swung the
handbell on the platform, sending clangorous shivers through
the hall; a few wild-looking figures rushed in at the entrance
door, eluded him frantically, and disappeared into the lobbies
adjoining their various class-rooms.

Five minutes later a mahogany door at the side of the model
steamship opened silently, and a pink face peered at the boys
for a few seconds. The light blue eyes behind eyeglasses asceti-
cally rimmed in gold, with lenses like twin half moons, seemed
to look right through each boy. The feeling produced in the
look of one so aloofly stern was not that of fear, but rather of
awe—the eyes under profuse white brows were distantly kind,
eyes bright with thought, straight with the intentness of a
panther. The door swung open, and Mr. Rore came entirely
out of his study, standing on the tessellated floor beside the
glass case; the fingers of his right hand all but hidden in black
knitted mittens, rested gently on its side. Below the high dome
of forehead with its sparse gray hairs his face was big, but not
heavy; the mouth hidden by the drooping moustache; his chin
pink and satiny. The rounded breadth of shoulder was obscured by the gathered rucks of a black gown; he was over six
feet in height.

'The new scholars. Ah, yes.' He spoke softly, as if addressing
somebody a long distance away, looking at them under his
semicircular glasses. 'Come in, all of you, and stand before my
desk. Your fates will be revealed to you. *Ad astra per aspera.*
Follow.'

Through the doorway they trooped, and ranged themselves
before his desk. A worn carpet, half the size of the floor, lay in
the centre of the room; behind the seated master a small fire
fumed dismally; through the diamond-paned windows could
be seen a few railed-in shrubs, and beyond, the asphalted
slope of the scholars' entrance. A small figure slunk past the
window, perceived instantly by those light blue eyes. Mr. Rore

sprang up, rapped sharply on the pane, and beckoned the miserable late-comer to appear at his study.

'Come heah, sah, double, double!' he commanded, while the figure broke into a half-hearted run and the line of new boys swayed in sympathy.

Moving quickly across the threadbare carpet, Mr. Rore swung open the mahogany door through which they had entered, and pressed a button. The late boy, white and with breath fluttering, appeared at the opening; Mr. Rore towering above him inquired the reason of his tardiness.

'My watch was wrong, please sir,' gasped the boy.

'No excuse. Name and form? Ah! Mr. Rapson. Give him my compliments and tell him to detain you after school. Ah! Portah!' as Crinkle appeared beyond. 'Portah! the main gates should be locked immediately after school bell. Don't let the omission occur again. Now double back to Mr. Rapson, and hard at it, hard at it!' to the boy.

The door closed silently, his gown swirled behind him, and he sat down at his desk.

'Let me see now. Yes—here are the results. Ah! yes. Devereux?' peering up before him. 'Ah, yes, an excellent paper.'

Devereux blushed.

'You will go to 4b. Mr. Rapson.'

With his blue pencil he made a minute mark on the list before him.

'Penny? Consistently excellent. 4b, I think, yes. Yes,' talking softly to himself.

Ten names were disposed of, and then he stared intently at the paper.

'Slater?'

The fat boy attempted the complex task of swallowing and answering together, with the result that a husky noise, half grunt, half sigh, came from his lips.

'You appear to be backward. And also,' he spoke slowly, 'in answer to question four, you have written that a nut named argichigo comes from Southern Africa. Will you elucidate for my benefit exactly what this commodity is?'

The fat boy shuffled his feet, and appeared to be fascinated by a knot-hole in the desk fronting him.

'Your memory stirs not? Let us award you time for recall. Maddison?'

Willie whispered acknowledgment of that name.

'Your paper is extraordinary. Is the boy ill?'

The terror on Willie's face lessened slightly, and a look of bewilderment came into his eyes.

Mr. Rore, peering intently at him under his spectacles, repeated his question more softly.

'Were you ill this morning? Come'—very softly and kindly —'do not be afraid. All of us get ill sometimes. Your face is pale. Are you ill?'

'Yes, sir,' he stammered, his palms flooded with moisture. 'I was very ill.'

'Ah, yes. I notice that only one answer appears to have been attempted. Is your headache bad?'

'No, sir, not now, thank you.'

'I am glad,' the Head replied courteously, and inclining his head slightly, 'but will you explain what are ichiargo nuts and momentoes?'

'I don't know, sir, honest to God, I don't sir,' stammered Willie in terror.

'How extraordinary, Maddison,' he said gently, his eye gleaming with humour. 'Interested as I am in research work, particularly in mathematics, the exact definition of such exports as ichiargos, argichigos, and momentoes has puzzled me. You did not see Slater's paper, I presume?' he queried, looking at Willie keenly.

'No, sir,' protested Willie, wondering if he would be caned.

'I see,' and he bowed his head suddenly on a paper on his desk. 'I fear that Slater and yourself must go to 2c. Your father explained that you were backward. He did not exaggerate.

And you must utter no more oaths, boy. Yes, Mr. Dimmer will receive you, with my compliments.'

Again he made a minute mark on the list.

'Now boys,' he said intently, 'you are new to Colham School. You will soon learn the traditions and mingle in scholastic association with your fellows. Remember all your days, that the only worthy thing in life is Work. The development of that mental power! Yes,' he went on, after a pause to allow the significance of mental power to have proper weight, 'it is your duty now to fit yourself for the conflict of a mature life. There are sharks and tigers in the world, boys. The ideal of a smug job after school is over most despicable! Work is the only Good. Mental power is the servant of Good. Mental Power! Make it your only aim! Develop that power! What boys agree? Show hands!'

Twelve hands wavered upwards and subsided.

'And sport. To keep fit, one must play. Play. Hard at it, always. Sport, a good servant, a bad master! You,' he fixed Willie with a swift glance, 'you should eat more pudding.'

He smiled with a grim aloofness, and pale smiles illumined momentarily the faces of the boys before him.

Ten minutes later they were merged into various classes, Maddison and Slater sitting attentively in the front row of the bottom form, while Mr. Dimmer, but recently a motor-cycling, gaudy-socked young man of 'Pothouse', Cambridge, inspired awe as he explained why King Alfred burned the cakes.

Chapter 24

THE DAYS of January ebbed slowly, and February's tide swung up the channel of the year. Willie and Jack, together with a boy called Margent and three flaxen-haired Cerr-Nores, used to catch the 8.35 train from the Halt near Rookhurst every morning, arriving at the market town of Colham at ten minutes to nine, sufficiently in time to reach school for prayers and the Latin hymn composed by the late Dr. Bullnote, D.D. This daily ceremony lasted for five minutes, when the various classes filed away into their form rooms, with the exception of a band of biggish boys composing what was known officially as the 'Special Class' and generally (especially among masters in the Common Room) as the 'Special Slackers'. The 'Specials' numbered about three dozen, their ages ranged from fifteen to seventeen years of age, and they were in their last term. As the members of this class, consisting of boys who either through lack of ability or an ingrained tendency towards mental prodigality, were considered by the Head master to be certain failures in life, becoming bank and insurance clerks, lesser Government officials or entering paternal businesses of trade after leaving school, Mr. Rore had decided to admit the existence of such subjects as book-keeping, shorthand, and business letter-writing. Nominally they were under the guidance of a junior master named Worley for discipline and instruction, but as that gentleman (whose hobby in life appeared to be the alternate growing and destruction of a wispy moustache) already had a full class of small boys to cope with, the 'Specials', sitting in Big Hall permanently, were left much to themselves. Finding the keeping of ephemeral debtor and

172

creditor accounts and the striking of faked balances wearisome, these youths had invented many diverse ways of passing the time. Those studiously inclined read minute novelettes; others made darts of penholders and nibs, fixing paper tails to the split extremities, and hurling them into the dimness of the ceiling, where some stuck. Others covered tennis balls with ink, and bounced them against the white walls of the hall, leaving what they termed *spugs* upon their surfaces. Periodically Mr. Rore would demand the names of any culprits who had thrown a ball, but without success.

Once, indeed, after a scornfully terse address by the Head, one boy had stood up and admitted that he had thrown a ball. He was congratulated for his 'sense of honour', and informed that his 'Spartan attitude was so worthy that he should welcome punishment.' The boy was caned, but on returning to the Hall all he said was: 'I never damn well thought he'd give me the whack, or I wouldn't have owned up like a fool.'

At three o'clock one afternoon Willie was sent with the compliments of Mr. Dimmer and a message to a senior house master named Beach, who took Latin for the upper school. Passing through Hall, he looked with admiration at the big boys whose voices had broken; and wondered how it felt to be left alone. Chapman called out: 'Why, here's Weary Willie. Where you off to, boy?' frowning and looking fierce.

'Going to Mr. Beach's for some books, with Mr. Dimmer's compliments,' replied Willie. So far he had avoided being seized upon by the great Dennis and Chapman.

'Ho, ho,' said his long-faced accomplice, directing gimlet eyes at him, 'going to Old Scratch, are you? Give him the compliments of the Specials, who permit you to go.'

'Yes, Dennis.'

'Dennis?' interrupted Chapman, 'say Mr. Dennis to him, and "Sir" to me. Go on!'

'Yes, sir,' quavered Willie.

The other boys sprawling at their desks laughed, and one

named Tyre called out. 'Leave the kid alone, Nosey. Hey you kid, hop it!'

'Come here, you,' hissed Chapman, frowning terrifically.

Willie, grateful for the support of one of the giants—the president of a secret society consisting of two 'Specials' besides himself, called 'The Society for the Abolition of Work and the Furtherment of Art'—ignored Chapman's order, and went away. Dennis called out: 'You wait, young weary Willie, you young skelington.'

Willie came to 5c class-room, knocked on the door, opened it timorously, and immediately a thousand faces, it seemed, rose up and regarded him. A gray-haired, elderly man sitting at a raised desk asked perfunctorily what he wanted.

'Mr. Dimmer's compermunts——' Here he swallowed suddenly, and coughed. 'And would you please lend him Meiklejohn, parts one and two.' While he was speaking a hum broke out over the class. Mr. Beach, whose gown was even more tattered than that of Mr. Worth, appeared not to hear it. He went to a bookcase, selected the volumes, and gave them to Willie. Meanwhile the hum had grown to a miniature hubbub. Suddenly Mr. Beach, blue of shaven chin, turned round and roared out. 'Quiet, I say, quiet!' with such suddenness that Willie dropped the books in alarm. Laughter rippled across the thousand faces, and he went pale.

'Quiet, I say, quiet!' shouted Mr. Beach. 'Bradley, come out here. I won't have this noise.'

The master dived into a corner, and emerged with a long black lath, with fragments of cloth adhering to it, that had once been part of a rolling wall map.

'Over,' ordered Mr. Beach. 'You, boy'—turning to Willie, 'go away. I don't want you. GO AWAY FROM ME!' he thundered, as Willie stared at his blue chin, too fascinated to move.

'COME HERE, BOY,' he bellowed a second later. 'Over.'

Willie, struggling hard to prevent himself from bursting into tears before the thousand grinning faces, went to him and bent over the desk. He did not know what the others knew, that Mr. Beach was the greatest humorist and sportsman in the school, and that his map-lath was one of his jokes. He made a great pretence of hitting a boy, and always hit the woodwork of the desk. To his surprise and the delight of 5c, Willie, after agony and fusion of senses in terror, burst into tears.

'New kid—wants his mother—soppy.' These and other terms were whispered.

'Don't cry,' urged Mr. Beach gruffly, 'that's not the way to get on.' He was sorry that his hoary joke had miscarried, and noticed that the boy before him—to judge by his face—was very highly strung.

'QUIET! All kept in till six o'clock to-night, translating Ovid,' he shouted.

'Oh, sir,' groaned the boys.

'Come and see me after school,' he said to Willie, softly, 'and don't be frightened of me.'

'No, sir.'

'Er—give Mr. Dimmer my compliments,' he exclaimed in an altered voice.

'Yes, sir.'

'If I have any more nonsense I will keep you in with Ovid,' he warned the class.

'Thank you, sir,' breathed the boys for the implied release.

'Er—quiet! Bradley, go back to your desk and try to look less like a cackling ninny.'

The boys laughed at this antediluvian joke, and the reading of Cicero's comparatively easy *De Amicitia* continued.

Willie closed the door behind him and crept back to 2c class-room. Dennis happened to see him as he passed, stretched out a red hand, grimy-nailed, protruding from a sleeve half-way up his arm, and in triumph called out—'Got you! Nosey, here's that cheeky yob, Weary Willie. Shall we send him into the Bird's study for the whack?'

'Oh, no, Mr. Dennis, I am sorry, really I am.'

The fright on his face only spurred the glee of his captor.

'Did you give Old Scratch my compliments, eh?'

'No, Mr. Dennis.'

'Oh, why not?'

'Stand him on the form for impertinence,' frowned Chapman.

The other members of the 'Specials' looked up from novelettes, futile but time-passing noughts-and-crosses, drowsiness and gossip, and regarded the scene with mild amusement.

'Go on, up on the form,' cried Chapman, his red face peering at Willie, whose own face was wan with agony.

Dennis twisted his arm playfully, and rucked his biceps with his fingers.

'Skinny skelington, bag of bones,' he taunted, holding his face near that of the smaller boy, who felt a revulsion when he saw his green teeth.

'Leggome,' he panted.

Dennis twisted again.

Willie blazed with temper, and calling him a name frequently used by the labourers of Rookhurst, which made the elder boys laugh and cheer him, hit him on the head with Volume I of Meiklejohn's History. Dennis clouted him heavily on the side of the head, and flung him on the wooded floor . . . a voice rang through the hall, and the class sank over exercise books.

'Come along, sir, come along! Give you that cane! Both of you. Double, double!'

Willie looked terrified, and wondered what would happen next. Dennis was apparently stricken with sudden awful deafness and a desire for work.

'Come along, sir, come along! Dennis, I mean! Pauper spirit! And you!' beckoning to Willie.

Dennis rose abjectly, and followed Willie into the study. Mr. Rore opened a cupboard and selected a cane.

'Now, sir,' he turned to Willie, 'how did it happen?'

Willie remained silent. For one thing, he was nearly numb

with terror; and into his head had come the thought that he must not sneak. Nothing that he had learnt during his month at school had produced this thought, he had gathered it from numerous stories in the *Thuddenblunder* series, maligned and forbidden as they always had been at home.

'Answer, boy. Your name?'

'Maddison, sir.'

'Ah, yes, I remember. You should eat more pudding! Dennis, why were you holding this boy?'

'If you please, sir, he hit me on the head with a book, sir, and I was holding his hands because I didn't want to be blinded, sir, as he was poking his fingers at my eyes. I wanted to get on with shorthand, sir.'

'Well, sir,' to Willie, 'did you hit him on the head with a book?'

'Yes, sir.'

'Well, well! Let me see, you have never been to school before?'

'No, sir.'

'And what form are you in?'

'2c, sir.'

'You could hardly be lower. When your father spoke to me he said that you were inclined to wildness. I gathered that your acquaintanceships had been mostly labourers and poachers. Howev-ah, you must learn not to hit inoffensive boys on the head with books. Come in!'

Someone had rapped on the door.

The President of the 'Society for the Abolition of Work and the Furtherment of Art' (who during school hours devoted his time to the feverish writing of a novel dealing with realism in the Quartier Latin in Paris—although he had never left England) came in rather nervously.

'Well?' said Mr. Rore peering at him under his semicircular glasses.

'If you please, sir,' replied the newcomer, 'I should like to say that this boy'—pointing to Maddison—'was entirely blameless. The whole class will bear testimony to that. He did not interfere—he was interfered with.'

He flushed intensely at what he inwardly considered elegant conciseness of expression, then asked: 'Have I permission to withdraw, sir?'

'You have, Tyre. You, Maddison, will return to your classroom.'

The Head liked Tyre, an earnest boy, he thought, and one who was wasted in the Special Class.

Dennis prepared fatalistically for the inevitable: was 'awarded' six cuts, interpolated with six requests to 'think, and not to let it occur again'; in the ordinary times he would have been 'awarded' four, but an extra was 'awarded' for telling lies, and the other for wriggling on the chair. . . .

After school, while Willie was talking to Mr. Beach about sparrowhawks and their habits, with an enthusiasm that took the old and beloved master to the beautiful years of his own boyhood forty years since, Chapman and Tyre had a fight in the fives court. Chapman had some knowledge of boxing, and was much heavier than his opponent, whom he beat after a fierce struggle.

Dennis hopped round him after the fight, jeering at Tyre, who with sudden rage knocked him down, where he lay nursing a long nose that bled almost as rapidly as a stuck pig, Willie told Biddy that night.

Chapter 25

TILL THE beginning of March winter bound the water meadows and the downs alike; never was there such terrible weather. Old Granfer Brown, the father of Big Will'um, would sit no longer in the sun of summers to come before the inn. The cold killed him, and they laid him beside his wife in the churchyard, near Jacob the shepherd.

The graven pattern of frost was not solved by the weak sunshine that sometimes came from the heavy sky. In Willie's garden snow lay over the flower beds and the lawns, and silence of the frore air showed how the birds had suffered. Indeed, the blackbirds, thrushes and hedge-sparrows that usually haunted its wilderness of wild and cultivated flowers had long since gone, a prey to starvation and, in their weakened condition, to owls, hawks, and weasels. One solitary robin remained, so tame that he would feed from his hand. In the morning a few chinking notes would tremble on the air; the ruddy stain of the feathers on his breast, puffed out to twice its actual size, show against the rimed branch of the pear-tree near his bedroom window. The robin seemed never to lose hope; throughout the icy solitude of winter his thin candle-gleams of song flickered through the dark lifelessness of the garden; maybe the golgothan legend was handed down in his race with that stain and its legacy of hope . . . he sang when the bloring wind rattled the branches, and whirled powdered sleet through the holly where he roosted.

Jim wondered as he walked about whether there would be any butterflies or flowers again. The buds on the trees that had released the autumnal leaves must surely be dead for evermore;

the founts of sap in their roots blasted by the frost. Yet every day behind the clouds the sun swept in a fuller curve; slowly its alchemic power increased. However black the winter, however cruel and indifferent the force that some men eulogised as beneficent Nature to living things, the future of summer had been assured by the species themselves. Nothing helped them except themselves. Under the snow lay the seeds, secure and still in their hard cases. Deep under the earth slept the unborn beetles and butterflies in their shells, awaiting sunrise and resurrection. From dot of seed and oval shell the scented petal and painted sails would arise into life. There was no scent or hue of petal in the seed, no pigment for colour-maze of wing in the caterpillar that had tunnelled in the ground last summer. Yet from intangible sunlight, dull earth—the decomposed fragments of life—and seed or minute egg, from these three would be enwrought the flower and insculped the wing: and with them, mightier still, would be the mystery called life.

It was during the seeming death of all things that Jim felt poignantly the loss of Dolly. He loved her, and yet hated himself for having destroyed his independent happiness. He felt that he loved her more when away from her; to dream of her at night; yet somehow it was different when she was with him. She had driven him away with scorn when he left the service of Mr. Norman to go into the wheatfields to the life he loved. And then Dolly, fickle and treacherous as he thought, had walked out with John Fry: he had seen them, with anguish in his heart, and yet. . . .

One morning the wind ceased, and through a rift in the cloud strata came a glow of sunshine. It glimmered for less than an hour, and that night the owls hooted with mournful insistence; three foxes were heard barking at once. Towards dawn a wind came from the south west; a wind less icy than before. Old men nodded their heads, and meeting in the lanes and at the inn at Rookhurst said that it meant a thaw at last. In the garden the robin piped tranquilly as ever. Gently came the wind all that day and the next night; in the woods, although nothing stirred *visibly*, the silence as of death gave way before sounds inaudible, less than a whisper—the air itself was softer, and made music that he felt rather than heard. The crust of snow, loosed from the hold of frost, became brittle; carts jolting along the lanes left tracks of a deeper brown, wads were cast from hooves. Before the soft insistence of the wind passed the tyranny of cold, till one morning Jim noticed with joy that the yellow bloom of the gorse was open to the sun. Swiftly the fields became fluid, the lanes filled with slush, rooks drifted thwartwise the wind with sticks in their beaks to their colony in the tree-tops. High into heaven fluttered a lark, another rose, they battled with crests upraised, singing the while. A week after the snow had gone the heart-shaped leaves of the celandine thrust themselves over the meadow grass; spiders' thrown lines gleamed in the sunshine; thrushes and blackbirds came from nowhere, it seemed, and sang in the bare oaks, or sought for spiders and worms. For days the brook overflowed into the water-meadow: duck, moorhens, and thousands of wild fowl passed overhead by day and by night. Once more the elms were suffused as with sunset haze, scattering the glumes of their buds on the sward beneath; gaily the chaffinch piped his sweet monotony of song; with mellow wildness the green woodpecker, dipping and rising in straight flight from coppice to spinney, spinney to covert, heralded the incoming of spring. Like great galleons ever sailing in cerulean waters argosy upon argosy of clouds drifted towards the unknown of the north-east, over the outlined and couchant downs. Already the migrant wheatears had come from afar; hoody crows, who had lived so easily during the black winter, beat across the North Sea to the pine forests of Scandinavia, followed by the clucking redwings and fieldfares.

One Wednesday afternoon Jack and Willie, released from school, determined to go on their first nesting expedition.

Willie carried a pair of climbing irons which he had traded that morning at school with a boy named 'Bony' Watson—although only twelve years of age he was nearly six feet tall. wore glasses, and was so thin when he turned sideways that it was reputed difficult to see him—in exchange for two hens' eggs, appropriately painted, that he swore were those of a peregrine falcon. In addition to these rare eggs, 'Bony' carried in his pocket a slip of paper with the following words upon it.

I promise to give Gordon Hereward Watson a jackdaw in May ready tamed and not thievy or merlicious singed Will Maddison.

(to which had been added in a shaky handwriting, with characters gaunt and bony as their writer:)

PS. The jackdaw must be a boy bird Boney Watson.

The postscript had been appended by the lank naturalist as a precaution that no increase should arrive after possession. As it was, his father suffered his various pets intolerantly; at any moment they were liable to be cast from the house; he declared that all his son's pets reproduced themselves inevitably and unnecessarily. He had taken two mice home one day—after a week both were discovered with family; the same thing happened with a guinea pig; also a white rat; and a rabbit.

The two friends crossed the field, passed under the rookery and entered the covert. Here yellow primroses flecked the woods, although the wind-flowers had not yet unfolded their star-droop of petal from the buds; a pegged rabbit's fur and piece of entrail marked where a gin, covered with grass, awaited those small hunters, the weasels. They passed leaf-brown pools; green shoots of bluebell tower arising from the dead leaves; solitary celandines. Vaulting a stile, they went along the clayey footpath by the side of a cornfield, coming to the outskirts of Colonel Tetley's garden.

From a tall fir-tree a black crow slid away, silent. Peering up they saw its nest, a large mass of twigs woven into the matted branches at the crest of the tree.

'A carrion crow, man!' said Willie, excitedly.

'We haven't got one, have we?' asked Jack.

'No. They're rather rare. But I say, what a swine of a tree to climb.'

All the branches for forty feet from the ground had been sawn off, leaving stumps protruding less than an inch from the bole. The bark was rough and scaly. At an immense height, it seemed, the bole divided, and higher still one branch went straight out. It was on this that the nest had been constructed. The tree was unclimbable.

Willie grimly strapped the irons to his legs. The iron passed under the boot, forming a bent spike on the instep.

'I shouldn't do it, man,' warned Jack.

'Pooh, it's easy.'

He hobbled to the tree, dug a spike into its bark, clasped the trunk firmly, and started to climb. After much effort he succeeded in raising himself six feet from the ground. The bark gave no firm grip for the irons, and his arms did not go even half-way round the trunk. Looking down, six feet seemed like a precipice. He came down again, panting.

'No good,' he gasped.

'Let me try,' said Jack.

'You'll be killed!'

'I can climb better than you, anyway.'

Willie turned his back and began to unfasten the climbing irons, throwing them on the grass. Jack adjusted them in silence.

Then he began to climb. Willie did not look up. He could hear the irons slipping in the tree, his friend's breath coming gustily, and he imagined that he had climbed about ten feet—no more.

When he did look up, Jack had reached the fork, and was

clinging to the branch tightly, and looking down with a white face.

'Well done, man,' cried Willie in admiration.

Jack did not answer.

'Does it look steep, Jack?'

He nodded.

'Come down, man. Don't mind about the eggs.'

'I can't!'

The crow had returned, and was flying with her mate high above the tree, croaking dolefully. Willie remembered the horror of Jacob on the downs at Christmas.

Jack had begun to swarm up the slanting branch. It was difficult work, for there was no grip for his hands. He determined to show Willie that he was not afraid of falling: that he was not a funk. The idea that Willie might be a funk did not occur to him. He felt no sense of superiority. To justify himself in his friend's eyes was his sole reason.

'Five eggs, fresh,' a voice called boldly from the heights.

'Bring 'em all, crows are no good.'

Jack removed his cap, put the eggs in it, and transferred it to his teeth. Then, carefully, he commenced to climb down. It was comparatively easy work till he reached the fork. From there onwards, however, he had a practically smooth bole to descend for forty feet, round which his arms would not go, upon which he could get no grip with his knees, and the spikes of the climbing irons hindered. Where they did find a grip Jack knew that they were liable to slip as soon as he put his weight upon them.

Two feet below the fork he stuck, clinging silently to the trunk. His nerve had given way, and he was fighting against the impulse to let go. Foolishly, he looked downwards, and saw what appeared like a tiny face looking up at him. He opened his mouth to scream, but no sound would come.

Then a variety of sounds seemed to surround him. A bluebottle with dazed, sluggish flight was buzzing aimlessly round

184

his head, a dog was barking somewhere, and from far away came the rattle of a train. From farther still came a voice that he recognised as Willie's saying: 'Oh, stick it man, stick it, man.'

The vision of himself falling to the ground and lying there after his back was broken passed from him. Although his arms ached and he was slavering over his chin and the dribble running down his neck, he determined to deliver the eggs safely. Moving his left hand downwards he felt one of the stumps, descending another foot. Gradually he worked lower. His back quivered, his muscles were trembling, his legs palsied. Then he stuck again, twenty feet from the ground.

'Don't worry, man,' called out Willie, who thought that he would fall any moment, 'If you leave go I'll catch you.'

Jack did not answer. He hung to the tree, by his finger-tips.

Willie braced himself, with open arms, determined to break his friend's fall. Any moment he would see the body dropping bigger and bigger. O, God save him, save him, he thought wildly.

A tall figure lurching down the side of the hedge between the park and the garden whistled softly to him. He looked round and saw the crowstarver.

'Jim, oh, Jim, come here, quick—oh, come.'

Jim leapt the hedge and padded swiftly towards him, seeing immediately what was required.

'I'm going to fall,' shrieked Jack.

'Keep hold, you young fool!' yelled Jim, as though in a great rage. He began swarming up the tree. He climbed like a cat, and soon reached Jack.

'Put ees fute 'pon head,' he ordered.

Jack kept still.

Jim climbed higher.

'Sit on ees head, wull 'ee?' he threatened.

Below, Willie watched with joy the slow descent, Jack resting on the head of Jim.

Soon they reached the ground, where Jack flopped exhausted on the grass. Jim was white and trembling; he put his hand up to his cheek, and then looked at it in amazement. Willie danced round, thanking Jim, telling Jack how clever and brave he was.

'And the eggs aren't broken either,' he chanted, 'Oh, Jim——'

He stared at Jim's face, down which blood was running. One of the spikes on Jack's feet had gashed a long wound in his cheek. He had climbed the tree by the aid of a power that had prevented him from feeling pain or stress.

The sun had lost its warmth, and they went homewards, insisting that Jim must come with them. Jack felt a hero, that is to say, he wondered however he could have climbed such a tree. Clemow and Hoys, their rivals at school, how they would envy the carrion crow's eggs! What a pity they had not been there to see him up in the awful heights!

Jim's cheek was badly gashed and was now painful. The boy was remorseful.

'You couldn't a-helped it,' said Jim.

Both Jack and Willie knew—as they discussed occasionally superficial things like marriage, the coming of babies, and courtships, as well as the important things like outwitting Nosey and Spotty, trapping and bird's-nesting—they both knew that Dolly was still 'mazed about Jim'. Jack had heard Dolly crying at night, and with his developing sense of fairness had only told Willie. Nor did he tease Dolly about it, as she no longer teased him. Although she sometimes went walking with big John Fry, they knew that it was only because Jim had quarrelled—'a winnicky grawbey courting a dawbaky drotchel', Biddy called them.

The grown man was therefore led to the farm by the small boys. Perhaps he welcomed the excuse, although he had gone to Dolly on Christmas night with a present and she had ignored him. Perhaps he wanted Dolly to see the wound upon his face, and to hurt her by letting her know how hurt he was. He spoke little, gazing on the ground and in the hedge, stopping to look at a bee crawling over a celandine, or to touch a shoot rising under the may-trees.

Dolly was pumping water when they went into the yard. Her face flushed, then paled. Jim looked at her, and joyed at the pallor, for it told him that she still loved him.

'Is there any warm water on the hob?' asked Jack, importantly, going indoors with Willie.

Dolly went up to Jim. She was trembling. So was Jim.

'Oh, Jim,' she whispered, 'where 'ave ee been? Ees poor face, look at that now. Oh, Jim, my dear, let me bathe it for 'ee, wull 'ee?'

She spoke so softly, her earnest eyes looking up into his.

'You said you didn't want to see me no more.'

'Oh, Jim, ee knew it was a-cause I loved ee.'

He laughed, and touched her cheek. 'Now I be going, so I'll bid 'ee good-bye, my dear.' He did not move.

'Oh, no, do 'ee stay, my darling,' whispered Dolly, breathing quickly.

The two boys were watching through the kitchen window. 'They've made it up,' announced Jack, grinning.

Willie turned away his face, and hastily brushed his hand over his eyes.

He stayed at Jack's house until after supper. Then he went home.

'Where have you been? It is nearly nine o'clock! How can you expect to learn and get on if you don't do your homework?' fumed his father on arrival. 'What's that, more birds' eggs? Give it to me. If this happens again I shall smash all your eggs and forbid you to go in the woods.'

So Willie spent the next hour and a half in learning unintelligible words by Shakespeare, and drawing a map of England, Scotland, and Wales, putting in the chief ports, capes, bays, rivers, and mountains.

That night in his room he blew the other crow's egg, which had been hidden in his handkerchief, and laid it carefully in his box, which he hid under his floor. He did not realise it, but he was hiding all the past joy of his life in that secret place; part of his soul which had not yet built its own tower.

Chapter 26

ONE WEDNESDAY after the Easter holidays Mr. Maddison
went to Colham to watch his son play football.

Willie felt as smart as a professional player in his new House
shirt and somebody else's boots. The boots were too small, and
too tightly laced; the shirt, a gaudy affair of orange and purple
stripes, too large. Overlong shorts made out of an old pair of
his father's trousers flapped round his knees. He was left wing
for 2b against a similar rabble from 2a, Jack with them. The
form master of 2b, Mr. Ellison, a long-faced man with flat feet
and eyes like buttons close together, was referee.

Willie felt uneasy about his father's beard. While they were
lining up his father smiled at him, waving his hand: Willie
waved back then glanced round, fearful lest the chaps
should see that it was his father. Father had an old tweed
hat on: had he worn a topper, like Mr. Dennis, the Mayor of
Colham, it wouldn't have been so bad! How terrible if
Dennis or Chapman saw him in that hat!

Mr. Ellison had not changed, with the exception of a pair of
football boots. His other boots he had left carelessly under the
pavilion verandah. From what transpired later, it was unfortunate that he had left them in such a conspicuous position.

The rival teams lined up. The ball was kicked off, and
immediately a multitude of small boys began to rush wildly
about.

From the point of view of the solitary spectator his son
chased the ball all over the field, but never kicked it: and
attempting to make up for this deficiency he yelled the whole
time: 'Pass man, pass—oh, pass, pass!' bumping violently into

smaller boys and endeavouring to charge them over; and himself getting charged over not a few times.

Willie thought that he was playing a fine game. He had given three boys a frightful charge, and sent Effish into the mud. He was so glad that father had seen him do it!

The monotony of the scene was interrupted a few minutes later by Effish accidentally kicking his crony Beckelt on the shins, and Beckelt, an Irish boy of hasty temper, punching him on the nose. Mr. Ellison ran up and shook Beckelt, who immediately sank to the ground, groaning mournfully and complaining that he had a pain inside him. Seeing that no punishment was likely to follow from an act that he regretted as soon as committed—although he felt a perfectly legitimate satisfaction from what he knew to be a fine straight-from-the-shoulder—the pain vanished after a little massage, and the game proceeded as before until the ball suddenly subsided into a flabby softness. Mr. Ellison examined it gingerly as though he thought that it might swell up and burst as suddenly as it had subsided, and discovered that the blade of a penknife was sticking through the casing.

'Who stuck a blade in his boot in order to puncture the ball?' he queried in a high, rapid voice.

'Not me, sir,' answered the boys.

'Very well, then, you will all have to pay for a new bladder between you.'

'Oh, sir,' they chorused.

Several boys began to nudge Jack, who looked round in desperation.

'Ah, Temperley, was it you?'

'No, sir.'

'Coo-coo!' several boys blew through their mouths, as though appalled by his deceit.

'Are you sure, Temperley?'

Jack stood on one foot and looked sullenly at the traducers of his character.

'Yes, sir.'

'You did do it, Temperley?'

'Yes, sir.'

'Why did you do it, Temperley?'

Jack did not answer.

'Go and ask the groundsman for another ball, Temperley, and tell him to charge your father with a new bladder.'

Jack went away, returning after five minutes with a new ball.

At half-time, Willie, with blistered feet in the small boots—someone had borrowed his own and left a smaller pair in their place—went to his father, taking Jack with him.

'Good afternoon, sir,' said Jack, attempting to raise a cap that was not there.

'Hullo, boys,' greeted Mr. Maddison, with an effort of jocundity, 'enjoying the game?'

'Oh, not so bad, sir.'

'What happened to the ball—a puncture?'

Jack looked quickly at his friend.

'The bladder wasn't pumped up securely,' Willie explained.

Those boys who were blessed with an abundance of pocket money had gone to the pavilion in order to buy slips of lemon to quench their thirst: not that their throats were parched, but it was the custom among the first and second elevens to suck lemon at half-time, and so the lower school did likewise although it was sour, and ginger-pop would really have been nicer. Those with scanty weekly doles refrained from purchase, albeit the sum needed for a quarter of a lemon was only one halfpenny; but a halfpenny was a halfpenny and would buy two ounces of American gums or a quarter of a pound of broken biscuits or *Comic Cuts* or an ice cornet in summer at Old Mother Vanderbergh's tuckshop at the bottom of the hill below the school.

'Are you having tea in the pav. afterwards?' queried Willie.

'No,' sighed Jack, 'no tin this week, for shutting the cat in the pantry where he ate half a chicken, the fool.'

'That's bad luck,' remarked Mr. Maddison, with the same effort of jocundity, 'you must come and have tea with us in the town.'

'Oh, thank you, Mr. Maddison.'

Willie looked at his friend with an expression on his face implying that their skill in trapping was not confined to the moldiwarps alone.

'How about a piece of lemon? You must be thirsty after your tremendous exertions.'

Mr. Maddison gave them sixpence, and the boys ran off to the pavilion.

'I say, your old man isn't so bad,' observed Jack.

'My Father's all right,' replied Willie rather shortly, and wishing he hadn't run him down so much to Jack. He felt rather a sneak.

'Although he is a terror at times, isn't he, man?'

'Oh, is he?'

'Well, you've often told me so, haven't you?' urged Jack, wondering why he was so inconsistent.

'Oh, shut up,' grumbled Willie.

'All right. But you said so, you know.'

They entered the pavilion where boys of all sizes were sucking liquids of various hues and colours from bottles that obstinately refused to emit those liquids on account of a round glass marble in the neck. Those versed in the habit of these liquids inserted skilful tongues with which the glass stoppers were pushed aside; but great skill was required, for too much tongue, as in home life, was liable to spoil the pleasure of the proceedings. Either it completely stopped the flow, or being withdrawn carelessly, allowed a sizzling gush to bespatter the face. Other boys were munching biscuits, purchased at what they considered the outrageous price of three a penny; many still clamoured imperiously for attendance, or pleaded obsequiously with the groundsman for the honour of being served, according to their different temperaments.

'Let's save the money, man,' suggested Willie. 'We can spend it on ice cornets later on.'

'Good bloater,' agreed Jack, which cryptic remark, in no way connected with fishing, was intended merely as an endorsement.

The whistle blew, and they returned to the field, his son giving Mr. Maddison four pennies with his fervent thanks. Willie was rather disappointed that his honesty in returning the change was not rewarded by its prompt division between them. Once more the teams lined up; again little boys rushed helter-skelter after the ball, kicking the air and butting one another like rams; cries of 'pass—pass' were shrilled on the air; the rabble surged round one goal and then for no apparent reason aimlessly transferred itself to the other. For a moment only did the game lose its terrible earnestness when Mr. Ellison's face got in the way of the ball kicked diagonally by one of the 2a backs, and the team laughed with outrageous delight. By the way Willie rushed at the opposing wing man it might have been imagined that he had nihilistic tendencies both towards the ball and his opponent, but his efforts wasted themselves always before he reached either. He had a dread of having his ankles kicked, and his three stone six pounds of bone, skin, hair, and boots made no impression on his weightier adversary and little upon the mud when he missed his objective altogether. Just as Mr. Maddison reached the climax of boredom and each individual member of the teams was thinking that his old superb form had returned, a long blast on the whistle announced that the match was over, and that 2a had won with thirty-five goals to twenty. A few enthusiasts remained on the field for practice, but the majority rushed into the pavilion, some for overcoats and caps; others to suck coloured liquids from thick glass bottles; others to hang around in the hope of being treated. Effish and Beckelt each with a second and a small following of sightseers retired to a distant corner for a fight.

There the unwilling principals hummed and haared, amid the encouraging remarks of the onlookers. Beckelt gave Effish his 'cowardies'—two feeble pokes on the chest, and Effish returned the compliment by 'doing his dags'—two taps on the ribs. After this ceremony both refused to fight, so they returned to the pavilion much relieved, just in time to see the unfortunate master who had left his boots under the verandah discover that they were full of water. Being possessed of tact, although to the casual beholder his button eyes belied any sagacity, he said nothing out loud about it but drained them carefully, as though to swill out his boots with water were one of his regular idiosyncrasies.

Willie was still a little apprehensive of his father's hat and long beard. He had been out with him seldom. It was the third time that he had been into Colham town with him; he had been up to London on one occasion, when taken to the Zoo, where his father had lost him and found him eventually in the monkey-house stroking a dead mouse. As far back as he could remember his father had worn the same hat.

His apprehension changed to extreme fear as they entered the tea-room upstairs and found that Chapman and Dennis were seated in one corner with two pig-tailed girls of about thirteen or fourteen years of age, evidently pupils at Colham High School for Young Ladies, where the girls, Willie had heard, were supposed to be 'frightfully hot'.

A silence overcame the quartet in the corner as they entered. Dennis leaned over and whispered to Chapman, who said 'Rather!' in a contemptuous voice, while the girls giggled. Then with all the nerve in the world, Willie thought, Chapman produced a gun-metal cigarette case, opened it with a flourish and said:

'Fag, Spotty?'

'Thanks, Nosey', grunted Spotty, as he took one, watched by Willie, while the girls laughed.

Mr. Maddison asked for bread and butter, cakes and tea; Willie asked for hot buttered muffins but his father said no, thinking them indigestible; Chapman immediately made a remark that was greeted with explosive merriment.

'Not old enough,' whispered Dennis hoarsely, at which they giggled again amid renewed whisperings, and one of the girls said admiringly of Dennis: 'Oh, I say, isn't he awful?' to her friend after each remark.

The bread and butter stuck in Willie's throat, and drinking a little tea to ease things he coughed suddenly and spluttered over the table. Jack laughed, his father looked annoyed, and the others became hysterical. The cakes arrived, with Mr. and Mrs. Norman, and Elsie. Amid greetings Mrs. Norman said: 'Hullo, Willie, dear,' who turned red and his heart began to throb inside as she kissed him. Everyone shook hands all round, and with a general moving of chairs, imitated by Chapman's party, made way for the newcomers. Willie looked at Chapman, who leered back at him; felt frightened; then noticed that the gimlet eyes of Spotty Dennis were directed upon Elsie. A rage surged in his heart when he saw him wink at Chapman.

The two men began talking, while Elsie's mother asked him how he liked school. Willie stuttered and told her that it wasn't so bad and could not help glancing at Chapman, who frowned tremendously and muttered with his lips; then turned to Spotty and grinned. Willie, with a bravado that terrified him afterwards and for which he could never account, added:

'It isn't so bad, except for the awful bounders there. Eh, Jack?'

'Yes,' answered Jack bravely, 'awful bounders.'

Plunging deeper, Willie went on:

'No manners at all, some of them. Get whacked by the Old Bird every day. Slackers, devilskins, funks, too.'

His father had not heard, but Mrs. Norman remarked the change in him, and thought that the tone of the school must be rather bad.

The pastry cook came in with a supplementary tray, and when the rattling of saucers ceased Dennis called out:

'Crumbs—the usual.'

Crumbs nibbled his pencil and made out the bill. All four rose to go. Outside the room they burst into laughter again— God knew what for, thought Willie—and a minute later, from the street, came a series of goat-like 'maa-aa-as'.

'The swine,' whispered Jack. 'I say, man, what a nerve you've got.'

They went back to Rookhurst together. Willie was in the wildest spirits during the short train journey, and astonished his father by the sudden vitality which had somehow come into him. The reaction, however, set in as soon as they parted at his gate, and he said good-bye; to enter the house and see about homework, which his father said he would look over. For an hour he struggled with history dates, but all that would remain in his head was *William the First ten sixty-six, William the Second ten eighty-seven*—and there he stuck; thinking about Elsie, and the owl hooting in the wood far away, and if the nightingale were singing in the hazel wands yet, and if Chapman—oh, lumme, he would get it to-morrow . . . *William the Second ten eighty-seven, Henry the*—oh, he hated the muck, damn history!

He made another effort, and attached to the memorised dates the fact that *Henry I* succeeded to the throne in 1100. Then he thought he would do arithmetic, but he could not concentrate on that: his brains *would* race. Again the owl called through the dusky April evening, and he went to the window and looked up at the stars flickering above. A great longing came to go out under them, to watch them winking in the lake, and see the new moon as it rose in the sky. . . . Father was coming!

As he lay in bed that night listening to the branches of the pear-tree outside rustling in the wind, Willie wondered if Elsie loved him back, and how Jack and he would be friends for ever and ever, and if Chapman would challenge him to a fight on the morrow. The thought made him shiver. However, he would think of Elsie's love as he fought. He would fight, even if he were knocked down! He wouldn't give up, however much it hurt.

It was two o'clock in the morning before he ceased to move and mutter in his bed; and he woke up in the morning feeling tired and dull.

Chapter 27

MORNING SCHOOL passed without contact with Chapman and Dennis, and by the time that lunch had finished Willie was in a state of profound apprehension. Jack had not called for him that morning; as he went towards the Halt he thought that he was probably ill, the lucky fellow. During the morning another thought had persisted that Jack was probably feigning illness because he was afraid: it was an unfair thought (especially as Willie had had many demonstrations that Jack was loyal and brave), but his temperament was exceedingly impressionable, with the consequence that his views were unstable.

The thought remained, and when after luncheon he sensed intuitively that the moment was not far off when Chapman and Dennis would seize him, he cursed Jack in his mind for a traitor. In reality, Jack, having eaten too many doughnuts, was at that moment groaning on his bed and wondering if the nausea of a bilious attack would last for ever. Even in his prostration he remembered his friend, and hoped that he would bite, kick, and scratch if they tried to whack him.

He hung about in Hall, where Mr. Worth was again on duty, wearing the same gown, looking as though it would sigh to fragments at a puff of wind, and correcting similar exercises. Willie looked at the pinned illustrations from the weekly picture papers, looked in the glass cupboards at the electrical apparatus that he would handle and understand in the far dim future. That morning by post he had received a letter from Elsie, the first one she had written to him. Many times he had read it in the train and surreptitiously in class, feeling a warm glow about his heart as he did so. Once more he took it from his pocket, after assuring himself that no boys were near.

Dear Willie—I hope you are quite well. I thought I would write you a letter. I have given Magdalene my doll to Cook's niece in Colham. How are you. Father is reading. Mother is writing a letter. How is your poaching hat? Father says come and see us when you like.

> *Believe me,*
> > *Always yours sincerely,*
> > > *Elsie.*

He was standing there, seeing only the bright mental picture of himself having tea with Elsie, when an arm reached over his shoulder, an arm in a sleeve half-way up to its owner's elbow, and a hand with bitten nails snatched the letter. Two arms were wound round his body, a hand was clapped over his mouth, and he was carried away into the playground.

The faces of the few boys hanging about or playing fives in a desultory fashion up against the walls and the class-room windows, brightened when they realised that something special was in store for them.

'Come along, all of us,' shouted Chapman, 'prisoner to be tried for his life.'

'Leggo my arm,' cried Willie to Dennis. 'You're hurting.'

'Ho, ho,' leered his captor, 'yew wait, Willie Soppy-Skelington. Slackers, skinned devils, and funks, are we? No manners, eh? You wait, young cocky-boy.'

'Yes, you wait, you slug-face, bag o' bones; awful bounders, eh?' mimicked Chapman.

'I didn't say it was you,' cried Willie. 'It was a joke, I swear it was, Mr. Dennis!'

'Here's the torture pit,' exulted Dennis, 'now for a trial.'

About a dozen boys had gathered round, some in silence, but most of them enjoying the spectacle of a 'rag'.

'Silence,' roared Chapman. 'Weary Willie. Is that your name?'

'Yes, Mr. Chapman.'

They laughed.

'Was that your old man with the face fungus and the billy-cock headgear?'

Willie did not answer.

'Answer,' hissed Dennis, rubbing his knuckles into his neck.

'Yes,' he almost whimpered.

'Say Sir.' A few boys tittered.

'Yes, sir.'

'What is your old man, a rag-and-bone merchant?'

'No, he's a gentleman,' snarled Willie, 'and not a bone merchant, or a grocer. Oo, get off my stummick you—oh shut up, I say, Mr. Chapman—Oo curse you—I mean I beg your pardon—Oo, oh, damn you to hell,' he shrieked.

'And you,' replied Chapman, putting his knee in Willie's belly, 'that's to teach you.'

'Now Spotty, read the letter!'

'Ho, ho, we'd forgotten that. Here it is.'

Spotty pulled the letter from his pocket, and a red rage came into Willie's heart. If he had had a knife, he would have stabbed his tormentor. As it was, his arms held, he lowered his head and butted Dennis in the stomach with a loud, high-pitched scream. Then he kicked Chapman on the knee, and after a minute of struggling was reduced to the state of being spread-eagled on the asphalt while Dennis knelt on his biceps and Chapman sat on his stomach and legs.

'Get off my stummick, I can't breathe,' he cried in an agony of tears and bitten lips. 'Oh you——'

Dennis gently oscillated up and down on his muscles and Chapman rapped his knee-caps with a ruler.

'Cads, bullies,' shrieked Willie, 'dam hell swines and rats.'

'It dam well serves you right for kicking like that'—observed 'Jumbo' Williams, a fat boy with a face like a pudding in a cloth swelled to bursting point. 'Serves you right!'

'It's going a bit too far,' dissented one.

'My God, he's strong!'

'Well, he kicked first,' retaliated Williams. 'Also little kids of the Lower School can't be allowed to behave like that in the Tuck Shop towards the Upper School. He'll have to learn not to do those things at Colham. This isn't a Board School.'

When Willie had been subdued Dennis read the letter, ho-hoing, while the others tittered and guffawed. The two boys—weighing between them eighteen stone—considered that his punishment was deserved. He had kicked.

'No honour,' sneered Chapman, 'dirty hoofer—mule kicker! Crowbirdslegs! Let's get some mud and stick him to the wall of The Bog!'

Perhaps the expression in the face on the gray asphalt, with the hair spread out, moved some feeling of shame, or pity, or fear in him.

'Let 'n go,' he ordered, 'Weary Willie won't sauce Sir Perce Chapman and Mister Alf Dennis again, no jolly fear. Such nasty swear words too! Next time it'll be The Bog wall!'

They got up and walked away, advising the others to leave him. They straggled off, till only one little fellow remained. He was slightly smaller than Willie.

'I say,' he quavered, looking at the other's tear-stained face, 'I say, are you hurt?'

No answer.

'I say, they've gone now.'

The face of the boy was almost like that of a girl—the skin delicate, the eyes gray and long-lashed.

Gradually the sobs ceased to shake Willie.

'I say, may I be your friend?'

Willie looked up at the other.

'I only came on Monday,' explained the boy. 'My name's Bryers.'

Trying to control his voice, Willie said: 'Oh, a n-new b-bug?'

'Yes,' admitted the other, realising fully his ignominy. 'But I saved your letter.'

Willie suddenly felt that he liked him.

'Where?'

'Here.'

'Thanks. I hate this school.'

'I don't like school either,' volunteered the new bug.

'I'm going to clear out, before I go mad.'

'Shall I come with you?'

'Yes.'

'Shall we run away to sea? To America?'

'Yes,' cried Willie.

They slunk out of the gate at the lower playground, and feeling daring, walked through Colham.

'I say, I do like you,' said Bryers, linking his arm in Willie's. 'You are brave. You fought those two all right!'

Willie had been thinking himself a frightful coward, but now he felt better. A big boy had said he was strong!

'Shall we be friends for ever and ever?'

'Aren't we going to America?' said Willie, 'then of course we will be.'

'Yes, rather.'

'Swear fidelity then, to Maddison.'

'I swear, Maddison.'

'Right. I'll go and get my catty, and bullets, my traps, and birds' eggs, and a bag of grub, with some samples of malted milk I've got, say good-bye to Jim, and then we'll go off.'

Joyfully they set out for America.

Chapter 28

THEY LEFT the town, and followed the road to Rookhurst. The houses left behind, Willie's spirit soared. Who cared any more for anyone? Not he! He and old Bryers were going, oh, right across to America, to join the cowboys on a ranch, and make friends with the Indians—glorious! Chapman and Dennis he would never see again . . . but how about Jack—but Jack was a traitor. Rupert would do instead . . . no he wouldn't—no one could ever be like Jack!

As they neared the village doubt began to gloom their plans. Rupert thought of his mother, and Willie, without knowing why, did not like the idea of leaving his father, and the woods and fields. No other woods and fields could ever be the same: and Elsie! He would love her all his life, he knew he would.

'I say,' he said nervously, 'do you think we had better go to-day?'

'It is rather sudden, isn't it,' replied Rupert, looking at the other boy anxiously. 'We shall be expelled if we do.'

'Oh, golly, I hadn't thought of that.'

'Don't let's go, eh?'

'All right.'

The day once more became filled with possible happiness.

'I know,' suggested Willie, 'let's go in the woods!'

'I say, how spiffing!'

'Not old Tetley's, though. My father sometimes goes to see him. There'll be a row if he knows I've mitched like this.'

'Do you think they'll discover?' asked Rupert, wide of eye.

This boy, thought Willie, was all right. He obviously admired him. If only he had his catapult to show him how he could knock a pigeon's egg off a gate at twenty-three paces!

'Not they. Can you get your mother to write an excuse? Say you weren't well. I can get Biddy, our housekeeper, to write one. She'll do anything for me.'

'I say, haven't you got a mother?' inquired Rupert.

'No, she's dead. I've got a father though. He's rather strict, but I can dodge him all right. Poo, easy!'

'My father's dead. He was killed in the Boer War. He was a sailor.'

'But they didn't have sailors in the Boer War,' contradicted Willie.

'Oh, yes they did. My daddy was a leftennan.'

'No,' disagreed Willie. 'I've got a book called *Valour and Victory*, and it tells you all about it.'

'But I'm sure it was the Boer War,' insisted Rupert.

'All right,' said Willie, with sudden generosity, 'only I think I'm right,' he added.

'I'm sure he fired a Long Tom, Willie,' pleaded the other.

'Oh, yes,' said Willie feebly, 'I remember. There's a picture in *Valour and Victory* of one. At the end, of course. You're right,' he conceded brightly.

'I was little at the time,' mentioned Rupert, gratitude in his voice.

'My mother died when I was born. The owls hooted,' announced Willie with pride.

'I was born on the ocean.'

Willie was silent at the thought that to be born upon the ocean and a father killed at battle was better than a mother dying because the owls hooted.

They reached the footpath leading to Turney's farm, and Willie said:

'I say, man, we must be careful here. My father might see us. Shall we go into Brogborough woods instead?'

'Yes,' assented Rupert, who would probably have assented if the Malay Peninsula had been suggested.

'Good bloater. That's a spiffing expression, isn't it? Temperley made it up. At least he said so, but I bet he read it in a book. He's an awful liar, you know, but can't he half climb a tree! Lumme, much better'n I can!'

'I say!' said wide-eyed Rupert admiringly.

They crept down a hedge, and approached the Brogborough woods owned by a retired bookmaker named Isaacs. Once only had Willie ventured in his preserves, and had fled in terror from the pursuit of a gamekeeper. Many pheasants were preserved, and four keepers were employed to keep trespassers out of the wood. Rumour among the village boys, whom Willie hated because they cheeked Jim and also because they 'pulled' birds' nests and had been known to stick thorns through a brood of fledgling robins in the lane, said that two of the keepers carried guns loaded with tin-tacks that they fired at the trousers of escaping marauders. Rumour from the same source also said that man-traps were set just before the first of October to catch poachers, but Willie had ceased to believe this more than two years ago. It had some distant semblance of veracity, since in the boyhood of Big Will'um's father man-traps had been employed, but that was seventy years before; and in the years preceding his death Granfer Brown's memory was muddled after a pint of 'Goliath' ale, with no sense of time.

An old notice board, nibbled by generations of wasps, was nailed to an oak-tree, bearing the warning:

TRESPASSERS WILL BE
PROSECUTED
BEWARE THE DOGS
By Order

They read it in silence.

'There aren't any dogs, I'm sure,' Willie assured Rupert. Rupert hesitated.

'Come on,' said Willie, jumping over the ditch, and holding

on to the rusted barbed wire, which was loose enough to be forced up and allow him to scramble gingerly underneath. The other boy followed, Willie held the slack wire up, and he crept underneath.

They were in the forbidden forest.

A magpie chattered before they had gone fifty yards, and they crouched in silence. A blackbird shrilled, and a wren commenced its 'tack-tack' warning.

'It's not a keeper,' whispered Willie, 'for wrens don't call out for a man. I expect we've disturbed an old owl. Come on, man, it's quite safe. Aren't the bluebells lovely?'

They went on, then paused to listen. Somewhere a nightingale was singing; around them warblers and whitethroats were uttering husky, jarring threads of song, all in ecstasy; winding in and out of the hazel wands, their vanes splashed with gold as they passed through a rift in the leaves where the sunlight came, humming gently, went the wild humble-bees, called from buttercup and heavy-odoured nettle by the chimes of scent pealed from the bluebells. Gladly Willie noticed that Rupert loved the same things that he did . . . if only Jack . . . a rabbit rushed away among the brambles, almost from under their feet; their hearts thumped as with tremendous whir of wings and hoarse, quick crowing a cock pheasant rose and flew away.

'I say,' whispered Rupert, smiling feebly.

Willie whispered that it was all right—somehow it was natural to whisper among the greeneries of the wood.

Warily the two boys crept along a path, beaten and imprinted with hobnailed boots, all leading the same way.

At any moment Willie whispered they might have to run for their lives. Walk on the toes, and watch out for dry sticks, lest they crack! Hush! Forward very slowly!

Round a bend in the pathway they came upon a small hut, with the door open. They retreated, and hid; crept out again, and tip-toed to the side of it. Peering in the cobwebbed window, they saw an old coat hanging on a nail, a besom broom, several pheasant cages—made of wood to trap hen birds—rusted gins, bottles, spades, and other things. Round the other side of the hut was a tall oak, and upon its bole were nailed things that made them gaze in silence. There were many dead creatures, hedge-pigs and cats among them, tier upon tier of them. Magpies and jays alternated with the brown kestrel hawks and crows. There were dozens of hawks, scores of weasels and stoats, all in various stages of decay and desolation. Of some only the head remained, others had been shot or trapped that morning, with blood clotted red on their paws and noses.

'What is it?' Rupert whispered.

'A vermin pole. Look, the owls!'

Tawny owls were there with the white owl. Their soft wings were bedraggled and drooping; the rains had soaked them, the sun bleached them; the orbits, holding once the soft and luminous eyes, were empty, the sockets hollow, filled with dust. Never again in the duskiness of a summer night would the tawny owls float over the mice runs, or answer quaveringly the mournful plaint of their mates with whom they had paired for life; the barn owls indistinctly white and with winnowing wings go over the cornfields under the moon, flutter vaguely among the tall stalks, rise again, and drift away.

Gradually those wings would grow more drab, the frail skeletons droop to the earth, fall into nothingness. Under the tree were bones and fragments of feathers, part of the earth. Death, how terrible and sad it was, thought Willie.

A scream came from somewhere near, and they clutched each other.

'What is it, Willie?'

'I don't know.'

'Let's explore.'

'Go carefully. Let me go first!'

Quietly they went towards the sound, but could find nothing.

Another scream, not so loud but hoarser, caused them to look to one side.

Upon a big piece of turf, supported three feet from the ground by four sticks, stood a jay. They went nearer, and saw that it was caught in a trap, that the jagged teeth had sprung together and broken the thighs. Its mouth was open, as though to breathe more air, its crest raised in pain. Its poor eyes looked at them wistfully, its poor breast fluttered. Blood had clotted the thin frailty of its legs; the bones were smashed.

'Oh, who did it to the poor bird?' cried Rupert.

'It's trapped,' said Willie, 'look, the keeper has put some rotten pheasants' eggs to tempt it, and hidden that gin underneath. Old Bob says jays don't rob nests at all, unless they are exposed and therefore deserted. Oh, the rotten cads.'

He went nearer, breathing fast. The jay screamed feebly. It was too weak to flutter its wings; it was dying.

'I'm going to kill it and put it out of its misery,' said Willie, and he pulled off its head, and then looked at the blood on his hands.

'I say, you do look pale,' said Rupert.

'Shut up, you fool!'

'I'm sorry, Willie.'

Willie wiped his hands on the grass, muttering: 'It's against the law. Jays are protected. I looked on the police board. It's all wrong. It's got to be stopped. The dirty swine.'

'Shall we tell a policeman?'

'A copper?' sneered Willie, 'aren't we trespassing?'

The other looked frightened.

'I will tell you what I'm going to do,' said Willie. 'I'm going to tear up every damhell trap in this wood, that's what I'm going to do! And what's more, no one shall stop me. No one! Do you hear? I'm not going to have my owls shot,' he shouted. 'I don't care for all the keepers in the world. They can—well, shoot me, if they like!'

Rupert followed him. Soon they found another trap, and

Willie hit the eggs with a stick. A metallic snap leapt up as the jaws were released; he pulled the platform to pieces and hurled the gin into the thick undergrowth.

'They'll stop me, will they,' he cried, laughing. 'I'll soon see about that. Come on, Bryers. Forward, I say. Ah! here's another. It's meant for a stoat, but no matter. That's it, he's sprung. Pull hard—up she comes. Chuck it over there, in that little pond. That's what I think of keepers. Forward, I say.'

Followed by Rupert, he went from trap to trap, wrenching them up. After a few minutes, they had destroyed eleven.

'Ha! one more, Rupey'—common idealism had apparently welded still more firmly their friendship—'that makes twelve. What do you and I care for keepers, eh? Nothing at all. Let them all come. I'll show 'em what it means to hurt my birds. How much do keepers enter into my calkerlations? Nothing at all!' he boasted. 'Now then, we'll rip this up—Oh, Billo man! Run, quick!' he cried, for an underkeeper had crept to within fifty yards of them.

They fled down the ride. Imagination sapped their strength, their mouths dried with the thought of capture. Willie took Rupert's hand and pulled him along, but steadily the thudding footfalls of their pursuer drew nearer. He shouted as he ran. 'Fred! Fred!' and at each bellow their hearts thumped sickeningly. Round the narrow path they ran, startling blackbirds which had been searching among the leaves. Rupert's feet moved slower and slower; his eyes protruded from his head in agony.

'I'm done, man,' he sobbed.

'Come on,' wailed Willie, pulling him along, 'he's dead beat himself.'

'Fred! Fred!' bellowed the keeper.

Someone shouted in front: 'Here I am.'

A keeper came out of a cross ride just in front, with raised gun.

They collapsed on the ground, gasping. Willie was sick.

Fred came up, and pounced upon them. He had once been a groom, and came from Wapping.

'I knows 'un,' he growled, 'lives in Rookhurst. I knows 'un. Young gent he calls 'isself, too.'

'Pullun traps up, they was, was they?'

'Come on,' ordered Fred, 'up t' see the Squire. Young gent, yer calls yerself, eh? Oh dear me, I'm not sorry I'm not in your shoes, my young toff!'

He took Willie's arm, and led him along. Willie wondered if he would be sent to prison. He could have shrieked with frenzy.

The two under-keepers led them before the owner of the estate, and by their appearance they might have been plucked from the vermin pole in the forest.

Chapter 29

Mr. Maddison looked at his watch, a gold hunter that had belonged to his father, whose intemperate habits in later life had been so confirmed that he had died of them. His two sons, John and Richard, were left to settle the debts incurred by his wastefulness. The elder son had been called to the Bar only two years when the old man died, but a love of country life and an inherent dislike for the strivings of men among themselves, but chiefly the frail health of his young wife, had prompted him to return to Fawley when in the natural order of things it passed to him. Three of the farms were lost in the foreclosure of mortgages, and, with the exception of about twenty acres of meadow land and the ancient beech forest, the remainder of the estate was sold to pay the death duties and the dead man's debts.

Mr. Maddison had a fear that the son had inherited the weaknesses of his grandfather, in whom a tenderness for animals and birds, and a spasmodic generosity existed side by side with the equal opposites of those traits. During his lifetime, Willie's grandfather would be intensely moved by a newspaper account of an Armenian massacre by Turks; most of his sympathy being given in the abstract, he had little for his wife and children, to whom he was frequently (and deliberately) cruel. The sight of a cat with a mouse gave him pain and stirred acute pity for the small biter; yet he hunted three days a week in the fox-hunting season, and until his debts grew too large he kept a pack of otter hounds. Easily upset, and having no real work to do, he was irritably disappointed by life; he drank to find release, and died in the vain search.

Pondering these things as he sat on the lawn that late afternoon, while the swallows twittered on the roof and the bees were at the peach bloom on the south wall of the stables, Mr. Maddison's mind went back to the past. It was an encouraged habit that now was natural to the lonely man. His brooding ceased when it occurred to him that the boy should have been home an hour before. He wondered if he were a bad parent: if Jenny were near, would she be reproaching him? Ah, no, Jenny would reproach no one; never had he known her say a hard thing about anyone. Jenny: the hundred times he had sat still and tried to speak to her, gripping the sides of the chair in his effort to force her name beyond the stars! Nothing had come of it. Was he a good father? How could he tell? By results, he had failed. Willie didn't appear to like him, was afraid of him. Why? It must have been his own fault, because the child came into the world when he himself was a grown man. Could a father shape his son's destiny? He doubted it. There was not much difference between the seed of a dandelion and the seed of a pink willow herb, but when they grew up there was all the difference. Something evolved in a child— heredity of temperament. Where had Willie got his temperament? Not from his mother or himself. His mother was like Stevenson's mate 'steel true and blade straight'. Willie was deceitful. He often said he hadn't got a catapult, but he knew otherwise. Yesterday at the football match he had said that the ball was punctured. Why, he had seen Jack adjusting the spike in his boot. An old trick, he had done it himself! No, the boy had the lying trait in him: it must, for his own sake, be stamped out: he was disobedient, too. He had no sense of discipline and that was most essential in a good citizen. He wanted to be proud of his boy. He wanted him to work hard, and win a scholarship to his old college. He was a little slacker, the kind that used cribs later on in school life. Rore was a good fellow: keen, idealistic. Seven o'clock, and Willie not yet home, unless he had sneaked in quietly: he was rather inclined to be a creepy-crawly boy. He must watch Willie carefully!

At this moment in his musings, his housekeeper came along the path by the untidy boxwood hedge, stumbled up the stone steps to the lawn where he was sitting, and called out tearfully:

'Oh, Mas' Madd'zun, the little lamb be in trouble. Mas' Eyesicks of Brogberry be here wid a keeper. Come at once, will ee, Mas' Madd'zun, little Willie be a-weeping.'

Mr. Maddison followed her, a great fear within him. Fidelis rose and swayed wearily along after him.

By the pump stood Mr. Isaacs, florid of face, clad in loose, hairy homespuns, a check cap on his head. The years had been unkind to him since he was a tick-tack and general handyman for Gordon Pweek, whose fortune, large as it was, was enviously rumoured in the big parasitical section of the racing world to have been eclipsed by that of his former tout. His nose, always large and with wide nostrils, had bulged in proportion to the quantity of port that its owner had swallowed, until it now spread over his face like a fungus on a dying tree. His ears were thick and red; so were his lips, and the folds of his chinlap. Seeing Mr. Maddison, whom he knew only by name, he broke into a strident denunciation of his son, who stood, with a dirty tear-stained face, between the under-keeper and his master.

'Yes, here he is, the scoundrel. Prison is the only place for him, I should think. And that's where he'll go, or my name isn't Sol Isaacs. Sorry for you, sir, but this 'ere boy's the limit. Hamstrung my birds' chances, sir, that's wot he's done, damn and blast him!'

Biddy stood by, looking as though she would rush forward and take Willie away. He looked at her mournfully. Mr. Maddison, his voice trembling and higher than usual, said coldly: 'I don't quite know what you mean, Mr. Isaacs. If you have any grievance, and wish to complain to me, I shall be glad if you will come inside the house. Nothing would be more distressing than to have a crowd collecting in my stable yard, attracted by your voice, and under the impression that a fight is in progress.'

The empty stables were two hundred yards from the lane, so it was most improbable that any crowd would collect there. Mr. Maddison's manner was due to extreme nervousness.

'Oh, that's your tone, is it? Then we'll soon see about that. I came here with the intention of allowing you to thrash your young rip'—(Willie began to weep again without any attempt to put his hands up to his face)—'but if you're goin' to do the hianmighty pater, I may as well take him to the jug straightaway. I'm on the bench, sir, and don't you forget it. I know the law; make no mistake about it.'

'Oh,' replied Mr. Maddison in tones as pale as his cheeks, 'I don't doubt for one moment your knowledge of law. Might I suggest, with deference to you in your, er, magisterial capacity, that it is usual before summing up to prefer the charge, to hear evidence, and give the accused a chance for defence?'

'Defence? Defence? Well, I like your blasted cheek,' bellowed Mr. Isaacs. 'What defence can a poacher 'ave?'

'Must you shout?' asked Mr. Maddison.

'Yes, sir, I must!' roared the other, 'you turn nasty, so will I, and don't you forget it!'

Mr. Maddison ignored his truculent manner, and they walked to the house.

'Mrs. Crane, I will call you if I require you,' he said to Biddy, who followed after the keeper into the hall.

'I should——' began Biddy.

'My keeper can come in, I suppose you've no objection,' asked Mr. Isaacs.

'If you want him to.'

'Well, I do want him to. Come on, Fred.'

'Coming, Squire!' replied Fred.

Biddy went back to her kitchen to have a good cry, and
Fidelis followed very slowly into the room.

'Will you sit down, Mr. Isaacs?'

'No, sir, I guess I'll stand.'

His voice was not so harsh in the sombre room, from the
walls of which portraits of dead and gone Maddisons looked
down on the uneasy group.

Blind Fidelis crept behind Willie and licked the back of his
knee. Willie's finger touched his nose—it was hot: Fidelis was
very feeble, and he was upset, knowing that he was in trouble.

'Now please let me know all about it,' said Mr. Maddison as
easily as he could.

'I think I'll ask my man to state his case,' replied Mr.
Isaacs, whose head, now that the check cap was removed,
resembled in shape and appearance a great, livid ostrich's egg.
'Go on, Fred. Cough up what 'appened.'

'I was in middle covert s'arternoon,' began the ex-groom in
a hoarse voice, 'when I 'eard a voice what I knew to be 'Arry's,
yellin' out for me. 'Arry's in trouble, I says to misself, wiv egg
poachers. So I lay quiet, knowin' that they was runnin' my
way. Well, I mean to say, there's too much of this sorter thing,
says I to misself, goin' on abaht among these ere rusticks. No
discrimination they ain't got, stealin' from a kind gent like
Squire Isaacs, an 'im a beak an' all——'

'A beak?' interrupted Mr. Maddison, yet knowing what was
meant.

'That's what I said, beggin' Squire's pardon. Well, I mean
to say, I lied doggo, until 'Arry's shouts got 'oarser. So I ups
and 'ops round the corner, and two boys immediately flings
'emselves on the ground, and starts a-whimpering. "Pullin' up
traps", says 'Arry, puffing an' blowin', wiv' 'is weak 'eart too.
"It's too much, Fred", he says, "my pore old 'eart won't stand
it——".' He paused in the flow of his speech, and looked
dramatically at Mr. Maddison—'Well, I mean to say, poor
'Arry looked proper groggy. "Pullin' up traps, all for devil-

ment?" I says, "'Ow many?" I says. "Dunno", 'e says, so we leaves it at that. All of them was pulled up, s'far as we could see. So I says: "Off to Squire Isaacs, 'Arry", I says. Well, I mean to say, in a manner of speaking, though we're 'ere now we were there then, and from them there woods to this 'ere 'ouse was done as quick as kiss yer hand.' Fred gulped after this eloquence, which had caused him, as he recounted afterwards, in 'The Cat and Gnatfly' inn, ' to sweat 'ot and 'ard'.

'You heard, sir?' boomed Mr. Isaacs. 'You heard what my man said?'

'However loud it may have been necessary to speak in your life otherwise, I can assure you that your remarks are perfectly intelligible to myself without shouting. My dog is old and weak: the noise disturbs him.'

This was literally true, but Mr. Isaacs imagined that it was meant only as an insult.

The face of Mr. Isaacs became more florid; his eyes protruded like those of a lobster; his nose assumed the hue of a tropical fungus growing on a dead tree.

'Wottyer gotter say about that young blackguard son of yours, eh? That's what I wanter know. Stand there cool and lofty as you please, but you're all going through it, now, don't you forget it.'

'Your voice is going through the walls, I fear,' replied the other, wearily, 'once more I must ask you not to bawl. It really isn't necessary.'

Willie's gloom began to lighten. Perhaps there was hope after all—he had expected Father to take sides against him! Fidelis licked his leg again.

'By God, I won't stand it, I won't stand it. No one has ever back-answered Sol Isaacs and not paid for it. You're backing the wrong 'oss when you rile Sol Isaacs.'

'Since in asking you to speak in an ordinary manner I am wasting my breath, I will ask my son to explain. But first of all, I understand your keeper to say that there were two boys. Where is the other?'

'Your boy is the one to blame. He admitted that himself. The other was smaller, and he has gone home. Led astray by yours. I only want one, to make an example.'

'Now, Willie,' said his father, 'what have you to say?'

After many hesitant beginnings, and between sobs, Willie explained that Rupert and he had gone in the wood 'to see the bluebells and had seen a jay'.

'But why weren't you at school?'

'I ran away, Father.'

'Why?'

'I don't know, Father.'

Mr. Isaacs interpolated some remark, but his father ignored it.

'Well, that is not the point at present. Why did you go in the wood?'

'For a lark, Father.'

'Who was the other boy?'

'Rupert Bryers, Father.'

'Who's he?'

'I don't know, Father.'

'Was Jack with you?'

'No, Father.'

There was a pause. Outside a thrush was singing in the cherry-tree. The door creaked, as though Biddy were listening, but no one noticed it.

'It's a considerable offence,' remarked Mr. Isaacs significantly, 'and seeing as how you question it, I'm now going to give him in charge.'

Willie began to weep silently. He had made up his mind to commit suicide. He did not want to live any longer. Perhaps if he hanged himself they would be sorry. He was glad that Rupert had escaped.

'One moment,' said his father, 'I understand that my son did great damage to your traps.'

'Oh, you're climbing down, are you?'

'At what do you estimate the amount of damage done?'

'Oh, dear no, money ain't the question. I'm going to law, I am.'

The board outside creaked again.

Mr. Maddison opened the door, and Biddy nearly fell in.

'Come in, Mrs. Crane. You may as well be here.'

Willie looked appealingly at her. She folded her arms, and fixed Mr. Isaacs with a terrible eye. Mr. Maddison went on:

'You said that no money would compensate the damage done, Mr. Isaacs?'

'I did.'

'But why?'

'We'll settle that when he's committed for trial,' pointing an enormous forefinger at the boy, 'reformatory, I think. Leading small boys astray. Playing truant. Destroying my jay traps. Oh, dear no, you don't compensate Solly Isaacs. I told you to go steady and nurse her along the rails. No money will square the damage, and don't you forget it.'

Biddy, her face like a fossilised apple, was about to speak, but Mr. Maddison held up his hand.

'Jay traps, Mr. Isaacs?'

'That's what I said.'

'I heard you. So did my housekeeper. That's why I asked her in. Of course, you realise that jays are protected birds?'

'You can't bluff me with any old buck. They're my birds, in my woods, and——'

'Please don't shout. Jays are strictly protected under the Wild Birds Protection Act. It is an offence to destroy them, although the law is practically inoperative owing to the lethargy of, may I say, without wishing to imply any criticism of yourself, our police and legal system. There is a society for the protection of birds, which would be interested in this case, I believe. You are a magistrate, you told me. You know the law, you also told me, or rather bawled at me. So do I. I am a barrister. I do not say that my son is blameless; it was very wrong of him to trespass, and do damage to other people's property. That, however, can wait. The point I want to raise is that of jays in traps.'

The under-keeper looked sullenly at the carpet.

'Damn rot,' said Isaacs, 'how'll you prove it?'

'Mrs. Crane is a witness of what you said. If you press the matter you will, I suggest, appear very ridiculous.'

'That doesn't alter the fact that your son is a rip who wants flogging.'

'That I cannot discuss with you, Mr. Isaacs. I apologise to you for his conduct in your woods, and I am perfectly willing to consider immediately any claims for compensation you may wish to make.'

'Compensation—my foot! If I catch your brat on my land again, I will flog the life out of him.'

'In that case I will have no hesitation in shooting you. Meanwhile I have more important things to consider, and perhaps you have, too.'

He went to the door, and opened it, and stood back. Mr. Isaacs thumped out, shouting that he hadn't heard the last of it, followed by his keeper.

'Now my boy, go and have your tea,' said his father to Willie.

'Yes, Father,' replied Willie, hopefully.

Left alone, Mr. Maddison dropped into a chair, and it was twilight outside when he rang for Biddy.

'I want to speak to Willie alone, Mrs. Crane, if you please.'

Biddy went reluctantly from the room, hostility in her eyes. A moment later Willie crept in, holding a history book in his hand to show that he had not been idle. He muttered to himself, as though engrossed with study: 'Agincourt, fourteen-fifteen, Agincourt, fourteen-fifteen, A—Agincourt——' and could not speak any further.

The dog Fidelis lay on his side, and did not move as he entered. His tail shivered, once.

'Why did you play truant, Willie?' asked Mr. Maddison.

The tone of his voice chilled the warmth and admiration that was new-born in the boy. While his father had been speaking to Mr. Isaacs, Willie had felt that he was saved. An impulse had come to him telling him to go to his father and kiss his hand, so great had been the relief. But he restrained himself because other people were in the room: in particular he did not want Biddy to see him doing it. The admiration had been increased because Father had spoken up for the birds. Wouldn't he tell the chaps at school!

The habitual reserve of Mr. Maddison, which had been encrusting his life and alienating him from his son, had cracked; it might have fallen off altogether at this crisis in the boy's life. But speaking coldly, asking him why he had played truant, the son's glow of affection died down: Father would never understand, he thought, the instinctive protection of falsehood coming to him. Quick! Quick! Think of something to tell Father! He could think of nothing: he began to weep.

'Why did you play truant, Willie?'

'I don't know, Father.'

'You always say that you don't know. Have you no excuse, no reason?'

'No, Father.'

'Well, you know what happens when people do wrong, don't you? You know what happened to Adam and Eve in the Garden of Eden.'

Even as he spoke, he felt that the matter was beyond him. What was the good of an allusion to an ancient parable that was thousands of years old, generations out of date—the literature of minds, good and idealistic maybe, but minds nevertheless in the infancy of knowledge?

'They behaved wrongly, and displeased God, and were punished. All sin has to be punished. You have behaved wrongly, haven't you?'

'Yes, Father,' he agreed, hoping to lessen any coming punishment.

'Then you must be punished.'

Mr. Maddison waited.

'Do you not see that, my boy?'

Willie hung his head. The gleam was gone, and all was darkness.

'Won't you tell me why you played truant?' he said, almost gently, and adding sharply (ashamed of his fancied weakness) 'or was it merely devilment? No lies, now.'

Willie looked on the carpet, and tried to balance on one leg. Even if he did tell about Chapman, and the letter . . . oh, no, he could never tell anyone about the letter.

'I am waiting for an answer, my boy.'

'I don't know, Father,' he said, almost desperately.

'Very well, then, I've given you a chance. Don't forget that. Now, if you please, you will go up to your room and get undressed. I am going to give you a thrashing, you will have no supper, and to-morrow I will go and see Mr. Rore. Perhaps he will be able to do something with you. Now then, upstairs you go.'

Willie turned, and went out of the room, ran quickly upstairs. He was going to be thrashed! Oh God up in the sky, save him from a thrashing! But God did not answer prayers; he had prayed before, and had always been thrashed.

Like a ghostly beckoning, a twig of the pear-tree was blown against the window pane.

Five minutes later Mr. Maddison went upstairs with a cane. Fidelis whined as he was shut in behind him.

He opened the door of his son's bedroom, and a gust of wind from the open window clashed it to. The branches of the tree outside seethed in the wind that had risen at sunset, an owl quavered mournfully in the windy darkness.

'Willie,' he called sharply.

There was no answer.

He looked under the bed. He was not there, neither was he in the cupboards—as he searched, the father remembered hiding there when he himself was a boy, playing hide-and-seek with other children—he was not behind the washstand.

'Willie,' he called, less sharply.

He went into the other bedrooms.

His son was not to be found.

'Willie!' The cry echoed through the house, but only the feeble scratching of old blind Fidelis at the door below and his thin whine of anguish answered in the solitude and the fear of his own heart.

In the kitchen Big Will'um was eating a meat pasty. Biddy was weeping quietly. Bob the terrier was asleep before the fire. The owl called again.

Midnight came and passed, but he did not return, and in the early hours of the morning the dog Fidelis died.

Chapter 30

The uncertain flickerings of the fire illumining dully the foliage of the fir-trees gave an impression of impenetrable blackness beyond. The flames rose in yellow stabs and with sudden ragged yawning of vermillion colour staining the night. Sometimes a gust of wind sweeping over the corn fanned its very heart to brightness, and glowing embers and sparks whirled over the ground.

The lovers who leaned against the turved dome of the hut had not spoken since first a tiny flame had curled round the sticks and the smoke hanging vaguely overhead had tarnished the little moon. Dreamily they looked into the fire. The auburn silkiness of Jim's hair touched Dolly's cheek; his arm was round her shoulder, and she held his other hand. Seen thus in the most romantic of all lights, the light by which ancient hunters wooed their mates centuries since while the coughing roar of lions shuddered the air in the fire-guarded caves, Dolly's face appeared to him with a saintly unreality. Her hair, brushed from a centre parting, lay smooth on her head and gathered in a loose knot at the nape of her neck, left serene the forehead limned above the dark eyes with uplifted curve of brow. The firelight lingered and glowed on her cheek, leaving a soft shadow under the cheek bone as the flames crouched low again. Her lips, red and parted slightly, seemed to be faintly smiling. She was with her lover, and she knew that her purpose would be achieved. Withholding herself from Jim with that nobleness of purpose, partially selfless, that comes only to those women to whom love is instinctively a power to help the loved one, she knew now that she could influence his life. Jim's murmured love lingered in her mind as she joyed in the touch of his head against her cheek, and that is why each leap of flame discovered anew the smile.

'Oh, li'l Dolly, you be my mother-maiden.'

'What be mother-maid, Jim?' she asked, just to hear from him what already she must have known deeply within her.

'My mother, as I minds her, long ago it be now, were someone who held me an' I felt safe and wanted to stop there.'

'What was ees mother like, Jim?'

'I disremembers, Dolly sweet, for 'twere when I were a child. All I minds were a warm mother wi' weeping eyes and hand that stroked my hair but she went away from me and never came back.'

Now she came closer to him, and laid her hand lovingly on his hair. 'Do ee mind ees feyther, Jim?'

'I minds he, but not very well, I minds he writing at a table in a dark room, and walking about, looking at the sky through the windy, but I disremember aught else.'

'Poor Jim,' she whispered.

'You be my mother, do ee know that, now?'

'Es mother, Jim?'

'L'il Dolly, when you were kind to me and came for walks with me, I were sad when ee were gone. Do ee mind it, now, that ee never kissed Jim?'

'Jim never wanted to kiss Dolly,' she murmured.

'I wanted to kiss ee, and not to kiss ee, Dolly,' he replied, stroking her brows with his hand, 'but I can't say for why. At first I thought ee might be a-mocking, do ee see. I couldna' understand for why a lovely dear like Dolly would a-want to love a moucher.'

'You bean't a moucher,' she said fiercely, 'you be my Jim who will a-get a reg'lar work, woan't ee now?'

' 'Es Dolly,' kissing her lips and feeling passion rising within him. She did not respond but seemed to lose her will, and to lie inert.

'Do ee mind a-kissing like that?' he asked, speaking more broadly as his blood quickened.

She touched his hand, clasped it, and held it against her heart.

'I love ee like a mother, Jim.'

He felt utterly restful. Nothing mattered now that he had Dolly. What were the stars and the glowing suns in the darkness, full of mystery, to the love of Dolly?

'I doan't a-love ee as a feyther, Dolly.'

'How do ee a-love then?'

'I loves fierce, Dolly.'

She kissed his hair, then laid her cheek on his head. And they remained so for many minutes, while the fire sunk lower and a little wind murmured in the firs.

Then Jim rose, and threw more logs on the fire.

'Be ee cold, Dolly?'

'Not with ee near me.'

He crept close to her.

'Dolly, will ee wed?'

'Knows I will,' she replied.

'Then kiss me.'

She kissed him.

'Jim,' she breathed, 'will ee do a favour?'

' 'Es.'

'Cut ees beard off ?'

' 'Es.'

'Will ee now?'

'If ee wants it.'

'Darling Jim.'

'Sweet li'l Dolly.'

'Shall see Mis'r Norman to-morrow, Jim?'

'Yes. Kiss ee agen.'

'Why does ee want to love me?'

As a sudden storm changes a landscape, so the sudden passion, the fierce desire of possession, had changed Jim. The listless, moody dreamer was gone, the dumbly incoherent thoughts of beauty fled, a man remaining that cared only for love. But it is decreed that men in whom is a mystic understanding and love of the wild are tied forever to loneliness.

'Hark ee, Dolly.'

He had suddenly raised his head. From far across the corn had floated a Voice, a Voice pure as the wan fires of the moon, a Voice seeming to express the sadness of beauty that was ever fleeting and elusive. It seemed to tell of all the springs that had passed with their sweet violets and windflowers, of the song that had been amid tragedies of the little unknown wild things. And now it sang with a tranquillity of longing, low and fluting, calling something beyond the trees, higher than the wind, changing to ecstasy, rising with passionate yearning, dying in wistful cadence, a Voice aiding the world-old struggle of genius to express the unknown, the longing for a fuller happiness, a loveliness of life for all things under the ancient stars. From the far thicket another Voice responded, and still another, till the darkness of night seemed laced with silver threads of song.

Once more the nightingales were among the hazel wands and ashpoles of the woods.

'Oh, Dolly, hark.'

' 'Tis only a bird, Jim Holloman.' Fear was in her voice.

'I knows, but doan't ee dream when he sings?'

His voice pleaded, as though beseeching her to think as he did. He spoke quickly, his words confused, and with broad accent. He was deeply stirred.

'Life be too hard for dreams, Jim Holloman.'

'Life's lovely, Dolly, though not so wi'out dreams.'

'Only love counts, Jim.'

'That's what nightingale be a-singing on. If I had singing voice I'd sing so to ee.'

'Dear Jim,' she whispered.

'Oh, listen to um. Dree on um, there be. They only

sing fur a few weeks, then their songs die. 'Tes like all life.'

'That be like courting, Jim, do ee see now. Love goes quick when you'm wed.'

'Not us, Dolly. I doan't a-love like another man 'ud love. It be like the wind, the way I love ee, for it goes on for ever.'

'A wind'll blow cold, Jim.'

He could think of nothing to say to that, so folded her to him and kissed at first gently, and then roughly. The warm softness of her was in his arms; suddenly he drew back and looked at her face in the flamelight. Her eyes stared heavily into his, bright with the first love of youth. With his hand he stroked her cheek. She turned her head and pressed wet lips upon it. With a sound that was almost a sob he wound his arms around her body and laid his mouth on hers. She struggled faintly, yet knowing deep within her that she did it only to prolong the joy that swept through her whole body. Wildly he claimed her for himself, crying that he would kill any man that looked at her. His sweet captive tried to hide from his kisses, but he would not be denied; he turned her head towards him and she kissed him quickly and shyly before hiding her face in his coat.

'Dolly, stop wi' me in spinney.'

'No, no, Jim. Not yet.'

' 'Es ee wull.'

'Not yet Jim. One day.'

He pretended to desire release from her arms. She pressed her body close to his, the nightingales were still singing. She was afraid of the desolation returning. Suddenly she pulled him over and took his head upon her bosom, rocking at the pain of her mingled pity and desire. Against her breasts she nursled his head, murmuring husky and rapturous words in her throat as though to a child. Jim caught her in so rough an embrace that she cried out. All the blood in his body seemed to be in his heart and trying to pierce his chest like a spearhead. In the struggle her hair fell over her shoulders in a loosened shadow, and he buried his face in it, breathing deeply—thrust it away with a savage hand in order to feel with his mouth the blood pulsing in her neck. A sob come from Dolly, she felt that if she were weak she would in her apparent victory lose everything. With nervous strength she forced him away with her arms; she saw his wild eyes staring at her in the firelight, then he had flung himself on the ground and lay with face hidden in his hands.

She looked at him, still on the ground. She yearned towards him, a tenderness overcame the desire with which her body throbbed. A flame leapt in the fire and gave to her dark hair and gleaming throat a humility as she knelt there. She swayed a little, her hand went to her eyes, she called his name brokenly and with yearning tenderness, but he did not look up.

'Jim,' she moaned, then bowed her head and wept. He sprang up and knelt beside her, speaking hoarsely.

'Doan't ee cry now, Dolly love, I durdn't mean to hurt ee.'

She looked at him with wet eyes, and smiled; touched his brow and kissed it with little gentle touches of her lips. He cherished her, and she grew softly warm in his arms, a virgin maid held by the man she loved, and to whom she would surrender herself. Jim saw that her eyes were larger with her love; leaf-brown pools in which the star of evening was drowned. Hoarsely he besought her never to leave him, never for a moment: she was his little thing, his little thing. She draped her long hair round his neck, and so they lay, now in ruddy firelight, now in shade as the flames sunk. Then again Dolly wanted to hear him speak of his love for her, and wished that he would treat her fiercely. She put her hand behind the collar of his coat, and stroked his shoulder.

But the moment had passed, and Jim had come to manhood. He was stronger than she, and she would follow. She would do as he asked. Her desire sank back. Whenever he wished to claim the right of his manhood and love, he would do so. She lay quiet and happy, holding his hands. After awhile she told him how she had cared always for him.

'Nothing ee could a-do would make me hate ee, dear Jim, I only want ee to be happy,' she whispered. 'If ee goes mouching all ees life, time'll come, Jim love, when ee'll be lonesome. No one else tried to show ee, 'cept me, did they Jim?'

He shook his head, feeling that she was like the blossom of the white-thorn when the buds were opening.

'When I saw ee so lonesome,' she went on, her voice low and beautiful, 'when I were little 'un, I felt sad for ee, Jim. I know'd ee was kind, gentle chap when ee saw us swummun' years agone in Witch Pool. That ould Biddy Crane told 'um all in village I were drotchel. 'Twasn't so, only just 'cause I were always happy and joking wi' the men. John Fry now, proper outish fool, he be! He called me a scarlet 'ooman 'cos I told 'um to go 'bout ees own work and let me be. Wanted to kiss me, John Fry did.'

'Called ee scarlet 'ooman, did ee?'

' 'Es, Jim. Be I?'

'I'll break ees neck, I wull.'

'Wull 'ee?'

'I'll knack his bliddy head off if I catch'n talking to ee again!'

The fire was burning brightly, the branches crackling and sending up floating sparks that drifted away and died suddenly into ghostly gray flakes.

'Jim, what be time? Missus Temp'ly doan't want me to be late.'

He looked at an enormous watch strapped on to his wrist, an American timepiece that he had traded for twenty rabbit skins in the market.

'Be dwenty minutes after nine.'

'Better be strolling.'

'Wait another ten minutes, wull ee?'

Conscious now of time that sped so fleetingly they sat dreaming by the fire. Sometimes a faint and high squeak pierced from above as the little flittermice risped with leathern wings in and out of the branches of the trees, while all around where the notes of field voles as they ran swiftly on the dried ancient leaves. A dog barked, his raucous howlings strangely distinct on the still air. Then a noise of feet running quickly came to them, and sounds of tearful gasping. Looking down the open sweep of field they saw a small dark figure labouring upwards as though exhausted towards the spinney. Once the tiny outline seemed to collapse, but picked itself up and spurred by fear of pursuit swayed and stumbled over the loose earth. As it drew nearer they could see that it was a boy, and soon afterwards heard that the boy was speaking to himself as if for encouragement and to inspire self-confidence. They watched him coming nearer, and then a voice that they recognised as Willie's panted:

'Go on, man, you're nearly there. He's there, I know he is, for a fire's burning. He won't split, I tell you. Jim won't split. They'll all be tracking you soon. Go on, man, it's not far, go on.'

When he reached the spinney he called loudly for Jim, and rushing forward knocked his head on the suspended length of train rail. With a moan he collapsed.

'Quick, ee be a-hurt,' cried Dolly.

They picked him up, sobbing and clasping his head.

'Someone hit me,' he cried, pretending; at the same time hoping he was seriously hurt.

'Now doan't ee a-cry,' said Dolly, kneeling down by the fire and holding him in her arms. 'Let me kiss it well then,' she crooned, laying her cheek against his face. In the firelight the eyes of the boy and the woman were dark and beautiful. Jim watched them, and his own eyes brimmed with love for both.

'There now, it'll soon be better, Li'l Will'um.'

Jim looked on with a great tenderness for Dolly in his eyes.

Soon the pain in his head lessened, and wildly he told them that he had run away, and that in future he was going to live with Jim. If Jim refused to have him, he would drown himself in the lake.

'But why 'ave ee runned away?'

'Father was going to thrash me because I sprung all the jay traps in Brogborough Wood s'afternoon.'

'Ah,' interrupted Jim, 'I knows. That ould ed-kipper, George Cog, be a ould rat.'

'Well, I went in there s'afternoon with an old friend of mine called Rupert Bryers. He's an awfully decent chap really. Well, when we got in the wood first of all we saw a vermin pole. And what do you think was on it besides hawks, jays, crows, cats, and magpies? Owls, yes! Millions of them. That made me pretty wild, I can tell you. So I said to Rupert: "It's time this was stopped". Then a scream rent the atmosphere and we found a jay. Oh, Dolly, its legs were broken! So we put it out of its misery and I said to Rupert: "We're not going to stand this, are we?" So we pulled all the others up and flung them away where no one could find them. Then a keeper appeared upon the scene, named Harry.'

'I know 'un,' growled Jim.

Willie's voice grew loud with an almost hysterical happiness.

'We were chased, At last, after a tremendous chase, he overtook us. Rupert was pretty exhausted, but I did not intend to give up without a proper fight, so used my fists and I can tell you I marked him pretty severely, for he isn't very big, as you know. Of course, he outclassed me, although he had absolutely no knowledge of boxing, and as you know I have had considerable sperience!'—Willie had: from collecting cigarette cards of the 'Famous Boxer Series'—'You remember how Jack and I outed those cads with the baby rabbit in Hangman's Mash last year? Well, since I've been to school I've been in strict training. I can't tell you how long the scrap lasted, but a low-looking cad named Fred appeared upon the scene, and of course we were overpowered. They took us to Mr. Isaacs, you know, that awful bounder who came two years ago. Well, he cussed and swore and said he'd send for the police, but I persuaded him not to'—Willie did not add that the persuasion was augmented by an uncontrolled prayer upon bended knees—'as I more or less explained that jays were protected birds. However, he would have his way, so he took me to Father, after sending him, Rupert I mean, home because he was sick and wasn't really responsible for what happened. Father soon sent the old cad Isaacs about his business and I thought he was very decent, but when afterwards he got ratty, I thought I would hop over to you. Don't split, will you Dolly, about where I am? Besides, its my birthday in two days time. Let me spend it with you!'

'But ee had better go back,' warned Jim.

'No, no, no,' cried Willie, beginning to sob, 'if you turn me away I shall kill myself. Father hates me, you know he does. I heard Biddy telling Big Will'um as I listened by the window that it was because I had killed my mother. I was the wrong way up when I was born. Jim, for God's sake don't send me back home!'

Dolly hugged him closer, her eyes wet at the thought of the boy without a mother, and the hate of a father against him because his mother had died so sadly.

Neither knew what to do.

Dolly asked what Jack would do without him. 'Jack be queer wi' sickness,' she told him.

With fear Willie asked if it were serious, and was relieved when told that it was a bilious attack.

'He gorged himself all right yesterday you know, at the tuck shop.'

Slyly Dolly hinted that Elsie would be miserable.

Willie was alarmed. Then people knew about it, he thought. How awful. What would her mother say? She would be awfully offended. He must pretend.

'I hardly know Elsie,' he mumbled.

'Ees a-told a bung,' whispered Dolly in his ear. 'Elsie's ees yungleddy.'

'She isn't.'

'Dolly's jealous,' she whispered, kissing him.

He wriggled away from her and sat down by the fire, feeling the misery slipping from him, and beginning to enjoy the adventure.

' 'Eed better go back to ees feyther,' repeated Jim.

'No, no.'

'They'll come and search for ee.'

'Then I'll hide.'

Soon Dolly said that she must be going. So after further doubts Jim said that he could stop there with him.

'When you are married can I come and live with you, please?'

Dolly said that of course he could.

'I'll stay here till you come back,' he called out to Jim, who was going to Skirr Farm with Dolly, 'and don't tell a soul, will you Dolly?'

She promised that she would keep the secret.

Left alone, Willie stared into the fire. Wild ideas formulated in the flames, dying as quickly. He would walk to the coast, and become a cabin boy. Or a smuggler. He would try for a job in the British Natural History Museum. Should he go and throw himself on the mercy—that was the idea—on the mercy of Mr. Norman. No, he would think that he had come because of Elsie, besides, hadn't he pelted his picture in the mowing meadow last year. Would Elsie be sorry if he never returned—he hoped so. He might die of exposure. A beautiful and sad picture of himself in a marble coffin being lowered into a grave while his father, standing by in a black coat and a top hat, came to him. In a sad voice the Vicar would say the burial service. Elsie would be sobbing into her hanky-fish, quietly and utterly broken-hearted. Jim would be there, and Dolly, while he would gradually be lowered into the earth . . . the picture was so acute that tears rolled down his cheeks. There was a lovely feeling in brooding on Elsie's wild grief at the graveside. All would be understood then. He would come to her in the wind at night, and tell her to forget him, and love another, and then he would go away on the wind over the downs, to the sea and the stars for ever. He thought himself into the leaves, and when the nightingales sang he forgot himself entirely.

The song came like the purling of a brook, like the spilled plashings of a fountain holding in thrall the moonlight, like the wind sighing in its dreamy sleep among the tall feathery grasses.

When Jim returned he found that the boy was sitting by the fire, staring into the flames, all his life in his eyes. They crawled into the shelter, and slept on the bracken.

Willie was aroused by a hand touching his foot. He was awake instantly, remembering where he was, feeling chilled.

'Come wi' me,' Jim whispered.

Outside the stars were still bright. Willie shivered. The ashes of the fire were flat and gray in the centre, and unburnt branches at its verge. They went to the edge of the spinney, and looked out over the sloping field of wheat.

No wind stirred, and solitude brooded over the earth.

'Look,' whispered Jim, pointing to the east.

Over the dark outline of the beech wood hung a star, a lustrous globe of radiance, larger than any star Willie had ever seen. They watched it in silence. Slowly it moved higher, glowing with softer and purer blaze as it was lapped by the light now flowing into the eastern estuary of heaven. It was neither white nor golden, nor would any colour describe it: the darkness paled before the spectral dawn. Looking up into the sky, he saw that the stars were keener than before. Light, mystic light, the life of the world, was flooding like an incoming tide into the dusked shallows of the dawn. Gradually the footpath through the field showed up; from among the corn a lark rose singing into the sky—he too had seen the Morning Star. Another and another fluttered upwards till it seemed that a dozen trickles fell from the overspilling font of sky. Then the church steeple loomed in the murkiness, and the vapour lying below in the watermeadows assumed a wandering and phantom semblance before the risen wind. A thrush flung clear notes from an oak outstanding in the covert; a pheasant crowed sharply. Immediately it seemed that the world was one great melody. As it rose higher the light-bringer shone with whiter fire; one by one the stars in deeper heaven grew wan and sunk into the waters of day. Like a motionless sea, light swept up the sky, purging it of darkness, glowing in the lofty empyrean, bringing life and joy to living things.

Jim turned away into the spinney. Willie followed without speaking: never before had he seen the dawn. The sun would not throw its beams from the east and lustre the beech-trees on the ridge for some time, so they crept into the shelter again.

They lay there half-awake till the tops of the fir-trees were touched by the sunrise. Then Jim crawled out and Willie followed, a great happiness coming to him as he saw the glory of the morning. No carts yet clattered along the road; three horses in a far field were galloping round the hedges, the thud of their hoofs came dully. No wisps of yacht-like cirrus or vast frigate cumulus were anchored in the heavenly roadsteads, the beauty of tidal light was seen without reflection on the snowy sails of the cloud galleons that had slipped their cables and drifted with the ebbing night to other firmaments. Walking down the path to the lake, they stopped to watch the dark specks that were larks straining upwards to their ideal and flinging down their jewelled loves to the earth. Never before had Willie felt that school and history lessons were so unimportant. He determined to be a moucher, like Jim, when he grew up. What was Elsie to him on a morning like this? No wonder Jim lived in the spinney!

A mist covered the still surface of the lake. In the centre many moorhens and coots were feeding, calling with melancholy 'cronk-cronk'. The broad leaves of the waterlilies rested placidly, green and cool, with copper undersides guarding the

235

aphroditean blossoms not yet foaming the waters. While they watched, a great gray heron sailed down and stood like the snapped and tindered stump of a birch-tree at the edge, waiting for a fish to pass near his beak. With a heavy splash a brown carp leapt among the lily leaves, rocking them. 'Can't never catch one of they,' whispered Jim. They moved from behind the beech-tree and in alarm the heron flapped away, his long legs stretched behind him. From a deep sullen pool that had received the tree's leaves for centuries Jim pulled his night lines, and to his amazement Willie saw that four big perch were hooked. They plattered on the ground, and raised their spiked dorsal guards; their deep sides were barred with black, and their fins crimson. Jim killed and cleaned them, while Willie lit a small fire with birch-bark. Soon the fish were sizzling on sticks suspended across the fire, and surely with the bread that Jim had in his pocket no fish had ever possessed a rarer flavour or been eaten with such relish.

Stamping out the fire, Jim re-baited the hooks and slung the lines into the pool. All traces of the meal were buried, lest a clue be given to search parties.

As the morning took more warmth and light to its freshness, Willie began to feel anxious. The adventure was so splendid that he realised its joy could not last for ever. He wondered how his bed had looked in the morning, and whether Fidelis had missed him, and whether Biddy had cried for him, and if Father was sorry. But these thoughts soon disappeared, to come again in the afternoon as with almost a piercing longing he watched Jack walking quickly along the road to Rookhurst. That night when clouds came up and cloaked the stars and the slip of a moon, he missed Jack acutely. He was sitting by the fire when he heard voices coming up the footpath; hurriedly he climbed a fir-tree, and crouched still against the bole, sweating when the sparrowhawk, that had a nest in the tree-top, flew off and made a noise with its wings. The voices came into the spinney, and with joy he recognised Jack's.

'He's gone,' it said. 'I would have sworn I saw him by the fire, too. Willie! Willie! Are you there? It's all right, I'm here with Jim!'

'Hullo, old man,' said Willie, casually, 'I'm just up this tree. Half a mo', I'll come down.'

Jack told him that the police had been told; that there was terrific excitement in the school. Chapman and Dennis had been up before the Old Bird, and it was said they would be expelled. There had been a terrific shindy. Rupert had told all the chaps how he, Willie, had pulled up the traps, with reckless bravery. But what was he going to do? Stay there? He'd better come back. Should he, Jack, join him, and stand by him? He was quite ready.

No, said Willie: he must bear it all by himself. After a few minutes Jack went away, promising to come back the next evening with some food. Later on that night it rained so hard that large drops oozed through the thick roof and splashed on his face, and he could not sleep. Jim came close to warm him, but his brain refused to allow him rest. The vision of prison came repeatedly before him; expulsion; a reformatory.

How far away seemed school now! For an hour his brain raced and involved him in innumerable terrors; then he slept. A weary, misty dawn dispelled the phantasms and presented a reality of sogged ground and wet drippings from the trees. Fear prevented him from going home. Jim left him in the morning to go into Rookhurst for food, and returned as the rain commenced again. Willie was drenched and his teeth chattered. A little pool of muddy water lined the floor of the dug-out. He began to cry at night, the rain ceased, and through tattered clouds the moon showed a ghostly radiance. Jim said that he would soon have him dry and warm, for they would go down to the quarry and lie on the hot stones near the limekilns. Willie slithered over the field, too miserable to heed the song of the nightingales, blackcap warblers, and cuckoos which were singing in the darkness.

The quarry was white with chalk, which was burned in large kilns for the lime to dress the fields. As they reached it they saw that one was burning; a lambent flame rose now and again, licked the darkness, and disappeared. Near the circular rim a glow beat upwards, a reflection from the white-hot lime. They lay on the stones, and soon a lovely feeling of warmth and security stole over Willie. Jim had slept there before. The hovering blue and red and gold flames rose like spirits in the night, and the boy watched them with dreamy contentment.

The two fell asleep. The wind dropped, and the quarry, sunk by excavations to a low level, was still. Palely the gas burned, like a will-o'-the-wisp over the marshes. It grew more chilly, and Jim crept nearer the rim, which glowed with the reflection of the fires below. Soon he lay near the lip of the crater. Willie lay with his head on his arm, still. Both breathed loudly.

The night was quiet and patient. A wind blew all the stars to shine, but the sleepers did not stir. The blocks in the kiln slid lower, the flames hovered feebly. In the darkness a mass of chalk, loosened by the wet, crashed to the floor of the quarry. The boy, sleeping exhaustedly, was not startled and awakened by it; nor did he hear a hoarse cry that ended in a wild shriek and slowly died away.

Just after dawn had drenched the clouds as with bloody stains, Willie awoke with a throbbing head and shiverings of his body.

He was alone. He ran to the shelter. Only a brown muddy pool remained in the dug-out.

'Jim, where are you, Jim?' he called, then went back to the quarry. He sat down and wept. His head throbbed.

All the morning he ran about, crying 'Jim! Jim! Please answer, Jim! Oh!' and then he would cry again. At last hunger and misery had their way, and thinking that Jim had gone away from him on purpose, he went home.

As he approached the house of Mr. Norman he wondered

how much surprise a sudden entry into the garden would create. He decided that Mrs. Norman would probably send him away, because now she would consider him an unfit person with whom to allow Elsie to associate. Although he had been away only three nights from home, it seemed like a lifetime. His face felt hot and puffy; his head still throbbed; he felt sure that his eyes were sunken, glowing like live coals, and his cheeks haggard.

Mr. Norman was standing by his rose-trees when Willie peered through the hedge. He was rather stern, he thought. Eagerly he looked for Elsie, but could not see her. He was almost surprised to see the garden unchanged.

'Blabbery—Blabbery—Bla—Bla—Blabby!' called a voice that he knew, and suddenly his throat was parched.

'Daddy,' it called, 'have you see Blackberry?'

'No, my love. Where is your mother?'

'In the back room, with Mary.'

Her voice seemed very cheerful to the boy peering through the hedge.

'Has she been in long?'

'Just come from Mr. Temperley's with Jack. There's no news of Willie.'

'Ah!'

Jack came out of the house, followed by Mrs. Norman, and Mary Ogilvie.

'Good-afternoon, sir,' he said.

'Good-afternoon, sir,' replied the artist. 'I hear you've come to tea. Pity you haven't brought your friend.'

The watcher was quivering with excitement.

'Willie?' said Jack. 'Ah, no, *he's* hopped it for good. Pity *I* didn't go with him.'

'Why, are you turned rebel too?'

A cunning look came over Jack's face, and looking on the ground he said: 'If only dear old Willie had waited for me! I think he's awfully brave to hop it like that. I wouldn't mind betting that at this moment he is in a decent uniform on a ship bound for America.'

Willie whispered 'Shut up, you fool', for he would look a fool when they realised in a few moments, that he was still in England.

'Well, I'm sorry for his poor father,' said Mrs. Norman, shaking her head, 'after all, he was rather a rascal. Stealing pheasants' eggs, so Cook told me. After all, there is a limit to boyish mischief. I wonder if the police will be able to trace him.'

Willie felt sick.

'No,' declared Jack, emphatically. 'I know Willie. Once he means to do a thing, he will do it. And as a matter of fact I wouldn't mind telling you that if I knew where he was I would follow.'

'Would you now?' asked the artist, in a serious voice. 'You'd get a bit torn and scratched if you tried, I expect.'

Willie withdrew his head suddenly, and looked about him. Had Mr. Norman . . . ? Someone was shuffling down the road. He saw the policeman. He immediately crawled through the hedge, and called out in a small voice:

'I say, here I am.'

'Willie!' cried Jack.

'Copper's coming, hide me quick!'

They bundled him into the house. Many questions were asked. Had he been home? How long had he been in that condition? He must change at once. He was sopping. He must have a hot bath. He was a naughty boy. They were going to drag the lake if he had not been found by this evening! (thus Mrs. Norman). Whatever had made him smash Mr. Isaacs' eggs? Why hadn't he come to them, they would have given him sanctuary? He was a bad boy to distress his friends and break their hearts (thus Mr. Norman, while Willie's heart leapt at the implication). Elsie looked at him with a new interest; Mary with a strained pitiableness of face.

They gave him a warm bath, and afterwards he was so drowsy that he was put in a spare bedroom and immediately fell asleep, to dream in the middle of the night that flame was all around him and Jim: shrieking with fear to awake and see a dim nightgowned figure padding with bare feet into his room, feel arms round his neck and a little husky voice murmuring in his ear.

'Oh, thank you, dear God, for making it only a dream,' cried Willie in relief, 'I was dreaming. It's nice to awake after that damhell nightmare. Coo, the flames! Elsie——' He pressed his face against the soft warm cheek.

'It isn't Elsie; it's me, Mary,' said a small voice by the bed, and the arms were withdrawn.

Mrs. Norman came into the room, and sent Mary back to bed, saying she must not go into other people's bedrooms, just as Willie was wondering desperately why Elsie had not come, but only Mary, whom he did not want.

Soon afterwards he awoke and found that it was morning. His head was better. Although light stripped the dream of its actuality, the memory of it lingered.

Dressed in his own dried and brushed clothes he went downstairs, ate very little breakfast, and returned home after saying good-bye to all except Elsie.

Biddy cried and sobbed over him, but his father went out of the house without a word.

IT WAS evening. The boy's face was washed. His hair, disciplined temporarily by water, was carefully parted. He knocked at the door of his father's room.

'Come in.'

Willie went in, and closed the door behind him.

'Well?' said his father.

'If you please, I have come to say that I'm sorry.'

Father did not answer at once. Willie looked at his face. He noticed that it looked very thin. His beard was straggly. Father was not angry. His forehead was frowning, but not his eyes. He had expected him to be angry, Father looked sad.

'I am glad that you have apologised, Willie. Then there is no more to be said. As far as I am concerned the matter is ended.'

Father spoke so quietly that he wondered what was the matter.

'Won't you forgive me, Father?'

No answer.

Willie tried to pick up a piece of paper on the carpet with his boots.

After a long time, Father said almost in a whisper:

'Come here, my boy. I have something to show you.'

He turned up the lamp, and went to his desk. Willie watched the jingling keys shining in the light. The lock clicked, the desk cover rattled up. He took out something.

'Come in the light, Willie.'

Willie went nearer.

'Look at this. It is your mother. She died ten years ago to-day.'

For the first time he looked at the photograph of his mother. A lump rose in his throat—not for himself or caused by the picture, but because Father seemed sad. Why was Father so unhappy? To please him he looked intently at the photograph, thinking that his mother hadn't been so bad looking, only what awful clothes she wore, her jacket all frilled at the shoulder.

'I loved your mother so much, Willie, that when she died everything seemed to finish for me. You are very young, and I wonder if you can understand. I suppose not. Perhaps one day you will.'

He felt awfully sorry for Father, and had to swallow.

'Your mother was so good,' Father whispered presently, 'and before you were born we talked about you. Somehow she knew that it was you being born, and no one else. And when she talked of you, and how fine a man you would grow up, I loved her all the more.' Mr. Maddison hesitated, lifted his brows, frowned, clenched his hand, and said in a level voice: 'You are only a child now, but one day you will grow up. Perhaps, too, one evening you will wait in a darkened room sitting before a fire, wondering if someone will live or die. And perhaps that someone you love more tnan anything will die and leave you a little son. Would you not want him to be good like his mother?'

'Yes, Father.'

'And if he wasn't, wouldn't you be sad?'

'Yes, Father,' he replied, quite unable to visualise the scene or its sadness. He realised that the way Father was talking meant that he was not to be punished; and he strained hard not to shout or move his feet. He began to dread that he would grin, because he was expected to be sad at what Father was telling him; not a laughing grin, but Father would not understand that. Oh, God, please don't let him grin!

'Well then, Willie, I want you to try to be a good boy, for your dead mother's sake.'

He looked at his son, who stared at the picture, thinking that the sleeves looked awful: that it was taken by Moore at Exeter, Devon: that it was faded: that——

'Don't be afraid to tell me things, Willie,' his father said rather hurriedly. 'Tell me the things you do. I've got a birthday book to give you, called *Our Bird Friends*.'

'Thank you, Father,' his son answered, wishing that Father hadn't bought it for him.

'Mind you get on at school. I've seen Mr. Rore and everything is all right. Now shake hands like a man.'

Twisting his body about, with head averted, the boy held out his hand. Awkwardly they shook hands. For a moment Mr. Maddison hesitated. Then he kissed his son.

Willie felt the rough hairs of his beard on his face, and smelled old tobacco. He pressed his cheek against the beard, and began to cry. He made no sound, keeping it all back behind his closed throat. He dared not breathe.

Mr. Maddison stiffened, and turned away. The little boy stood still hanging his head.

'Well, that's all, I think. Good-night, old chap. And don't worry any more, will you?'

'No, Father. G-good n-night, Fath-er,' he whispered, with puckered face, and shook hands again, and went out of the room, closing the door behind him. He forgot the book.

Just outside the window a robin was singing pensively, hidden in the branches of the pear-tree, piping his sweet vespertine ode in the shifting twilight. The father went to the window and looked at the young moon wandering with the corse of the old one towards the western rafters of heaven, and his sigh breathed a dim blur upon the window pane.

JUNE—NOVEMBER, 1920

END OF BOOK ONE OF
The Flax of Dream

NOTE

THE FOUR Books (of childhood, boyhood, youth, and early manhood) making the work called *The Flax of Dream* are

The Beautiful Years

Dandelion Days

The Dream of Fair Women

The Pathway

with the pendent 'celestial fantasy' (as Maddison himself described it) entitled

The Star-born

ZENITH

☐ The Way of a Transgressor	Negley Farson	£2.95
☐ A Child Possessed	R. C. Hutchinson	£2.50
☐ Days of Greatness	Walter Kempowski	£2.95
☐ The Beautiful Years	Henry Williamson	£2.50
☐ Dandelion Days	Henry Williamson	£2.50

HAMLYN PAPERBACKS

GENERAL FICTION

☐ The Patriarch	Chaim Bermant	£1.75
☐ The Free Fishers	John Buchan	£1.50
☐ Midwinter	John Buchan	£1.50
☐ A Prince of the Captivity	John Buchan	£1.50
☐ The Eve of Saint Venus	Anthony Burgess	£1.10
☐ Nothing like the Sun	Anthony Burgess	£1.50
☐ The Wanting Seed	Anthony Burgess	£1.50
☐ Mildred Pierce	James M. Cain	£1.50
☐ Past All Dishonour	James M. Cain	£1.25
☐ My Father's House	Kathleen Conlon	£1.50
☐ Pope Joan	Lawrence Durrell	£1.35
☐ The Country of Her Dreams	Janice Elliott	£1.35
☐ Secret Places	Janice Elliott	£1.35
☐ Letter to a Child Never Born	Oriana Fallaci	£1.00
☐ A Man	Oriana Fallaci	£1.95
☐ The Bride of Lowther Fell	Margaret Forster	£1.75
☐ Marital Rites	Margaret Forster	£1.50
☐ The Big Goodnight	Judy Gardiner	£1.25
☐ Who Was Sylvia?	Judy Gardiner	£1.50
☐ Duncton Wood	William Horwood	£1.95
☐ Styx	Christopher Hyde	£1.50
☐ Passing Through	Guida Jackson	£1.25
☐ A Bonfire	Pamela Hansford Johnson	£1.50
☐ The Good Husband	Pamela Hansford Johnson	£1.50
☐ The Good Listener	Pamela Hansford Johnson	£1.50
☐ The Honours Board	Pamela Hansford Johnson	£1.50
☐ The Unspeakable Skipton	Pamela Hansford Johnson	£1.50
☐ Kine	A. R. Lloyd	£1.50
☐ Dingley Falls	Michael Malone	£1.95
☐ Highland Fling	Nancy Mitford	£1.50
☐ Pigeon Pie	Nancy Mitford	£1.50
☐ The Red Raven	Lilli Palmer	£1.25
☐ Cocaine	Pitigrilli	£1.50
☐ An Inch of Fortune	Simon Raven	£1.25
☐ Celestial Navigation	Anne Tyler	£1.00
☐ The Clock Winder	Anne Tyler	£1.50
☐ If Morning Ever Comes	Anne Tyler	£1.50
☐ Morgan's Passing	Anne Tyler	£1.50
☐ Searching for Caleb	Anne Tyler	£1.00

CRIME/ADVENTURE/SUSPENSE

☐ The Blunderer	Patricia Highsmith	£1.50
☐ A Game for the Living	Patricia Highsmith	£1.50
☐ Those Who Walk Away	Patricia Highsmith	£1.50
☐ The Tremor of Forgery	Patricia Highsmith	£1.50
☐ The Two Faces of January	Patricia Highsmith	£1.50

FICTION

CRIME WHODUNNITS

☐ Some Die Eloquent	Catherine Aird	£1.25
☐ The Case of the Abominable Snowman	Nicholas Blake	£1.10
☐ The Widow's Cruise	Nicholas Blake	£1.25
☐ The Worm of Death	Nicholas Blake	95p
☐ Thou Shell of Death	Nicholas Blake	£1.25
☐ Green for Danger	Christiana Brand	£1.10
☐ Tour de Force	Christiana Brand	£1.10
☐ The Long Divorce	Edmund Crispin	£1.50
☐ A Leaven of Malice	Claire Curzon	£1.50
☐ King and Joker	Peter Dickinson	£1.25
☐ A Pride of Heroes	Peter Dickinson	£1.50
☐ The Four False Weapons	John Dickinson Carr	£1.25
☐ A Lonely Place to Die	Wessel Ebersohn	£1.10
☐ Gold from Gemini	Jonathan Gash	£1.10
☐ The Grail Tree	Jonathan Gash	£1.00
☐ The Judas Pair	Jonathan Gash	95p
☐ Spend Game	Jonathan Gash	£1.25
☐ Blood and Judgment	Michael Gilbert	£1.10
☐ Close Quarters	Michael Gilbert	£1.10
☐ Death of a Favourite Girl	Michael Gilbert	£1.50
☐ The Etruscan Net	Michael Gilbert	£1.25
☐ The Night of the Twelfth	Michael Gilbert	£1.25
☐ Hare Sitting Up	Michael Innes	£1.10
☐ Silence Observed	Michael Innes	£1.00
☐ There Came Both Mist and Snow	Michael Innes	95p
☐ The Weight of the Evidence	Michael Innes	£1.10
☐ The Tanglewood Murder	Lucille Kallen	£1.50
☐ The Howard Hughes Affair	Stuart Kaminsky	£1.10
☐ Go West, Inspector Ghote	H. R. F. Keating	£1.50
☐ Inspector Ghote Draws a Line	H. R. F. Keating	£1.10
☐ Inspector Ghote Plays a Joker	H. R. F. Keating	£1.25
☐ The Murder of the Maharajah	H. R. F. Keating	£1.25
☐ The Perfect Murder	H. R. F. Keating	£1.10
☐ Sweet and Deadly	Freny Olbrich	£1.25
☐ A Fine and Private Place	Ellery Queen	£1.00
☐ The French Powder Mystery	Ellery Queen	£1.25
☐ The Roman Hat Mystery	Ellery Queen	£1.50
☐ The Siamese Twin Mystery	Ellery Queen	95p
☐ The Spanish Cape Mystery	Ellery Queen	£1.10
☐ Murder for Treasure	David Williams	£1.50

CRIME/ADVENTURE/SUSPENSE

☐ The Killing In The Market	John Ball with Bevan Smith	£1.00
☐ Five Pieces of Jade	John Ball	£1.50
☐ In the Heat of the Night	John Ball	£1.00
☐ Johnny Get Your Gun	John Ball	£1.00
☐ The Cool Cottontail	John Ball	£1.00
☐ Then Came Violence	John Ball	£1.50
☐ Opalesque	Bernard Boneher	£1.50
☐ Tagget	Irving A. Greenfield	£1.35
☐ Holding Pattern	Alistair Hamilton	£1.35
☐ Don't Be No Hero	Leonard Harris	£1.25
☐ The Blunderer	Patricia Highsmith	£1.50
☐ A Game for the Living	Patricia Highsmith	£1.50
☐ Those Who Walk Away	Patricia Highsmith	£1.50
☐ The Tremor of Forgery	Patricia Highsmith	£1.50
☐ The Two Faces of January	Patricia Highsmith	£1.50
☐ The Valkyrie Project	Michael Kilian	£1.50
☐ Acid Test	Colin Lewis	£1.50
☐ The Traitor Machine	Max Marquis	£1.25
☐ Einstein's Brain	Mark Olshaker	£1.75
☐ The Last Prisoner	James Robson	£1.50

FICTION

CRIME/ADVENTURE/SUSPENSE

☐ Masterstroke	Marilyn Sharp	£1.75
☐ Air Glow Red	Ian Slater	£1.75
☐ Sledgehammer	Jasper Smith	£1.25
☐ Deadline in Jakarta	Ian Stewart	£1.25
☐ The Seizing of Singapore	Ian Stewart	£1.00
☐ The Earhart Betrayal	James Stewart Thayer	£1.50
☐ Jenny's War	Jack Stoneley	£1.25
☐ Bloodwealth	Blair Stuart	£1.50

HORROR/OCCULT/NASTY

☐ Death Walkers	Gary Brandner	£1.00
☐ Hellborn	Gary Brandner	£1.25
☐ The Howling	Gary Brandner	£1.25
☐ Return of the Howling	Gary Brandner	£1.25
☐ The Sanctuary	Glenn Chandler	£1.00
☐ The Tribe	Glenn Chandler	£1.10
☐ Croak	Robin Evans	£1.10
☐ Transplant	Daniel Farson	£1.00
☐ The Quick and the Dead	Judy Gardiner	£1.00
☐ The Unbegotten	Bill Garnett	£1.25
☐ Rattlers	Joseph L. Gilmore	£1.00
☐ The Nestling	Charles L. Grant	£1.75
☐ Slither	John Halkin	£1.25
☐ The Unholy	John Halkin	£1.25
☐ The Wicker Man	Robin Hardy and Antony Shaffer	£1.50
☐ The Skull	Shaun Hutson	£1.25
☐ The Beast Within	Edward Levy	£1.25
☐ Night Killers	Richard Lewis	£1.25
☐ Parasite	Richard Lewis	£1.25
☐ Spiders	Richard Lewis	£1.25
☐ Parasite	Richard Lewis	£1.25
☐ Spiders	Richard Lewis	£1.00
☐ The Web	Richard Lewis	£1.10
☐ Gate of Fear	Lewis Mallory	£1.00
☐ The Nursery	Lewis Mallory	£1.10
☐ The Book of Shadows	Marc Olden	£1.25
☐ The Spirit	Thomas Page	£1.25
☐ The Summoning	John Pintoro	95p
☐ Bloodthirst	Mark Ronson	£1.00
☐ Ghoul	Mark Ronson	95p
☐ Ogre	Mark Ronson	95p
☐ Plague Pit	Mark Ronson	£1.00
☐ The Scourge	Nick Sharman	£1.00

NAME ....

ADDRESS ....

....

Write to Hamlyn Paperbacks Cash Sales, PO Box 11, Falmouth, Cornwall TR10 9EN.

Please indicate order and enclose remittance to the value of the cover price plus:

U.K.: Please allow 45p for the first book plus 20p for the second book and 14p for each additional book ordered, to a maximum charge of £1.63.

B.F.P.O. & EIRE: Please allow 45p for the first book plus 20p for the second book and 14p per copy for the next 7 books, thereafter 8p per book.

OVERSEAS: Please allow 75p for the first book and 21p per copy for each additional book.

Whilst every effort is made to keep prices low it is sometimes necessary to increase cover prices and also postage and packing rates at short notice. Hamlyn Paperbacks reserve the right to show new retail prices on covers which may differ from those previously advertised in the text or elsewhere.